Also by Cassandra Page

The Isla's Inheritance trilogy
Isla's Inheritance
Isla's Oath
Melpomene's Daughter

CASSANDRA PAGE

www.cassandrapage.com

Cassandra Page
www.cassandrapage.com

Cataloguing-in-Publication data available from
the National Library of Australia www.nla.gov.au

ISBN: 9780994445919

Set in Bookman Old Style 10pt

Book and cover design by KILA Designs
www.kiladesigns.com.au
Cover images: ©Thinkstock / Ghetea Iulia / Jordan McCullough

To Nathaniel. Always and forever.

I lay me here to sleep;
No nightmare shall plague me,
Until they swim all the waters
That flow on the earth,
And count all the stars
That appear in the sky!
Amen.

Chapter One

"So, um, I've never done this before. Visit someone like you, I mean." The man swallowed, Adam's apple bobbing.

Way to make me sound like a prostitute, pal. But his reaction was hardly unique. I extended a hand. His palm was sweaty despite the cold outside, his handshake weak. Ew. "I'm Melaina. Why don't you take a seat, Mr Heaney?"

"Sure. Okay. Call me Larry." He struggled out of his jacket and hung it on my hatstand, which swayed like a drunk. One of these days it would collapse in a pile of cheap timber and overcoats, but apparently not today.

I flashed my dimples at him as we sat on my battered armchairs, each of them wearing an orange throw rug like a shawl to hide the bare patches on their shoulders and arms. The chairs were at right angles with a corner table between them. Nice and cosy. Larry didn't relax, though, his spine straight and his shoulders tense.

"Why don't you tell me why you're here?" I asked.

"My Aunt Mim organised it. I think she knows the lady out front." He waved towards the door he'd come through, which led to the storefront of Serenity's New Age Gifts. I rented the room in back. "She's a bit batty to be honest, but her heart's in the right place."

I assumed he meant his aunt, not Serenity ... although the description fit either way. I nodded for him to continue.

He spoke in a rush, as though that would make it less embarrassing. "I've been having these recurring night-mares, and I tried sleeping tablets but then I couldn't wake up, which was *worse*, and the doctor referred me to a psychologist, but I rang them and they said it could be months before I get in." The lamplight flashed off the lenses of his glasses, partially obscuring his bloodshot eyes. Fatigue lined his face. I guessed he was in his mid-twenties, a little older than my twenty-one, but it was hard to tell. "Honestly, I'm desperate."

"I can see that," I said. He bristled despite my attempt to soften my tone, and I cringed inside. I didn't have enough customers that I could afford to drive them off. "Look, Larry, I get it. You don't really believe I can help you. You wouldn't be the first customer to feel that way. So I'll tell you what—if I can't do anything for you, the appointment's free."

He blinked brown eyes that would have been nice, if the whites hadn't been spider-webbed with veins. He was clearly trying to figure out the catch.

"Scout's honour," I added. *Or Girl Scouts. Whatever.* "What have you got to lose?"

"Nothing, I guess." His fingers worried at the throw rug's fringe, where it hung over the arm of the chair.

"Okay, what do I do?"

"The first thing I need you to do is relax. Would you like a cup of herbal tea?" He looked as if I'd offered him a ferret in a sock, eyebrows shooting towards his hairline. It was the most animated expression I'd seen from him yet. "It's my own blend. Lavender and chamomile, and a few other things. Nothing illegal or dodgy. It'll help you relax."

"Okay. I guess."

The pot was already brewing on top of the freestanding drawers in which I stored my minimal tools of the trade. Candles. Essential oils. A rainbow of small crystals Serenity had given me as a "rentiversary" present. A half-eaten bag of individually wrapped caramels. Herbs in little bags, neatly labelled with stickers. A few CDs of the sort you'd expect: rainforest noises, the ocean, whale song.

All flimflammery, of course. Except the caramels.

I laid a couple of mugs out—when a customer's nervous, it's a good idea to have a cup too, so they don't think you're poisoning them—and picked up the pot. It was made of clear glass, and the lamp's reflection glowed in its surface like a candle flame.

Then the glow was obscured by a figure that moved past it, heading towards me. It moved like a ghost. Or an angel.

I jumped, nearly dropping the pot.

"Uh, do you have any allergies?" I asked to cover my reaction. I scowled at the pot and its interloper, pouring carefully. It—he—looked like a reflection, but I knew if I turned around, the space behind me would be empty.

"No. Well, cut grass gives me hives."

Well, empty except for Larry.

The pot had been brewing long enough that the tea

had started to turn bitter, so I stirred a spoonful of honey into both mugs and brought them back to the table. "Give it a moment to cool. I have to grab something. Won't be a second."

Larry nodded, eyeing the steaming mug with a frown. I slipped from the room.

"Is everything okay, dear?" Serenity stood on top of a short stepladder that looked as though it might buckle under her weight. It wasn't that Serenity was fat, although she was definitely on the chubby side. It was that she was more than six feet tall, and had shoulders as broad as a football player's, with hips to match.

The stepladder was a plucky thing, though. It was up to the task.

"Yeah," I said. "Just got to pee."

"You should've gone before he got here."

"Yes, Mum." I sighed. Then I crossed my eyes at her.

"I'm not your mother," she said, shaking a candle at me—but a smile tugged at the corner of her lips.

The shop's bathroom was small enough that when you sat on the toilet the sink was practically in your lap. The smell of potpourri tickled my nose as I closed the door and turned to the mirror, hip cocked. My reflection didn't stare back. "What the *hell*, Leander?" Serenity talked to herself all the time and wouldn't think anything of me doing it, but I lowered my voice so my words weren't easy to make out. She'd definitely raise an eyebrow if she thought I was talking to someone else.

"Is that any way to greet a friend?" The man in the mirror smiled. He was dressed in an elegant green tunic embroidered with gold thread: colours that perfectly echoed the gold-flecked green of bright eyes. Vain creature. His

skin was the same golden brown as the honey I'd stirred into my client's tea, a tan I'd have to work to maintain. Only I'd probably get cancer doing it.

Most striking, of course, were the wings. The forewings flared out from his shoulders, the smaller hindwings from a hand-span lower down his back. They were shaped like a moth's and coloured soft grey, like those of a dove. Or a pigeon. A rat of the sky.

"If I'd dropped that pot I'd be burned from the waist down," I said. "Don't sneak up on me."

The Oneiroi pouted, hands resting under his strong chin in a cutesy pose that didn't suit him. "I thought you'd be happy to see me. It's been months."

I ran a hand through my hair. I was never happy to see Leander anymore. In fact, after his prolonged absence I'd hoped he'd found something better to do than bother me. But it wouldn't do to tell him that. "What do you want?"

"Do you have time to talk?"

"No, actually. I'm with a customer. Which you damned well know, spying from the teapot."

"Are you going to see your mother soon?" His tone was casual.

"Soon. Tomorrow, probably. Why?" I worried at a fingernail, and then dropped my hands to my sides, not wanting him to see my agitation.

It didn't work, and his eyes hardened at my feigned ignorance. "You know why."

"I guess I do."

"So you'll tell me if she mentions your father?"

"Uh huh." *No way.* "Can you get out of my mirror please? I need to do secret girl things, and I don't want you watching."

He laughed and stepped out of the frame like it was a webcam. My own reflection, now revealed, appeared perfectly normal. Pale blue eyes, heart-shaped face. Black hair, pixie cut, now sticking up at the front. A streak of cobalt blue in my fringe—and, damn, I wished my eyes were that same bright shade. A silver nose stud, small and discreet.

I saved the bigger piercing for family gatherings. It drove my uncle wild.

I flushed the toilet so Serenity wouldn't get suspicious and headed back onto the shop floor. There, I cast around for something to borrow, to explain my absence to Larry. My gaze settled on a cluster of amethyst. "Can I borrow that?"

Serenity raised an eyebrow. She knew my thoughts about props, even if she didn't agree with them. "Why?"

"Larry needs all the Zen he can get."

"Sure. But if you break it—"

"—I bought it. Yeah, yeah."

The cluster was big. It would have fit comfortably in a gorilla's palm, so I carried it in both of mine. I was tall, but not that tall. And I couldn't afford to buy it.

Larry was sipping the tea when I re-entered, forehead still furrowed. "You were a while." His tone was flat.

"I *said* I wouldn't be a second." I pushed the lamp back and squeezed the amethyst in next to the coffee mugs.

It startled a laugh from him. "Touché."

We made small talk—yes, it had been a particularly cold winter so far, with snow on the Brindabella ranges; no, I hadn't had problems with ice on my car since I

didn't have a car—and sipped our tea till he had unwound enough for me to do my work. I suspected it wasn't the tea that calmed him down as much as a conversation that didn't involve anything "new age".

What can I say? I'm a people person.

"Okay," I said. "This process is actually pretty straight-forward. I just need you to close your eyes and relax."

He put his mug down. "Should I take my glasses off?"

"Only if you want to."

"I'd rather not." His ears flushed pink.

"My housemate has glasses," I said. "She hates taking them off in public too."

"Yeah." After hesitating a moment longer, Larry closed his eyes, resting his hands in his lap. I started my patter, keeping an eye on those curled fingers. Slowly, as I talked him through taking deep, even breaths, his hands loos-ened, curving into a more natural arc.

When they did, I leaned over and, as he was inhaling deeply, blew gently onto his face.

He fell asleep between one heartbeat and the next, head lolling back against the throw rug as if he'd nodded off during the football after too many beers. A faint snore escaped his lips.

"Aw, I thought I was really interesting company," I muttered to myself. Even Leander wasn't hanging around anymore. The only noise in the room was the faint tick of the oil heater against the wall.

But I hadn't bored him to sleep. The fact is, as a half-Oneiroi, I had some power over sleep and dreams. Near as I could tell, the Oneiroi were nature spirits ... although Leander, at least, would object to such a mundane descrip-tion. They lived in the realm of dreams. Usually they couldn't get out, which was why they were so determined to track down my father, Ollie. He shouldn't have been able to impregnate Mum. Simple as that. He'd been on the run ever since. Apparently he'd broken some Oneiroi rule or other. Or maybe they wanted to find out how he did it, so everyone could have a half-human kid.

Still, I was glad they hadn't taken it out on me, at least not directly. Leander had been assigned as my minder when I was a little girl. I'd been furious when I'd discovered my "imaginary friend" in the mirror was actually keeping tabs on me. I hadn't really gotten over it.

Hold a grudge? Me?

I closed my eyes and looked into Larry's dreams.

I was expecting to find a tortured psyche, an aspect of his subconscious manifesting itself there. Daddy or mummy issues, arachnophobia, anxiety, even garden-variety stress: I'd seen them all at one point or another. I couldn't fix his psychological issues, but I could put a temporary block on his dreams until his doctor's referral came good.

That was what it usually was.

What I found was a *thing*.

The creature was an amorphous black cloud about the size of my torso. Greasy as a burger shop floor, it had yellowing eyes and writhing tentacles ... if tentacles could be covered with fine hair and worm into your skin like something from a bad horror movie.

I'd seen manifestations of people's nightmares before, more times than I could count. But this wasn't part of Larry. It was an interloper. A blight.

"Hello," I said.

The blight hissed like a feral cat over a broken-backed

lizard that wasn't quite dead. Around us, the dreamscape resolved into a rolling hillside, distinctly Australian in its gentle undulations. No sharp-edged peaks here. The grass underfoot was withered, not by the summer sun but by the blight's corruption. A single eucalypt wept tears of black sap. Clouds loomed, obscuring the vast sky.

I wouldn't have picked Larry for the rural landscape type. *You can never tell.* "You're an ugly little grease-ball, aren't you?"

The blight's eyes were flat, uncomprehending and angry. I wasn't going to be able to goad it into letting go. And I didn't want to attack it while those tentacles were embedded in the reddish dirt beneath the tree. What if one of them tore off? That could result in residual bad-ness for Larry, like leaving a bee sting under the skin to spit toxins long after the bee has died.

Still, the blight was only small. I could take it.

I gathered myself, concentrating, and flexed my power like a muscle. As the power gathered, something with the shape of moth wings flared at my back, casting a shadow onto the ground before me. Then they faded like writing on cheap, waterlogged paper.

I grumbled. They never stayed. I would've liked to have wings, even if it was in dreams.

Oh well.

The creature, slavering at the overt sign of power, with-drew its tendrils from the soil and lunged at me, boiling and chittering. I was a much tastier meal than Larry.

Hands outflung like a comic book superhero, I threw a bolt of power at the creature. It saw too late, tried to dodge … but I caught it square in the middle of what would have been its chest if it'd had one.

It screeched and died, turning to oily mist that dissipated like smoke.

Feeling weak, I sat for a moment in the grass, looking at the blasted landscape. The eucalypt already looked perkier; at least, it wasn't dripping sap anymore. Larry's dreamscape would probably heal on its own now the parasite had been destroyed. But he was a paying customer. I'd better do some repairs before I left.

Maybe tonight he'd dream of kittens. Or sex kittens, if that was his thing.

Lucky Larry.

Serenity came back to check on me after she'd locked up the shop, eyebrows lifting when she saw me slouched in my armchair, feet up on the empty one. Larry had left hours before. "Melaina, honey, are you alright?"

"Tired," I said, a caramel sticking to my teeth. The sugar helped with the weariness. Although it wasn't doing as good a job today as it usually did. I didn't often evict blights.

"These sessions take so much out of you. You ought to charge more." She eyed my boots disapprovingly. It wasn't the purple laces that bothered her; it was the shoes-on-furniture thing. But to hell with it—they were *my* dilapidated second-hand armchairs, not hers. Besides, my boots, one of my few self-indulgences, were probably worth more than the couches.

"I charge what I can charge." I shrugged. "I don't have

a medical degree or anything."

"You could've done," she said, collecting the empty mugs. Once again, she sounded like my mother should. Only my mother hadn't criticised me for dropping out of university two years before, whereas Serenity brought it up every chance she got. She had kids my age, but they didn't live in Canberra and, in their absence, she'd taken me under her floral-clad wing.

"Yeah, and I'd never have paid off the debt after," I said.

"You could once you got a job as a doctor."

"A psychologist."

"Whatever." She sniffed.

I'd gone to university for a whole semester before I realised the degree was basically the same thing as my drawer full of candles and crystals: parlour tricks, something to hide what I did from the world.

The crystals were cheaper.

Speaking of which … time to change the subject. "Thanks for the loan of the amethyst. It was really helpful. And it's not even a little bit broken."

I handed it back to her. *She* was able to cradle it in one hand, empty mugs dangling off the fingers of the other.

"Do you have any clients tomorrow?"

I shook my head, standing and stretching. My vertebrae popped.

"Do you want a shift?"

"Morning or afternoon?" I suspected she was offering the work out of pity. Some weeks I could barely afford to hire the room from her, let alone pay my half of the rent for the flat I shared with my best friend.

She shrugged. "Whichever suits." Yep, definitely a pity shift.

I wanted to say no, that I didn't want to inconvenience her. But I also wanted to eat. So I smiled when I thanked her, taking the mugs back. The least I could do was clean up after myself.

Chapter Two

After my shift the next day, I caught the bus out to Wattle Tree Park to see my mother, gazing out the window at low-rise offices and shopping arcades interspersed with bare-limbed trees that shivered in the wind. The nursing home was set on a large block of land among the native trees from which it drew its name. It was early winter and the trees were a drab greenish-brown—but at least they had leaves, which put them one up on their non-native cousins. And in a month or so, the wattle flowers would bloom and the trees would be covered in tiny yellow balls of fuzz: a hayfever sufferer's nightmare and the first harbinger of an Australian spring. Two sides of the same flowery coin.

A high brick wall gave the grounds some privacy. The offices on either side of the home were only a couple of storeys high, so inside the grounds it was peaceful despite the rumble of nearby traffic. I let myself in the pedestrian gate before stuffing icy fingers back into my jacket pockets.

The rent-a-cop in his heated booth barely glanced up from his paper. A burly footballer glared at me, mid-sprint, from the front page.

It was a pleasant nursing home, one of the best in Canberra. Uncle Ian, Mum's brother, was generous when it came to her care. His generosity towards me, on the other hand, had dried up when I'd reached the end of high school. Probably because he wasn't legally obliged to care for me anymore.

Serenity thought I'd dropped out of university to spite him. I hadn't, but it was a pleasant side-effect.

The sunlight was thin, doing little to warm the air as I stomped up the path to the building. At least the wall reduced the chilly wind gusting off the nearby lake to a whisper. The grounds were deserted except for an old man wearing a brown bathrobe over thick flannelette pyjamas and boots. He studied a tree trunk intently. I hoped he was wearing thick socks. The frost-seared grass under the trees glistened with dew.

At least it almost never snowed in Canberra. Thank god.

A blast of warm air greeted me at the door, heating working overtime to counteract the cold draft that followed me in. I sighed with relief and signed in at the desk. The receptionist on duty told me my mother was awake and in the rec room. I smiled my thanks and went looking for her.

At this time of day the hall, carpeted in a peach-fuzz pink that I think was meant to be restful, was crowded. A few elderly ladies and one man were gathered around a large LCD television whose volume was turned up too loud, projecting the chiming and cheering of an obnoxious

game show. Others knitted, read battered paperbacks, chatted, sipped drinks. A few listened to music up the other end of the hall, a jazz tune I didn't recognise.

My mother sat by the window in a long, white night-gown, gazing out at the lawn.

She stood out like a daisy in a field of grass: her hair was long, unbound, and the same jet-black as mine. It hadn't yet gone grey like that of most other residents. Her pale skin bore only the fine wrinkles of middle age—the middle age of someone who didn't spend a lot of time in the sun. She'd been in a home for almost as long as I'd been alive. Longer than most of the elderly residents.

Thinking about it made me sad. And that made me cranky. "It's mid-afternoon, Mum," I said. "You should be dressed."

"Hello, dear." She smiled, lifting her cheek to be kissed.

"Hi." My voice sounded flat and, hearing it, I told myself to get a grip as I sat in the window seat opposite her. There were one or two others still wearing pyjamas, like the guy in the garden. Besides, it wasn't Mum's fault she was so detached from the world.

It was Dad's.

"I brought you some chocolate."

She clapped her thin hands with delight, as though my offering was the finest Swiss confectionary rather than a cheap assortment from the supermarket. Pulling the cellophane off, she put the box on the sill between us, inspecting the range with pursed lips.

"How have you been?" I asked.

She shrugged, choosing an anonymous blue-wrapped chocolate. "Nothing changes here. You?"

"More or less the same. I had an ... unusual client yesterday." I glanced around and lowered my voice. Given the volume of the television and the fact that most of the residents were wearing hearing aids, I was pretty sure no one would be able to overhear. "He had a blight infestation."

"Oh?"

"I haven't seen one in almost a year. Has Ollie ever mentioned them to you?"

She shook her head. "I can ask him if you like?"

"If you happen to see him," I said, glancing at the reflective surface of the windowpane. There was no sign of Leander. But I'd never been sure that was a guarantee of privacy. Maybe it really *did* work like a webcam, where he could be "off camera" but still hear the conversation.

He'd never confirmed either way. For obvious reasons.

"Leander's back too." I scowled at my reflection.

Her faraway gaze sharpened. She'd used to like my imaginary friend, till I discovered his real agenda. Now she hated him, rightly viewing him as a threat to her husband. Or partner. I don't think Mum and Dad ever did marry. I mean, how could they?

"What did he want?" she asked.

"The usual."

"And will you give it to him?"

I shook my head, looking down at my hands. I'd never met my father and he wasn't exactly my favourite person, but Mum loved him. I couldn't deprive her of that.

I wasn't sure she'd survive it.

"He loves you, you know."

At first I thought she meant Leander. *Ugh.* Then I realised she meant Dad, which wasn't much better. "Uh huh."

"Really, sweetheart, he does. He would come to your dreams the way he does mine, but—"

"—it isn't safe." I'd heard all this before. I was long past the point where I cared that he was putting his own safety ahead of meeting his daughter, getting to know her. Even if it meant her instruction in the ways of the Oneiroi came from Leander, a stranger with his own agenda, and what she could glean from the clues in dusty library books and on Wikipedia.

Okay, maybe I was only mostly over it.

Mum gazed at me with sad, hazel eyes. I forced a bright smile and reached past her to steal one of the chocolates. "Almond. My favourite!"

We chatted for an hour about my life, since hers never really changed. When she began to yawn I glanced at my watch: it was only three o'clock. I waved at one of the nurses, who hurried over, pushing a wheelchair.

"Time for bed, Ms Armstrong?" he said as he approached.

She nodded, eyelids heavy.

Ewan had been working at Wattle Tree Park for years and was well versed in my mother's peculiar condition. He was a few inches taller than me, with dark brown hair bleached blond in a single, thick stripe from his short fringe back to the nape of his neck. I had mixed feelings on the hairdo, depending on how charitable I was feeling at the time.

Today I thought it made him look like a skunk.

"You didn't get her dressed?" I glared at him as he half-lifted my drowsy mother into the wheelchair. She hung loose-limbed from his grip.

"I didn't see the point." He smiled apologetically, tucking Mum's slippered feet onto the chair's footrests. I grabbed the chocolates and followed him as he pushed her out of the rec room and down the corridor. "I'm sorry, Melaina, but it's a lot easier to care for her needs when she's in a nightgown. And we do put her in a clean one, morning and evening."

I grumbled. He was right. And it wasn't like she cared.

My mother was happiest when she was sleeping.

After years of fruitless tests, the doctors had declared she had chronic hypersomnia, a diagnosis of the symptom rather than the cause. What it meant was that she slept a lot. In her case, around seventeen hours a day—at least twelve hours overnight and then naps during the day to recharge as she grew exhausted. Some doctors believed she had underlying chronic fatigue syndrome; others, like her new one, thought it was a result of posttraumatic stress disorder.

But she and I knew she slept because it was the only way for her to be with my father. Like all Oneiroi, he couldn't walk in the waking world. To Mum, the time she was awake in our world was equivalent to the sleep of most people: seven hours she had to put up with in order to function. She was truly alive when she was dreaming and with him.

I loved my mother, but Dad was a selfish bastard. He'd taken her from me before I'd even been born and had never given her back.

Jaw clenched, I helped Ewan lift Mum onto her bed and we arranged her limbs as if she were an oversized doll. Although she and I had similar builds, Mum was lighter than me, her muscles lacking definition due to her sedentary lifestyle and birdlike diet. He laid her on her back, arms across her chest, but I frowned and

reached past him to put one hand up under her cheek. It looked more natural that way. Less funereal. She was already breathing deeply, a smile curving her lips.

Ewan stepped back. When he spoke, his tone was reassuring. "She really is doing well."

"Compared to what?" I asked, my voice sharp. If Mum were awake she'd chide me.

Ewan didn't take my bad mood personally. "Compared to my other sleeper."

There was an old man in the home who slept twenty-four hours a day. Was that technically a coma? I had no idea, but the nurse's comment made me feel ungrateful. At least I got to talk to Mum sometimes. If I timed it right.

Oblivious to my thoughts, Ewan continued, "Her physical fitness is pretty good for someone as inactive as she is, though I admit she still gets exhausted easily. But she's staying awake an hour or so longer a day than she was six months ago."

"Really?" That surprised me.

He nodded, making a note on a chart that had been tucked discreetly underneath a small pile of magazines on the tiny table. "Yup. Doctor Willis didn't mention it?"

"Nope. But he doesn't work for me, does he?"

"Well, no, I guess he doesn't," Ewan said.

Something about his tone made me frown at him. "Is there anything else the doctor isn't telling me?"

Glancing at me, Ewan put the chart down and crossed to the door, closing it. The jingling from the television down the hall fell mercifully silent. He folded his arms across his chest, his gaze weighing me up. I tried to smile but nerves jangled in my stomach, making the expression feel forced. So I gave up and scowled. "Spill."

"Doctor Willis has been talking to your uncle about drug treatments," Ewan said slowly. "He was surprised they hadn't been tried before. When I overheard them, they were talking about antidepressants."

"They haven't been tried because she doesn't want them," I said.

"*I* know that and *you* know that." Ewan pointed from himself to me and then shrugged.

"Uncle Ian has power of attorney over her." I clenched and unclenched my fists, the beginning of a headache pinching at my temples. "Has he authorised it yet?"

"No. And he can't, unless she grants him enduring power of attorney, which I understand she hasn't. Her medical treatments are still her decision."

"Good."

"But he can put a lot of pressure on her to agree."

I must have looked determined or pissed off—probably both—because Ewan shifted from foot to foot. "Uh, hey, you didn't hear any of this from me, okay? I could lose my job if they find out I discussed confidential information with you."

I had been contemplating charging over to my aunt and uncle's place, but his comment brought me up short. I gritted my teeth and then sighed. "Okay."

He smiled, miming wiping sweat from his brow. He was kind of cute when he smiled. And really not *that* skunk-like.

I resolved to say something to Mum next time I spoke to her. If she didn't already, she should know what was going on. I wouldn't put it past my uncle to ask her to give him the authority to make her medical decisions without explaining why, and she was so scattered she

might well agree. He would do it out of love for her; he wasn't a monster, just arrogant. Uncle Ian knows best. And, for as long as I'd been alive, he'd found Mum's passive existence frustrating at best and infuriating at worst.

I understood how he felt. But I couldn't support forcing her to change.

Ewan moved past me to close the curtains so the sun wouldn't shine into Mum's face as it inched down the pallid sky. Then we walked side-by-side out of the room.

"So why did you?" I asked, speaking in a quiet voice, even though the corridor was almost deserted, the television sounds from the hall distant. I couldn't shake the feeling someone was listening in on our every word. He'd made me paranoid.

"Tell you?" he murmured.

I nodded.

"Because I think the patient's wishes should be respected, no matter what," he said simply.

"Good answer."

"Excuse me? Nurse?" A middle-aged woman stepped out of the rec room as we approached. She wasn't one of the residents if her flyaway hair and a brightly patterned coat Serenity would've been proud of were anything to go by. She was also cradling a miniature poodle in one arm. The unexpected sight of it made me blink. "May I have a word?"

"Of course," Ewan said. He turned to smile at me, and I smiled back. Maybe he wasn't that bad after all. "See you next time."

Chapter Three

"*Is* he cute?"

I nearly choked on my beef and black bean.

Jen and I sat on the end of my bed. My flatmate wore a loose T-shirt, bright cat-print pyjama pants and a worn cardigan that used to be blue but had faded to the colour of a foggy morning. I was still in my jeans and jumper after my visit to Mum, although I'd swapped the boots out for two layers of socks.

We were eating dinner in my bedroom because it was the only place in the apartment where there were no reflective surfaces. The furniture was timber, the bedside lamp colour-coated metal. I'd even taken the light fitting down and put it in the top of the linen cupboard, so the room was lit by a bare energy-saver bulb whose exterior was a matte white. It was a pain mounting the fitting for rental inspections, but I wasn't willing to risk being spied on while I was sleeping. Or naked.

So whenever Jen and I wanted to discuss anything

Oneiroi-related, we did it in my bedroom.

"Well, is he?" Jen prompted.

"Ewan?" I gasped, choking down my Chinese.

"Duh. Who else?"

"Why? Are you interested?"

She tipped her head to the side, blond ponytail swinging. "No. Maybe. I don't know. Are you?"

"No!"

Jen raised her eyebrows behind her black-rimmed, rectangular glasses. They framed the blue-grey of her eyes and made her look like a cute librarian. "I've just never heard you say anything nice about him before now. I thought maybe..." She shrugged.

"He's never really done anything nice before. We wave politely while I snigger about his haircut behind my other hand."

"It's that bad?"

"He looks like a brown and blond badger." At least I'd promoted him from skunk.

"A cute badger?"

"He's alright, I guess. Not my type. He might be yours, though." I considered it, eating another mouthful of the savoury beef. "Do you want me to see if he's single?"

She took a bite from a spring roll and chewed thoughtfully, staring at the poster on the wall. It was a print of an oil painting: a wet pavement mirroring the trees and streetlights above, done in vivid yellows, greens, purples and oranges. I liked it because the colours were cheery despite the rainy night it depicted.

The irony of my having a painting of a reflection in a place where I avoided real ones wasn't lost on either of us.

"Sure, why not?" Jen said with a lopsided shrug. "If

he is, give him my number. I'm curious to see this legendary haircut, and what have I got to lose?"

"Your virginity?" I winked. She poked me in the arm with a chopstick. "Ow!"

"You deserved it," she said.

I grinned, unrepentant. "I know."

"So did you ask your mum about the blight?" Jen was the only one I'd ever told about my peculiar family history, the only one other than me and my mother—and the Oneiroi, I guess—who knew the real reason she slept so much. My flatmate hadn't believed me at first, but my ability to walk in her dreams had provided some pretty conclusive evidence. And she enjoyed the perks of reliably good dreams.

I nodded. "She didn't know anything. She's going to ask Ollie."

My poker face must have failed me, because Jen's expression grew sympathetic. "Have you ever considered going into your Mum's dreams? To ask him yourself?"

"I tried it once." I stabbed a piece of beef. It slid straight off the end of the chopstick back into the bowl. "I was thirteen and had just found out about Leander being a spy. I was furious."

"And?" she said.

"And it didn't work."

She blinked. "Why not?"

"I think he's put some sort of protection around Mum's dreams. It was like a wall. I could tell she was behind it, but I couldn't get in."

"It makes sense. If Leander could waltz in there any time he liked, he wouldn't need to harass you. He'd harass your mum instead."

"Yeah. She wouldn't be able to protect herself from him changing her dreams either. Ollie would be doing time in an Oneiroi prison by now." Another stab of the chopstick. "If I do ever get to talk to him, I want to find out how he did that. 'Cause Leander can still waltz into *my* dreams. Although he hasn't for a while, thank god."

Despite my mixed heritage, I still dreamed. But, like my mother, I was a lucid dreamer: I knew I was dreaming and could alter the dream if it didn't suit me. Because it was my dream, it didn't cost me anything to do it either. It defanged my nightmares, and meant my dreams were usually pleasant.

Unless I got a gatecrasher.

That night, seeking to escape the winter chill, I conjured up a summer beach. The sun shone down yellow rather than white, as if I were wearing sunglasses. The golden sand was soft and squeaked, pleasantly warm between my toes, as I walked down to the sighing waterline. A breeze scented with saltwater and hot eucalyptus stirred my hair against the nape of my neck and caressed my bare belly and arms. I wore a bikini, and the towel wrapped around my waist draped down my long legs.

The beach was deserted, the only footprints my own. Perfect. I unhitched the towel, let it drop to the dry sand beyond the waves' foam-laced fingers, and stepped into the briny water.

"You look good," a voice said behind me.

I whirled, almost falling into the water. My arms flailed, ungainly, as I caught my balance. "Leander!"

He wore emerald green board shorts that clung a little too tightly to his thighs, and his chest was bare so I could admire his lightly muscled physique. If I wanted to. Which I didn't. His wings fanned gently in the breeze, stirring up eddies in the sand. Locks of warm brown hair brushed the top of his shoulders.

"The one and the same. Have you missed me?" He puffed out his chest as my gaze ran over him. Leander was pretty and he knew it. If he could, he'd trade his grey moth wings for something vivid. Butterfly-like.

"No," I said.

"Not even a little bit?" His smile said he didn't believe me.

I folded my arms. The bikini that had been entirely appropriate a moment ago now seemed scandalously bare. I considered conjuring up a more concealing outfit—perhaps a nun's habit—but didn't want to give him the satisfaction of knowing he bothered me. "What do you want?" It was the same question I'd asked him the day before, and I suspected I'd get the same answer.

His wings drooped, but he regrouped fast. "Aren't you going to ask me where I was all these months?"

"Where have you been?" I picked up my towel and shook the sand out of it. He stepped back to avoid the scattered grains.

"I got summoned back to Greece by the Morpheus."

That got my attention; the towel fell still in my hands. Even the waves paused in their slide up and down the beach, casting a hush over the little stretch of coastline. "The god of dreams?"

He snorted a laugh, wings quivering like an insect in a pollen-gathering ecstasy. "No. Where did you hear that?"

"Oh, you know, ancient Greek myths about the Oneiroi. I can't imagine why I'd want to read *them*." I rewrapped the towel around my waist, tucking the ends in tightly

so it wouldn't fall open.

"Well, you can't believe everything you read." He flicked a few grains of sand off his shoulder.

I clenched my jaw, counted silently to ten, and then asked, "Who is Morpheus?"

"*The* Morpheus. It's a title, like a king. He's our ruler. When there's a queen it's the Morphea, but we have a king at the moment."

"And what did His Majesty want?"

"Ollie. Your father. He wanted to know why I hadn't caught him yet."

I knew it. Hands on my hips, I narrowed my eyes. "And now you're here to ask me for help?"

He nodded, not even having the good grace to look embarrassed.

"Honestly, you've got some nerve," I said. "He's my father. What makes you think I'm going to turn on him to help you?"

"My charming personality and our long friendship?" When I didn't return his smile, it melted like an ice cube on summer bitumen. His expression grew solemn, mouth turning down at the corners and eyes losing their sparkle. "Also, common sense. Your father's apprehension would benefit you too."

"How do you figure?"

"You'd get your mother back." He stepped forward to take my hands in his. Shocked at his words, I let him. His fingers were almost as warm as the sun-kissed sand. "It's not like he's earned your loyalty. What's he ever done for you?"

"Nothing," I said, then bit the inside of my cheek. Why had I said that? I hated admitting any emotional weakness

CASSANDRA PAGE

to Leander. I didn't trust him not to try exploiting it. "But Mum loves him," I added quickly.

"She loves you too. And Ollie monopolises her time, denies it to you."

I removed my hands from his grip. "That may be true—"

"It is."

"—but there's one thing I learned early, and that is life's not all about me. Taking Ollie from Mum would be selfish."

"What have either of them done to earn your self-sacrifice?" he murmured, running a thumb over the back of my hand. "Have either of them shown anything other than selfishness themselves? Did they ever give up what they wanted for the sake of their daughter?"

I turned away from him to stare out at the horizon. Storm clouds were brewing, responding to my mood. A breeze rushed towards the shore, whipping the caps of the waves into a white froth that inched further up the sand. The ocean's now-icy fingers snatched and tugged at my toes, sucking the sand from beneath me.

"Don't act like you're pushing this because of me, Leander," I growled. "You're being as selfish as you accuse them of being. We both know you don't want to do this to help me."

"I do. We would both benefit."

"Well, even if I wanted to help you, I couldn't." I clenched my hands into fists at my sides. "I don't know where he is. I never have. Now get the hell out of my head."

"Melaina..." He stepped forward to stand beside me. From the corner of my eye I saw him tense as a rush of cold water slid across his feet, but he didn't flinch.

"I mean it, Leander. Don't make me throw you out."

"Can I ask one thing before I go?" His voice was subdued.

"Don't expect me to answer it."

"You read books to learn about us. Why didn't you ask me?"

Surprised, I turned to face him, thinking he was mocking me. "It's not like you've been forthcoming with your motivations in the past."

His exotic emerald eyes, which I'd once found so appealing, were shadowed with regret, like the green heart of a jungle. "Are you ever going to forgive me for that?"

"I'm not sure. It's not every day a girl finds out her childhood friend was only pretending to be her friend because he was chasing her father." I tried to keep my tone light but the betrayal was there, under the surface.

"That wasn't the only reason." His shoulders slumped and guilt stirred in my chest, an unwelcome ache.

But before I could say anything, he left.

Chapter Four

"See you, Melaina! Thanks again."

I waved goodbye to the last of the class to leave: a first-time mother hoping deep breathing would get her through labour contractions. I'd never had a baby, but I didn't like her chances. I did, however, admire her optimism.

I locked the shop door behind her and turned the sign to CLOSED. Serenity was sick, so she'd asked me to run her weekly meditation class. It wasn't exactly my area of expertise—I was more of a tai chi and yoga kind of girl. But I'd needed the money, and the customers seemed happy enough. Apparently my visualisations were excellent.

I did a quick check of the store, turning out the lights and double-checking the windows out the back, even though they hadn't been opened in months. Serenity would have said I was being paranoid, but I didn't like locking up on my own, especially after dark. I'd already emptied the till earlier and put the money into our little

safe for the night. I glanced at my watch and sighed. If I left now, I'd make the quarter past nine bus. It would be a long trip home.

Most of the shops in the arcade were long-shut by this time on a Thursday night, faint security lighting lending the mannequins in a clothing outlet's window a sinister look. The bottle shop was still trading, but as I strode past, hands stuffed in pockets, I saw the store was empty. The eighteen-year-old working the register texted busily. I pulled my coat tighter and wrapped my tartan scarf around my neck till my reflection in the store window looked like a cloth-bound turtle. It had to be below freezing already. At least there wasn't a wind shoving frigid fingers through the gaps in the fabric.

The streets in this part of the city were lined with deciduous European trees whose naked branches reached for the sky, trying to catch the stars in their bony grips. A few autumn leaves that hadn't yet been swept away gathered in gutters or rattled along the street in my wake.

Miraculously, the bus arrived on time. I swung on board and took a seat halfway back, pulling a battered paperback out of my satchel. There were only two other people on the bus: a teenage boy plugged into an iDevice and an older woman in a supermarket uniform. She gazed out the window, her breath fogging the glass.

As the driver was about to shut the door, a man stumbled aboard, the sound of his boots hitting the metal stair audible over the growl of the bus's engine. I guessed he was in his mid-to-late twenties, and his clothing was … odd. Had he dressed in the dark? He wore crisp flannel pyjama pants paired with a woollen coat that had fallen open to reveal an untucked business shirt. His dark brown hair was askew, as though he'd just scrambled out of bed, and his eyes were glazed. If it weren't for the drug-addled expression, he'd have been attractive.

The man dumped a handful of coins on the tray. The driver frowned as he issued the ticket.

I pretended not to watch as the man stumbled up the aisle, but I didn't relax until he'd passed me, sitting two seats back. The older woman looked across at me, clenching her jaw and raising her eyebrows. I shrugged slightly. It was a free country—well, $4.60 if you paid the cash fare—and if the crazy man wanted to ride the bus he was allowed.

It was hard to read my book though. I couldn't help imagining the man's eyes fixed on the back of my head. My skin prickled with anxiety.

I was grateful when the bus finally rumbled onto the main road near my apartment, and even more grateful when I was the only one who got off. I glanced back as the bus pulled away from the curb and saw the strange man staring at me from the rear window.

Shivering, I hurried between the seventies-era blocks of flats, climbing the flights of stairs to our little two-bedroom apartment.

Jen was curled up on the couch with a furry blanket across her knees. She liked the blanket, saying it reminded her of her parents' cat. I'd never met the cat in question, and wondered if it was really big enough to cover her entire lap.

"How was work with the hippies?" she asked, stifling a yawn and straightening her glasses with a finger. She looked as if she'd been dozing over the magazine spread open on the blanket rather than reading it.

"Good." I slung my bag down beside the couch and went into our tiny kitchen. The room was "open plan", which was real estate agent for "part of the same room and only separated by a counter".

"Most of them aren't hippies," I said, putting the kettle on. "You'd be surprised how many regular folks we get."

"Closet hippies, probably. Literally. Closets full of tie-dyed flares and peace signs and whatever."

"You're just jealous."

"Totally." She grinned. Jen was in her third year of a medical degree. That was how we'd met; my degree and hers shared some early units. But she wasn't as uptight as some of the other students in our classes. Well, her classes, now. Her sense of fun was one of the reasons I loved her.

"Want a cup of tea?" I asked.

"No thanks. If I have any caffeine now I'll be up all night." She turned a page of the magazine and then covered a yawn with one hand. Fresh polish gleamed on her nails, a brilliant green that reminded me of Leander's eyes.

"If you want a cup I could help you get to sleep afterwards," I said.

Jen blinked. "That's sweet. But I'll do it the regular way, thanks."

I paused, carton of milk in one hand. "Sorry, was that weird?"

"Nah." She smiled. "I'll take you up on it at exam time. All those energy drinks make me crazed."

I laughed. "Speaking of, you should've seen this guy on the bus tonight." I told her about the man and his eccentric dress and vague expression, only exaggerating

33

a little for effect.

But she didn't find the story amusing. Her lips pursed with concern. "I wish you wouldn't catch the bus after dark."

"It's fine." I tried to sound reassuring, but her frown was sceptical. She mothered me almost as badly as Serenity did. "Besides, what choice do I have? I can't afford a car."

"You could borrow mine."

"How? Work's in the opposite direction to the uni. And there's no way I'm driving your car so *you* can catch the bus home."

Grumbling, Jen took herself to bed shortly afterwards. As soon as I'd finished the tea, the hot drink finally dispelling the winter chill from my belly, I did the same.

But the memory of the man on the bus stayed with me, so I double-checked the front door before I went to sleep.

Someone's hands wrapped around my throat.

For a fleeting second I thought it was a strange twist to my dream—Jen and I had been shopping for hippy clothes she could wear to her graduation ceremony. I tried to dismiss the sensation, but the dream wouldn't change.

Then I woke up with a gasp. *I wasn't dreaming.*

The clock radio cast the only light in my room. It was enough to see the black silhouette of someone above me. They knelt on top of the blankets, straddling my body,

their weight holding me down. Their hands hesitated on my throat, almost reluctant.

I screamed.

The intruder's hands clamped down.

Shit! Someone was trying to strangle me.

I writhed. My arms were trapped beneath the doona by my attacker's weight. I bucked my hips and thrashed my legs, freeing my feet, but I couldn't swing them up far enough to kick the hunched form.

Spots danced across my vision. I tried to exhale into my assailant's face, to put him to sleep with Oneiroi magic, but couldn't get a breath. Couldn't breathe. I was going to die—

The door flew open and dim light spilled into the room, showing that the silhouette above me was distinctly male. "Jesus!" Jen took one look at the situation and darted in, snatching up my bedside lamp and yanking the plug from the wall. She swung the base at my attacker's head. It connected with a meaty thump. When he didn't immediately let go, she swung again.

Jen used to play cricket. She had a good arm.

The man tumbled to the side, sprawling across my doona. Motionless.

I gulped one breath—the sweetest I'd ever tasted. Another, almost as good. Then I scrambled out from under the blanket, away from the unconscious figure.

"Are you okay?" Jen asked, her voice trembling as much as I was.

"Yes." I held one shaking hand to my throat and reached for the light switch with the other.

Light filled out the shadows, and Jen and I stared for a long moment. "That's your crazy man from the bus, right?" she said finally.

I nodded. He was dressed in the same assortment of clothes he'd been in when I saw him earlier. His muddy boots were messing up my doona cover.

And he'd tried to strangle me. My throat burned with the memory of his grip.

"The things you'll do to get a man in your bed." Jen's laugh sounded brittle. I couldn't even muster a smile. She handed me the lamp. "I'm going to call the police. If he moves, hit him again."

"What if you killed him?" I rasped as she left the room. It was hard to tell through his dark hair, but I thought he had the beginnings of a lump forming just above his temple.

"Good. Self-defence," Jen said from the corridor, her voice hard. The phone beeped as she turned it on.

"Ask for an ambulance too," I called after her. The words hurt my throat and I coughed. That hurt even more. Jen talked in an urgent tone to someone on the other end of the phone.

I stared at my attacker, gripping the lamp tightly. He appeared less crazy with his eyes closed. If I ignored the head injury, he looked as if he'd fallen asleep halfway through changing for bed, the tousled hair more appropriate in a bedroom setting than it had been on the bus. Faint stubble speckled a strong jaw and his soft lips were open slightly, relaxed, showing a glimpse of white teeth.

Was he breathing?

I couldn't tell, and the upturned collar of his coat obscured his throat, so I couldn't see whether he had a pulse. As much as I had no fondness for the man who'd tried to kill me, I didn't want someone dying in my bed

either. If he did I'd have to burn the mattress and linens, for a start, and I couldn't afford to replace them.

Plus I didn't want my best friend to be tried for murder. Manslaughter. Whatever.

Grimacing, I walked around the foot of the bed, the lamp cable swinging into my legs at each stride.

Please don't wake up. I licked my finger and placed it underneath his nose, in front of those parted lips. Warm air puffed onto my fingertip; I sighed with relief and pulled my hand away, frowning at the man. He smelled of soap. And his hair was clean. That wasn't how I expected a drug-addled attempted murderer to look.

He really *did* seem as if he was sleeping.

I took a step back, so the wardrobe door pressed against my shoulders, and closed my eyes. Then I touched his dreams.

I had only the faintest impression of the setting: an older house with worn linoleum tiles and faded wallpaper. And then, bellowing with pure fury, something leapt at me.

I jumped back, almost tripping over my feet, and yanked myself out of the dream just before the huge black creature ensnared me with jellyfish tentacles crusted with poisonous barbs. My ribs thumped hard into the wardrobe handle. There'd be a circular bruise there tomorrow. I'd have quite the collection.

"What the hell?" Jen appeared in the doorway, drawn by the thump. She held the phone idle in her hand, its light gone out. "What were you doing?"

"He wasn't awake." I swallowed hard to stop the cough before it started. My hands trembled even more violently now than they had when she'd first saved me.

She frowned. "Maybe you should sit down. The police will be here in a couple of minutes."

"I mean he wasn't awake when he attacked me. Jen, I think he was sleepwalking. He's blight-ridden!"

Chapter Five

I huddled on the couch, Jen's furry blanket on my lap and a tea towel-wrapped ice pack against my throat. My flatmate sat beside me, her gaze locked on my face. The paramedic had told her to make sure I stayed conscious, and she was taking the responsibility seriously.

The apartment was crowded, and I was glad the cold had convinced me to wear flannelette pyjamas to bed. In summer I slept in a T-shirt and underpants, if that.

One police officer examined the door to the balcony, which was wide open, dispersing all our carefully hoarded heat in an icy blast. The paramedics and the other officer were in my bedroom, loading my unconscious attacker onto a wheelchair-like contraption they called a "stair chair". When they wheeled him out, angled backwards so only the chair's back wheels touched the ground, I saw they'd strapped him in. A neck brace encircled his throat. His eyelids fluttered but he didn't wake.

Did the blight know what was going on? I'd never seen one that big before. I didn't know what it was capable of.

"He definitely came through here," the senior constable said, coming back in from the balcony. A man in his thirties, he'd introduced himself as David Nelson. Thankfully he closed the glass door behind him, although there was an expression about bolting horses and stable doors that seemed fitting.

"But we're two storeys up," Jen protested weakly. The sliding door's latch had been broken for months; we'd reported it to our landlord but nothing had been done. Until now we hadn't been too worried about it, relying on our elevation to protect us.

Not anymore.

"He climbed. He must have been pretty determined. Do you know him?" Nelson's tone was gentle, but his eyes were a steel grey that reminded me of handcuffs, making me feel unaccountably guilty as they regarded me. I was sure he wouldn't miss anything.

I shook my head, removing the ice pack for a moment. Jen winced, seeing the bruises on my throat. "He was on my bus. I think he followed me." My voice sounded husky, as if I were a pack-a-day smoker.

"Which bus was that?"

I gave him the route number and time, and he jotted it down in a notepad he'd pulled from his top pocket.

"And you'd never seen him before that?"

I shook my head again, grimacing as my fresh bruises protested.

"Did you want to come down to the station tomorrow to make a statement so we can press charges? Or can you do it now?" He glanced at his watch, and I read the

display on the DVD player behind him. It was after two in the morning.

I swallowed. It hurt. "I don't know if I want to. Make a statement, I mean."

Jen and the constable both stared.

"He's clearly crazy or something," I said, avoiding my flatmate's gaze. "Would you pressing charges result in him getting medical treatment?"

"It might," Nelson said, although from his pursed lips I wasn't sure he believed it. He glanced at his colleague, who waited by the front door.

I looked at my flatmate. "Can he press charges against Jen?"

"Don't you hold back because of me," she said, hands on her hips. "He was trying to kill you. Of *course* I hit him."

"Quite," the constable agreed, smiling slightly. The expression crinkled the skin around his eyes, softening his appearance. "Here, let me give you my details. You can always call tomorrow if you change your mind."

He wrote down his name and direct phone number on a blank sheet of paper and ripped it from the notepad, handing it to Jen.

After they'd closed the front door—Nelson locking it carefully before pulling it shut behind him—I smiled wearily at my flatmate. "I think he likes you."

"What?" She blushed. "No, he just—"

"Why'd he give you his number then? Rather than me?"

"Because your hands are wet from the ice pack?" she said.

"No, they aren't. Tea towel." I waggled one chilly hand at her as proof.

"Shut up, that's why. Besides, he was a bit old, wasn't he? He had grey hair here." She touched her temples thoughtfully. She'd clearly paid more attention to Senior Constable Nelson's appearance than I had. Then she stiffened as she realised what I'd done. "Don't change the subject, Melaina. Why aren't you pressing charges against that lunatic?"

"I told you, he's blight-ridden. And I don't think he was awake when he attacked me." I leaned my head back against the couch and closed my eyes, shivering a little.

"So he was, what? Sleepwalking?" Jen moved from my side and there was a click as she turned the heater on. It was an old electric wall heater that cost a packet to run, so we tried not to use it if we didn't have to. But I didn't argue. I'd been in walk-in freezers warmer than our apartment was now.

"I think so."

"And he sleep-caught the bus before sleep-climbing onto our balcony?"

I didn't blame her for her sarcastic tone. I wouldn't have believed it myself if I hadn't felt the pure fury of the blight when I'd touched the man's mind.

"Okay, maybe not sleepwalking in the traditional sense," I said, the warm air blasting across my frozen fingertips. The smell of heated dust itched my nose. "But I think the blight was in control. The guy may not even know what he did. It doesn't seem fair to charge him if that's the case."

She sat down beside me and I opened my eyes. Her expression was dubious. "What are we going to do then?"

"Tonight, sleep." The ache in my muscles went bone deep. "Tomorrow, I don't know. Try and figure out who he

is so I can attempt to drive the blight out of him, I guess."

Jen chewed her lip for a moment, her eyes narrowed as she pondered something. Shoulders dropping, she sighed. "His name is Brad Peterson."

I stared. "Do you know him?"

"No." Her lips twitched with amusement. "But his wallet was in his coat pocket, and I heard the cops talking about it when I went to the bathroom. They didn't know I was listening."

"You sly witch." I started to laugh, but it turned into another cough. "Ow."

"Now, in exchange for that piece of information, you're going to sleep with me tonight." Jen batted her eyelashes.

I stared at her, open mouthed.

"Your sheets are muddy, and the paramedics told me to monitor your breathing, so you can sleep in my bed. Just don't steal the covers." Her eyes twinkled. "Why, Melaina? What did you think I meant?"

A few minutes later, after Jen had wedged a broom handle in the track behind the balcony door so it couldn't slide open, we settled down into her queen-sized bed. The sheets smelled familiar since we used the same washing powder, but also faintly of Jen's apple-scented body wash. It was a comforting aroma, soothing my jangling nerves.

The last thing I saw before I fell asleep was Jen's watchful eyes, counting each breath I took.

43

When I woke, the window was on the wrong side of the bed. For a moment I was confused, fatigue clouding my thoughts, but then I remembered. I wasn't in my bedroom. The other half of the bed was empty.

I touched my throat gingerly with one finger and shivered. Last night had been a close call. If Jen hadn't been home, or hadn't heard me scream...

The sound of her voice approached. That's what had woken me, I realised foggily. She came into the room, my mobile pressed to her ear. She'd left her blond hair out today and it fell in waves halfway down her back. "Hang on a sec, I'll put her on."

I sat up, stretching. The muscles in my arms and torso ached, a counterpoint to the throbbing in my throat. Then I took the phone, glancing at the display. MUM. I stared at Jen, wondering what she'd told her. My flatmate sat on the edge of the bed, smiling innocently.

Everything then. Crap.

"Hi Mum." I tried to sound cheerful rather than resigned, but it didn't work.

"Oh sweetie, are you alright?" I couldn't remember the last time she'd sounded this engaged.

"I'm okay."

"Jen told me what happened—"

"Of course she did," I said.

"Why didn't you call me last night?"

"Because it happened at two in the morning and we were fine. I didn't want to wake you." *As if the staff could have, even if they'd tried.*

"Jen said you were injured."

I gave Jen a dark look. "Nothing serious. A few bruises."

"She also said you didn't want to press charges against

the guy that attacked you."

I ran my free hand through my hair. It was a mess. My longing for a shower was physical, like a compass point drawn north. "Did she tell you why?"

"No..."

"The guy who attacked me was blight-ridden. I'm pretty sure the blight was in control at the time. It was probably trying to avenge the one I beat up the other day." I met Jen's gaze, but she pulled a face and turned away, removing a shawl draped over her dresser mirror to check her makeup.

My paranoia about reflections was contagious.

"Well, then." Mum paused. I could almost hear her thinking. "That makes sense. Are you going to try and help the poor man?"

"Yeah. We're going to the hospital later to see if we can get rid of it."

"Jen's going with you?" she asked.

"I think so."

"Good. She's got a good head on her shoulders."

Gee, thanks, Mum. "Did you ask Ollie about blights? I've never seen one that big before," I said.

"Uh, yes, I did. That's one of the reasons I called you." She hesitated, and then a male voice spoke, asking if she was finished with breakfast. Her reply was muffled. She must have covered the phone.

When she spoke to me again she picked her words carefully. "They're parasites. Transmitted via eggs."

"Was that all he said?"

"No."

"But you can't say anything else right now?"

"That's right, honey. Next time you come and see me,

we can talk some more."

I closed my eyes, exhaling slowly. It was frustrating, but there wasn't anything I could do about it right now. "Okay. Oh, hey, you said one of the reasons you called. What was the other?"

"Oh, it doesn't matter now," she said, sounding embarrassed.

"Mum..."

"It's just that your uncle wanted to change some of the arrangements for my care, and I wanted to talk to you about it."

Ice crystallised in the pit of my stomach, and I was grateful to Ewan for his warning. "He suggested you give him enduring power of attorney, didn't he?"

There was a long pause on the other end of the line. "How did you know?"

"It doesn't just cover financial stuff, Mum. If you grant it he can make medical decisions for you. Like whether the doctor can give you antidepressants or caffeine pills or god only knows what else."

"He wouldn't do that!"

"Then why do you think he's asking for it?" I said, trying to keep my voice gentle. "Doctor Willis wants to try a drug treatment program. Uncle Ian knows about it. I'm sure he thinks it's for your own good." My words reminded me sharply of my conversation with Leander about self-ishness. Uncle Ian wanted his sister back, regardless of her wishes. It seemed everyone was trying to "help" some-one else for his or her own self-centred reasons.

Maybe that was how the world worked.

Apparently, someone trying to kill me the night before had put me in a cynical mood. I shook my head to dislodge

the negative thoughts, staring at the curtained window without seeing it.

I realised we'd both fallen silent. "Are you there?" I asked, feeling bad that I had upset her.

"Yes ... yes. I think you're wrong about your uncle." But the quaver in her voice gave lie to the words.

"Maybe I am," I said, "but I'd still suggest not giving him that enduring power of attorney."

"I'll have to think about it." She stifled a yawn. "Listen, I have to go. Promise me you'll take care if you go to the hospital."

"I promise. Love you."

"Love you too."

Chapter Six

A shower helped. Fortunately Jen had been up for hours, because I used all the hot water washing the grime and my bad mood away. Jen loaned me a soft scarf. My woollen ones were scratchy against my tender skin, but I didn't want people staring at the bruises, which were starting to blossom a purplish-blue. Then we drove to the hospital in her beaten-up old car.

It wasn't hard to find Brad Peterson's room. The staff were happy to give us his room number, especially because Jen had the presence of mind to buy a small bunch of flowers before we asked for directions.

On his floor, she peeked into the open door of each ward as we passed. What was she doing? Finally she grinned. "Perfect." Inside, a woman who had to be in her eighties lay in her bed, leg in a cast. She watched a tiny television mounted on the wall in a listless, glassy-eyed fashion, but roused herself and frowned as we entered.

"Do I know you?"

"No, ma'am," Jen said. "I just wanted to ask if you'd like some flowers to cheer this place up?"

The woman's smile brightened the room so much that she didn't really need the flowers anymore. But we gave them to her anyway.

Once we were back in the corridor I gave my friend a puzzled look. "What was that all about?"

"Well, I don't want to give the flowers to the guy who tried to murder you, do I? Why not cheer someone up who looks lonely?"

I hid my grin behind my hand.

The smile dropped off my face, though, as we approached the room we'd been directed to. The door was open and there was no sign of a police guard. But then, I hadn't made a statement, which meant they might not be able to press charges—so should there be? I didn't know. My stomach flipped, quivering with nerves, even though I knew Peterson didn't intend me any harm when he was awake.

Well, I was pretty sure, anyway.

Maybe.

Jen took my hand. "You don't have to do this if you don't want to."

"If I don't, he could be back tomorrow. I have to deal with the blight. But do I *want* to?" I shook my head, uneasy. "Not really, no. It was freaking huge."

"If he tries anything I'll hit him again. Does that make you feel any better?"

I laughed softly. "A little, yeah."

"Okay. Let's go."

She led me through the open door like a mother leading her child.

The room had two beds, the one closest to the window

screened by a drawn curtain. Peterson was in the one closest to the door. He and his visitor, an attractive brunette not much younger than him, looked up as we entered.

"If you're here to visit Maggie, she's asleep," the woman said, gesturing to the closed curtain. Her other hand gripped Peterson's as if it were a bird that might fly away.

He looked at me, no light of recognition in his eyes as his held an ice pack to the side of his head. Without the crazy look he'd had the night before, he looked handsome, if pale and tired.

Jen raised her eyebrows at me expectantly.

"Uh, no, actually." I paused and swallowed, hoping to clear the rasp from my throat. It didn't work. "We're here to see him. Brad."

"Do I know you?" he asked.

Jen laughed. The sound had a hard edge I was pretty sure was outrage.

"Not exactly," I said, fidgeting with the end of my scarf. "What do you remember about yesterday evening?"

"Not a damned thing," he said. His eyes widened. "Was it you that I...?"

"Little bit. Yeah."

He sat in stunned silence for several beats of my heart—although it was racing, so maybe that wasn't very long at all. Then he said, "I'm sorry. For whatever I did." The remorse and self-loathing that tightened his jaw and made his voice hoarse seemed genuine.

Jen didn't care. "You tried to strangle her."

"I don't remember!"

"So you say." She scowled.

"Jen." I put my hand on her arm. "I believe him. I told you, he wasn't in control." Biting my lip, I glanced at the

man in his hospital bed. I wouldn't normally go into the more … unusual details, but I couldn't risk him refusing to let me help. "It was the blight."

"The what?" Peterson said, jerking upright.

Eyes widening at his sudden movement, I suppressed the urge to flee. Jen noticed anyway. She stepped forward protectively, her free hand balling into a fist.

"How about we all take a breath," the brunette said hastily, "and start again? My name is Belinda and this is Bradley. Brad." Belinda and Bradley. Cute. "And you are?"

"I'm Melaina. And this is Jen," I said when it became apparent Jen wasn't going to speak.

"Hi. Why don't you make yourselves comfortable and tell us what you're talking about?"

There weren't any extra chairs near Brad's bed. Jen crept behind the closed curtain and borrowed one from the sleeping Maggie. "We'll put it back when we leave," she whispered in response to my raised eyebrows. "Now sit. You're still injured." She narrowed her eyes at Brad pointedly.

He lifted a stubble-covered chin, but a blush shaded his ears and his throat turned scarlet. Clearly he didn't know whether to be offended or ashamed.

I sat, grateful she'd put the chair at the end of the bed where Brad couldn't easily reach me. As much as I knew he hadn't been in control last night, the memory of those strong hands crushing the breath from my throat was powerful enough to make my hands shake. I folded them in my lap.

What if the blight was able to knock him out the way I could, and then take over? The thought made me queasy.

"Tell us what happened," Belinda said.

"I woke up and Brad was sitting on my bed. On me." My voice was flat as I fought to keep the remembered panic from my voice. "He tried to strangle me." I lowered the scarf for a moment, to show them the bruises. They both gasped and Belinda's free hand touched her own throat. I doubted she was even aware of the gesture. But her other hand stayed in Brad's.

"So I hit him with a lamp," Jen said with satisfaction. "Twice."

"Then we called an ambulance," I added.

"And the police." Brad's brow furrowed as he glanced from me to Jen.

"Well, yeah," Jen said. "You climbed up two storeys and broke into our apartment, then tried to kill her. So, you know, police."

"I didn't give them a statement," I added weakly.

Brad blinked, seeming to consider that as he dropped the ice pack onto a side table. "Why are you here?" he said eventually, voice weary and shoulders drooping. "If it's to get an apology, you've got one. If it's to hate me—" His eyes shifted to Jen, who clenched her jaw. "—I'd prefer you left. You can do that from elsewhere."

"I'm here because it wasn't your fault," I said, my gaze steady on him. "I don't hate you. And I can help."

"Why?" he said.

"To make sure it doesn't happen again. And because it's what I do."

"She's a regular superhero," Jen said with a grim smile that didn't reach her eyes. They were narrowed behind her glasses as if she was thinking about belting Brad with the chair. Maybe she was.

"Help? How?" Belinda leaned forward, wide eyes intent

on my face.

"You've been sleepwalking for a while, right?" I asked. "Having blackouts, waking up somewhere other than your bed?"

Brad grimaced and then nodded. I don't think he liked admitting his weakness to me. Maybe to anyone.

Still, he'd confirmed my suspicions—his blight had moved in a while ago, made itself comfortable. Grown fat on his nightmares. "It's because you're blight-ridden," I said. He raised an eyebrow, so I added, "Possessed."

He barked a laugh that contained exactly no humour. The fingers of the hand Belinda wasn't holding curled in the hospital blanket till the knuckles turned white. "You're an exorcist?"

"Not exactly. Blights aren't demons. They're spirits." *As far as I know.* Best not to add that.

"Right," he said, and I was surprised one word could be so heavy with scepticism.

"There's no religion to what I do, only skill. I'm a dream therapist." That was the title Serenity had given to me when I'd first rented the back room of her store. It sounded less flaky than some of the alternatives, but Brad narrowed his eyes anyway. "I've done this before. In fact, I drove a blight out of a client a couple of days ago. His wasn't as ... established as yours, though. He was having nightmares, not trying to kill people."

"Brad used to just have nightmares. Didn't you?" Belinda said, looking at the man in the bed. He nodded reluctantly. "Why don't you give her a chance? Maybe she can help."

"What qualifications do you have?" he asked.

I didn't need psychological training to read between

the lines. He was calling me a liar. "I have experience."

"Brad..." Belinda said softly, her eyes pleading.

"No," he said, releasing her hand to rub his face, his fingers scraping over new stubble. Then he met my gaze. His irises were a brown I would have described as "warm" under other circumstances. "Look, I'm sorry about what happened. But I need medical help. From medical doctors. Not voodoo magic. Now, please go. I have a rotten headache."

I stood, shoving my fists into the pockets of my jacket. My nails dug into my palms so hard I knew I'd leave a line of crescents, but I didn't seem able to stop myself. I was outraged and embarrassed in equal measure. Brad was lucky I didn't practice voodoo right then. Still, I managed to keep my voice even when I spoke. "I'm sorry you feel that way."

I turned to leave but Jen hung back, her eyes as hard as a frozen lake. "Sorry about the headache," she said in a voice that contained no signs of remorse, "but if you come back to our apartment I won't just hit you next time. I don't care if you're not the one in control."

"Let's go," I said, dragging her out of the room.

"I can't believe the nerve of that guy," she declared as we walked along the corridor to the lifts. A nurse glanced up at us from her station. Jen lowered her voice. "I mean, you're trying to help him."

I ran a hand through my hair, then examined my palm. Yup, crescents. "I *have* to help him. If the blight has it in for me, he'll be back."

Jen stared at me, eyes wide. "Definitely?"

"I'm pretty sure. The blight targeted me the first time. It wasn't random—it followed me home from the store.

Where I treated Larry."

She swore. "So what do we—"

"Hey, wait!"

We turned. Belinda hurried down the corridor after us, heels clicking on the tiles.

"I'm sorry about Brad. He's a stubborn arse sometimes."

"We noticed," Jen said before I could speak. I gave her a reproachful look. Usually *I* was the tactless one. "Is Melaina the first person he's hurt?"

"That I know of," Jen whispered. "He needs help. We both know it. But we've tried psychologists and doctors, and none of them have been able to do anything. We're desperate!" She wrung her hands, a gesture that telegraphed her anxiety more clearly than her words did.

"He said no," I pointed out.

"Well, yes. But I want to know…" She hesitated, then said quickly, "Do you need his permission?"

"Yes."

"That's not true, Melaina," Jen said, teeth flashing in a sudden grin. "You could just—*poof*. Put him to sleep, and then deal with it."

Belinda blinked.

"Yeah, but it wouldn't be right."

My flatmate put her hands on her hips and stared at me, her smile sliding away. "That is the dumbest thing you've ever said. You just told me the blight will try and get you again. Next time it might actually kill you. What if it attacks while you're alone? Or brings a knife? A gun?"

I nodded reluctantly. My throat throbbed after the amount of talking I'd done, the pain grimly underlining what she was saying.

"Maybe it's time to get over the ethical squick-factor

of it and get it done?" Jen turned to Belinda, her earlier hostility towards the woman apparently forgotten. "When does he leave the hospital?"

"Later today. We're just waiting on the doctor to all clear the head injury so he can be discharged." Belinda managed to say that without giving Jen a reproachful look. I was impressed at her restraint.

"Can you get us into his house?"

"We share a place, so yeah," she said. Her face was pale. Was she reconsidering approaching us? "What do you need?"

Jen glared at me till I answered reluctantly. "Nothing. He doesn't need to be asleep when I get there, although if you don't want him to boot us to the curb it might be a good idea if he is."

"Can you come over tonight?"

I chewed my bottom lip. What was the alternative? Lying awake every night waiting for Brad to sneak or smash his way into our apartment and try again? Wondering if next time the blight would come for me at work? Or try to run me down on the street?

Next time he might succeed in killing me. Or hurt someone else. Jen. Serenity. *My mum.*

Jen was right. Ethics be damned.

"We'll be there."

Chapter Seven

We pulled up out the front of Belinda and Brad's house at just after eight that night. Belinda's call to say Brad was asleep had come sooner than we'd expected, although it wasn't really a surprise when I thought about it. Hospitals weren't exactly the most restful places in the world. The beds were uncomfortable, and nurses came in at all hours of the night to take your pulse, give you pain medications or just to poke you to make sure you were breathing.

Plus he'd been busy beforehand, what with the attempted murder.

We were about to get out of the car when my phone rang. It startled me so much I dropped it into the foot well and had to dive for it before the message bank picked up.

UNCLE IAN (H), the display read.

Peachy. I stabbed the answer button harder than I needed to. "Hi. What's up?"

"What's *up*?" Uncle Ian's deep voice boomed in my

ear, making me wince. "I spoke to your mother. She told me what happened. Why didn't you call?"

That surprised me. It wasn't that my uncle was a monster, but he had never been particularly warm towards me. I guess I hadn't expected he'd care much.

"Sorry, it's been a crazy day." It wasn't even a lie. "But I'm alright."

"Good. Have you spoken to the police yet?"

"Yeah. Last night." Another not-lie. I was two for two!

"If you need a lawyer, your Aunt Lacey can recommend one."

"Nah, I don't think I'll be needing one," I said, my gaze straying to the front porch of Brad's house. If he decided to sue me for what I was about to do, I might. But then, what would he tell the court? That I entered his dreams without permission? It didn't seem likely. And it wasn't like we were breaking into the house. We'd been invited.

"Well, let me know." There was a pause, and then he said, "Listen, what are you doing tomorrow for lunch? Why don't you come over?"

"I could, I guess." I squirmed in my seat. Meals with my uncle and his family were always awkward. He and his wife disapproved of what they thought of as my "alternative phase". I couldn't explain without outing myself as a half-Oneiroi, and they wouldn't believe it even if I did.

"Excellent. I want to talk to you about Davina's treatment." Then he clarified, as though I might not know whom he meant. "Your mother's."

A cold feeling crept over me, entirely unrelated to the frigid air breathing condensation onto the car windows. "Okay. Look, I have to go." The house's porch light was

on, shedding a yellow glow over the bricked entryway. The narrow window beside the door framed Belinda's silhouette.

"See you tomorrow at eleven-thirty?"

"Yup."

After I hung up, I stared at the phone for a few moments. The cold feeling had settled into my stomach, forming a nauseating lump. That was the real reason Uncle Ian had called. The attack last night had given him an excuse, something to get me to lower my guard. Had Mum told him I'd mentioned the antidepressants? That would definitely explain it.

My stomach churned, and disappointment tasted bitter on my tongue. For a moment I'd thought he cared.

"Are you okay?" Jen asked. "What was that about?"

"My uncle wants me to come over tomorrow for lunch so he can pressure me to convince Mum to take drugs she doesn't want," I said, shoving my phone into my pocket with unnecessary force.

"Are you serious?"

"Yeah. I wish I wasn't."

I took a few deep breaths of the icy air as we walked up the path to the house, my breath fogging in front of me as if I were a dragon letting off steam. With the toe of my boot, I scuffed a blade of grass that poked through a crack in the concrete, turning it into a dark smear. I wished I could do the same to my uncle ... but I needed to focus now. I could concentrate on my outrage later.

The house was in a nicer part of a fairly average suburb. The rent here was probably double what Jen and I were paying for our little apartment. My wannabe assassin or his girlfriend must have a well-paying job.

We climbed several stairs to the concrete porch, which was lined with potted plants. A couple of wicker chairs sat beside a small table.

Belinda held the screen door open and urged us inside, closing the door on our heels. "Sorry," she said in a low voice. "It's freezing out there."

Jen and I both sighed with relief, removing gloves and coats. Acting out of enlightened self-interest, I left my scarf on. I wasn't ashamed of the bruises around my throat, but it might make Belinda uncomfortable, and I didn't want her throwing us out before I'd done what we came to do.

"You have a lovely home," Jen said with a pleasant smile.

"Thanks," Belinda said, showing us into the lounge room. Jen and I sat together on a worn leather couch. "It's our family home."

"Your..." Jen frowned. "Yours and Brad's family?"

Belinda nodded, taking the other seat. "Our parents left it to us, and we both live here. We thought about selling, but..." She shrugged.

"Oh," I said, feeling stupid.

"Oh?"

I glanced at Jen, and she raised a manicured golden eyebrow at me. I was on my own. "We sort of assumed you were a couple, actually."

Belinda's eyes widened, horrified. How had I not noticed they were the same shade of brown as his? "Brad and me? Ick! No! He's my brother."

"Well, I know that *now*," I said with an apologetic grin. "Where is he?"

"In his room. Would you like a coffee or anything?"

I shook my head, but Jen accepted the offer. I wished she'd said no so we could get onto dealing with Brad, but reminded myself we had to keep Belinda on side to get this done. Accepting her hospitality was definitely more diplomatic than walking in the door and demanding I be taken straight to his room. "I thought you couldn't have caffeine at night," I teased Jen instead as Belinda moved around in the kitchen, visible through an open doorway.

My flatmate's gaze, when she turned to me, was sober, her smile having slipped away. "I want to be alert for this. In case, you know..."

"It'll be fine," I said.

"Are you sure? You did say it was a big blight."

"Of course I'm sure."

I suspected Jen didn't believe me—I know I didn't—but she kept silent. Her support was reassuring. She wouldn't be able to help me fight the blight in Brad's dreams, but if he got out of bed and tried to hurt me physically... A mental image of her beating Brad over the head with his tallboy made me snort a laugh. Jen gave me a curious look, but I shook my head at her as Belinda returned, holding two steaming mugs. Jen's had a picture of Garfield on it.

I fidgeted as the two of them sipped their hot drinks and made small talk, folding my coat over the arm of the chair. The pocketful of caramels bulged on one side, a pointed, plastic-wrapped reminder of why we were here.

The truth was, I'd never dealt with a blight as big as Brad's before. I wished I'd asked Leander about them when I'd spoken to him. But, of course, I hadn't seen him since Brad had attacked me, and I hadn't had a reason to ask him beforehand.

Maybe he was hanging around now.

"Excuse me," I said, interrupting a conversation about landscaping, "do you mind if I use the bathroom?"

"Of course not," Belinda said. "Second door on the left."

"Thanks."

The back end of the house was dark. One of the bedroom doors, the one at the far end of the hall, was closed. Brad's room, presumably. The door loomed large before my eyes as I hesitated at the top of the corridor, wondering whether to turn the light on, or whether that would wake him. Was he a sound sleeper? Was the blight?

My hesitation reminded me of a time when, as a teenager, I'd stayed up late reading a Stephen King novel and then had to turn on all the lights to go to bed. I shook my head, feeling like an idiot, and hurried down the corridor to the bathroom.

But I did sigh with relief when I locked the bathroom door behind me.

The bathroom was done up in a cream-and-peach pattern that didn't seem to suit the house's current occupants. The vanity glittered, empty except for a faux-timber soap dispenser. I turned the tap on to cover the sound of my voice, feeling a pang at the waste of water, and leaned in close to the mirror. My reflection loomed back at me. The scarf hid the bruises around my throat, but I still looked like a person who'd had a fright: my skin was paler than usual, and my eyes had dark rings under them, as though I hadn't slept well. Which, of course, I hadn't. The blue in my fringe seemed to glow in the light.

"Are you there, Leander?" There was no answer. I repeated his name a couple more times. Finally, I grew

frustrated. My sharp expletive fogged the mirror. "Come on, you overgrown insect. Turn up when I need you for a change!"

If anything would have brought out the Oneiroi, it would have been an admission that I needed him for anything. But he still didn't appear. I guessed he wasn't there after all.

"Damn," I whispered, turning off the tap.

The sound of quiet footsteps in the corridor outside the room made me jump, whirling to put my back against the basin. My heart leapt into my throat.

Then there was a tap on the door. "Are you okay?" a voice asked. I exhaled with relief. It was Jen.

"Holy crap, don't scare me like that!" I opened the door.

Jen had turned the hall light on, and the glow illuminated her wide-eyed expression. "Like what, exactly?"

"I thought you were B..." Belinda was standing behind Jen. I amended what I was about to say. "The blight."

"Well, I'm not." She raised her eyebrows archly, but also reached out to squeeze my hand. "Anyway, we're ready if you are."

I nodded and we turned to face the closed bedroom door.

Chapter Eight

$\mathcal{I}$ stood back as Belinda turned the handle, easing the door open and creeping into the bedroom. Jen and I followed.

This was the first time I'd snuck into a guy's bedroom, and here I was doing it with two other women, one of them his sister. I felt like I should be holding a glass of warm water or a permanent marker, so I could execute a prank of some kind.

Except my heart thumping in the back of my throat tasted of fear rather than excitement.

Light from the hallway spilled into the room. Our shadows danced on the wall and the carpet muffled our creeping footsteps.

Brad's room reminded me of my own, although it was larger. The basket of clean, unfolded clothes was similar, as were the casually discarded shoes by the wall, and the side table piled with books. His bedside lamp looked newer than mine, though. And less dented.

Jen's gaze strayed to the lamp and her eyes narrowed with satisfaction. I hoped Belinda didn't notice.

When I turned my attention to the bed, I froze. It looked as if a spider had attacked Brad, tangling him in its web. Already fresh in my mind, thoughts of the monster from *It* made me shiver … until I realised Brad had tied his left ankle to the foot of the bed with a length of soft white rope. His leg protruded from the blanket at an uncomfortable angle. It was a sign of how tired he was that he'd managed to fall asleep anyway.

I reminded myself I wasn't the only one who hadn't slept much the night before. My fear of Brad attacking me, blight-ridden, must pale in comparison to his sickening awareness of his own actions. I wasn't sure how I'd have coped with it, especially if I believed as he did that it was caused by mental illness rather than supernatural interference. What would it be like to look at yourself in the mirror and wonder if you harboured subconscious, murderous urges?

Sympathy moved my feet where determination hadn't. I tiptoed over to stand by Brad's head. Jen was a reassuring presence at my side. I glimpsed her hands, curled into fists, only partly hidden by the long cuffs of her jumper. Belinda, chewing her lip, stood by a chest of drawers.

I leaned over the bed.

Brad's eyes flew open, flashing with rage. His hands launched towards my throat. Jen swore. Belinda gasped.

And I exhaled quickly, breathing Oneiroi sleeping magic.

For a moment I thought it wasn't going to work, that the blight was immune to my talent. Brad's hands wavered by my throat, fingers working the air. The fury slid from his face, leaving only puzzlement. Then he collapsed back against his pillow, sound asleep.

"Thank god," Jen whispered, her voice cracking. From the corner of my eye, I saw her ease her hands back down to her sides.

"You can talk normally." My voice was steady, despite the adrenalin fizzing in my veins. Go me. "He should stay under now."

"He was going to..." Belinda slumped against the drawers. Even though she understood what her brother had done, I guess the reality hadn't sunk in. Till now. Her eyes were wide, horrified, and the hand pressed to her lips trembled.

"I know," I said, smiling to soften my words. "Look, you don't have to stay here. Jen, why don't you take her back out to the lounge? I don't know how long this will take. It could be half an hour, or more."

"I should stay," Belinda said. "For Brad."

Jen nodded, giving me a dark look. She clearly didn't appreciate me trying to send her away.

"Alright, then. Let's get this show on the road."

Now Brad was safely in a deep sleep, we arranged the room to our satisfaction. I turned on the bedside lamp. His sister fetched a couple of dining chairs so Jen and I could stay right by the bed; Belinda then kicked off her shoes and climbed onto the blanket to sit beside her brother, taking his hand.

"This is so weird," she said. "He used to do this for me when I was sick."

"He's older?" Jen asked.

Belinda nodded. "I'm twenty-five and he's twenty-eight.

I had pneumonia when I was a kid and he barely left my side."

The two of them continued their quiet conversation as I leaned forward to study the sleeping man's face. His jaw was clenched, even though the rest of his body was limp. The blight fighting my compulsion, or him fighting the blight? There was only one way to find out.

"Here goes." I reached into his dream as quietly as I knew how.

I found myself in a small, cold bedroom, dimly lit by what thin light managed to penetrate the cloudy window. A single bed with a wrought-iron frame stood against a wall. Floral wallpaper, scattered with feeding butterflies, peeled away from the plasterboard like flaking skin. A small suitcase sat at the foot of the bed, the lid open to reveal a small child's clothes. The rest of the room was bare and the door was closed.

I held my breath and listened. A faint sound arose from below, vibrating through the stained carpet under my feet. *Thump. Thump-thump.* The blight? Or Brad?

Creeping over to the door, I opened it, willing the rusted hinges not to squeal.

To my relief, they complied.

The hallway stretched out before me. A bare bulb shed a dirty light that spilled into the bedroom, revealing that the stains on the carpet underfoot were oily and black. Blight ichor. The wallpaper was not just peeling but torn in long strips, as if it had been lashed with a cat-o-nine-tails. An oval picture frame lay on the ground. I picked it up. An older couple smiled sweetly back at me through the cracks crazing the glass. She had her hair in a bun; he grinned toothily, still handsome despite the wrinkles. Laugh lines creased the corners of his eyes.

Wondering who they were, I returned the photo to its hook. Glass pattered to the carpet like rain.

Several other doors lined the corridor, all shut. I briefly listened at each—nothing—before moving to the stairwell.

The sounds were louder now, definitely coming from below. Thumping. A snarling, slathering sound. And a faint whimper. The blight *and* Brad.

Time to prepare myself for a fight.

I'd considered this beforehand, mindful of the barbed tentacles I'd glimpsed during our last encounter. Now I conjured myself a set of heavy motorcycle leathers: a black jacket and long pants, reinforced at the joints. Blue lightning bolts licked down the outside of each sleeve, a touch I hadn't consciously willed but that made me smile. A pair of heavy boots and my outfit was complete.

I considered giving myself a weapon, but decided against it. I'd never learned to fight with one, and if I gave my energy form then it could be taken from me. I didn't have that much to waste. Conjuring my armour had already left me lightheaded.

Steeling myself, I started down the stairs, trying to move as quietly as I could in motorcycle boots. I held my breath at each step, easing my foot down. *Now is a time when wings would be really handy.*

When I reached the landing, where the stairs doubled back on themselves, I was able to see into the room below.

It was an open plan kitchen and dining room that might have been a pleasant, homely space under other circumstances, but a blight infestation wasn't showing it at its best. Ichor dripped off benches and fixtures as though someone had sprayed the room with oil from a fire hose. The walls had been torn open in several places, revealing dark cavities filled with wiring and flakes of insulation. The light fitting bore several broken bulbs that resembled shattered glass eggs, and the windows were coated with grime, giving the room a gloomy cast. Something unsightly bubbled on the stove. I averted my eyes before I looked too closely.

Most of the chairs had been smashed to kindling. The sole survivor was positioned at the table. In the chair sat a small boy dressed in high-waisted jeans and an *Inspector Gadget* T-shirt. He cradled his arms against his chest, and his left ankle was bound to the metal leg of the table by a short length of wire. It bit into his flesh with rusted teeth.

Brad. Dreaming of his childhood.

Those same chocolate-brown eyes looked up at me, helpless and terrified. There was no recognition there.

"Help me!" he cried, his voice high with fear.

So much for the element of surprise.

With a hiss like escaping steam, the blight moved into view, as slow and inevitable as a glacier. It placed itself between the boy and me, boiling like a cloud of volcanic ash. Its eyes, the colour of tobacco stains, were as large as dinner plates. Tentacles hung below its central mass like an obscene jellyfish, barbs protruding from them at regular intervals.

The blight hadn't driven the tentacles into the floor of the house to feed on Brad's mind. It had corrupted this place so thoroughly it didn't need to.

We locked eyes and the blight hissed again. This time I made out a word. "*Oooneeeeiiiroiiiii.*"

"Not quite." I felt the shadow of wings flaring at my back as I attacked, hurling a plasma-purple bolt of power.

The blight struck at the same moment, a half dozen tentacles lashing out. Several were burnt away by my attack. The creature shrieked, high and furious.

One tentacle, singed, coiled around my forearm. The barbs bit into the leather. They didn't make it to my skin, but my arm was trapped.

The blight reeled me in, a fish on a line. My boots slipped and skidded on the stairs, trying to gain traction. I had to walk down or risk overbalancing. I took a reluctant step towards the creature. Then another. My heart thundered.

The blight laughed, a sound like sucking mud.

"Like hell," I growled.

The blue lightning bolt on the trapped arm flashed briefly to life. Electric fire rushed along the outside of my arm, superheating the air. The exposed skin on my hand was uncomfortably warm, but the tentacle blackened and fell to the carpet, charred cartilage and ash.

Triumph flared in my heart, even as a wave of weariness left my limbs feeling heavy.

"Look out!" Brad cried.

A dozen more tentacles flew towards my face.

I threw my arms up—*should have conjured a helmet too!*—and several tentacles crisped and fell. The rest wrapped around both arms and yanked.

I fell forward with a scream. My boots thudded against the linoleum tiles, jarring my knees. I used the momentum

of my fall, twisting sideways and yanking on the tentacles. My body weight swung the blight ponderously through the air. Hovering, it was unable to brace itself. It slammed into the wall beside the stairwell. Plasterboard shattered. Tentacles loosened and I wormed free, the sleeves of my jacket shredded by the barbs. Strips of leather hung loose like flapping skin.

I ducked under the dining table, slashing at the wire-bound table leg with the flat edge of my hand, imagining my fingers were razor-sharp.

The dream complied. The wire split with a twang, freeing the boy's ankle, and a wave of dizziness shook me in its grip like a dog with a rat, punishing me for yet another change to the dreamscape.

I couldn't keep this up. I had to end it.

When I could see again, Brad was kneeling under the table, shaking me by the shoulder. "Lady, hurry! It's coming!"

The blight had pulled itself free of the wall and was drifting closer, its stately progress at odds with the writhing tentacles beneath it. Sallow yellow lights flickered within its clouds, an obscene thunderstorm. "*Braaad-ddlleeeey*," it hissed.

"Stay behind me," I said. "Now … *go!*"

We scrambled back on hands and knees, the filth on the floor caking my palms. The tentacles whipped forward again, targeting Brad. I kicked the table over, blocking their way. The barbs slammed into the laminate tabletop like darts.

I didn't wait to see whether they'd punched through, jumping to my feet and looking around for a weapon.

My gaze fell on the bubbling pot of ooze on the stovetop.

I snatched it up, hurling the contents at the seething mass of the blight's body. It screeched, infuriated, as the scalding liquid passed into its cloudlike form, followed by the hot metal pot.

Its smouldering eyes turned from Brad back to me. I hadn't killed it, and I'd pissed it off. Goody.

It yanked its tentacles free of the table and came towards me. As soon as it was in range, it lashed out again. I grabbed at the tentacles with my bare hands, ignoring the sharp thorns lacerating my palms. Yanking hard, I pulled the blight towards me. Slick with my blood, the tentacles almost slithered free, but I clung on. The blight roiled closer. I held the bunched tentacles over the sickly yellow flame that had been heating the pot.

And willed the gas to an inferno.

I leapt back, knocking Brad to the ground. My body shielded us both as the gas exploded, taking the blight with it in a fiery blast. Glass shattered; my hair crisped and burnt; smoke stole the air from my lungs.

"Melaina? Melaina!"

I couldn't breathe. I couldn't...

Chapter Nine

"Oh god. They're burning up."

Something cool and wet draped across my forehead. I flinched and opened my eyes. A bright light glared down from above. I closed them again, a headache blossoming behind my lids. I felt hung over and feverish. An awesome combination.

"Ow." Was that croak me?

"She's awake!" Jen's voice. "Melaina, honey, are you okay?"

I tried to speak but my voice broke. Someone lifted my head, and wet my lips with water. I swallowed, tried again. "Is my hair okay?"

"What? Yes, it's fine. What happened?"

"Did you get the blight?" another voice asked.

"Burned it all up," I said, my eyes scrunched shut. My voice slurred, as if I was drunk. "Why's it so bright in here?"

"Hang on." There was a click, and blessed darkness

73

descended. I peered through my lashes cautiously.

Jen leaned over me, holding a tepid facecloth to my forehead. Belinda was to my right, fussing over someone else. Brad? The hall light was still on, but the room was dark, so I couldn't read their expressions.

My hand twitched on the blanket. Blanket? I turned my head cautiously. Yup, I was lying next to Brad on his bed. Good thing he wasn't trying to kill me again, because I was as weak as a day-old kitten.

He moaned, lifting a slow hand to his forehead.

"How do you feel?" Belinda asked him.

"Like I've been hit by a truck. What happened?"

Her gaze fell on me, and Brad turned his head to see what his sister was looking at.

"I dreamed about you," he said, a frown creasing his forehead.

I wanted to make a wisecrack about how he flattered me, but I was too tired. "I know."

"You fought the..."

"Yeah."

"You burned my grandparents' house down."

So that was the couple in the shattered photograph. "Sorry about that. At least it wasn't real." I looked up at Jen. "Can you get my coat? There are caramels in the pocket. They'll help."

"Right." She climbed off the bed. I clenched my jaw, nausea surging as the mattress rocked.

Judging from Brad's expression, he didn't feel any better.

"What can I do?" Belinda asked.

"Some painkillers would be nice," Brad replied. I gasped my agreement.

Once they had left the room I heaved a sigh of relief, closing my eyes. I was so tired. And cold. I shivered.

"I thought I told you not to help me," Brad said.

I opened my eyes again, meeting his gaze. He was close enough to me that, if I hadn't been exhausted, it would've felt strangely intimate. His expression was puzzled rather than angry, eyebrows drawn and lips a flat line. "You did," I said. "I ignored you."

There was a long pause—long enough that I closed my eyes again. Then he mumbled, "Thanks."

"You're welcome," I mumbled back.

Belinda and Jen returned, bustling around the bed. Belinda gave us each a couple of painkillers, helping us to sit so we could take them. The water was cool from the tap, heaven in my parched mouth. I downed the small glass but, when I asked for more, Jen shook her head. "Not with that fever. Drink too much at once and you'll hurl."

I wrinkled my nose but stopped complaining, munching my way through a couple of caramels before lying back down. I insisted Brad do the same.

Soon his breath settled into the slow rhythm of deep sleep. I willed my limbs to move, but fatigue dragged them downwards and it wasn't long before I followed suit. And this time my sleep was dreamless.

The fever was gone when I woke. So was Brad.

I blinked up at the strange ceiling: my second in two

days. A faint line of wan light crept in along the top of the curtain rail. It was morning already? I glanced at my watch. Just before seven. Ugh.

I propped myself up on my elbows and looked around. I was still dressed, although someone had removed my boots and thrown a crochet blanket over me. It was tangled around my legs.

Footsteps in the corridor made me look towards the door. Brad tiptoed in. When he saw I was awake, the corner of his lip tightened in a grimace. "Sorry, did I wake you?"

I shook my head.

"I was getting socks. My feet are cold."

"Be my guest." Then I laughed at myself, giving him permission to get his own things from his own room. He smiled back, sharing the joke. He grabbed a pair of balled socks from the top drawer and sat on the bed to pull them on. "Have you been awake long?"

"A little bit. Your friend is asleep on the couch, so I've been hiding in the kitchen." So that was where Jen was. I opened my mouth to apologise for taking over his home, but he waved the words away. "It's alright. Besides, the kitchen has coffee." I must have brightened, because he stood and offered me his hand. "Want one?"

I hesitated for a moment, the memory of that hand choking me fresh in my mind. A shadow flickered in his eyes and he started to pull back but, before he could finish the gesture, I took his hand and let him help me to my feet.

My teeth were furry from going to sleep without brushing them. The caramels hadn't exactly helped. "Can I use your bathroom?"

He gave me a lopsided grin. "You came into my house uninvited—"

"Belinda invited us!"

"—and into my dreams uninvited—"

"Fair."

"—and *now* you're asking my permission?"

"Well. Yes. Better late than never, right?"

He chuckled. "Help yourself."

After taking care of what my aunt would have called "necessities", I splashed some water on my face and ran wet fingers through my hair. My clothes were rumpled from sleep, but there wasn't much I could do about that. My breath, however... I peeked into the vanity. Mouth-wash! Bingo!

Minty fresh, I padded up to the other end of the house.

Jen lay curled on the couch, covered with another crochet blanket. She had one hand under her cheek, while the other curled in a loose fist beneath her chin. Her face looked vulnerable without her glasses, which had been placed neatly on the coffee table.

Reassured she was okay, I slid open the door to the kitchen as quietly as I could and stepped inside.

The room faced northeast and the sun, sliced into bars by the vertical blinds in the window, did its wintery best to lend everything a warm glow. It was the opposite of the grime-encrusted kitchen from Brad's dream the night before in almost every way: clean, homely, and free of flying, tentacle-wielding monsters. Except he too had a pot on the stove. The air smelled of honey and vanilla.

"Better?" Brad asked from the refrigerator, looking over his shoulder at me.

"Mostly." I sat on a stool at the breakfast bar, swinging

one foot.

"How do you have your coffee?"

"White. One sugar."

Brad bustled around the kitchen, making coffee in between stirring the contents of the pot. The sight of good-looking men doing domestic chores always made me smile, and Brad definitely looked good, even with a healthy crop of stubble, and wearing shabby jeans and a knitted jumper that appeared to be an old, comfortable favourite.

When he handed me the mug I wrapped my hands around it, soaking in the heat through my palms. The kitchen was warm, but looking at the frost-covered branches of the tree outside the window made me feel cold.

"Porridge?"

I laughed, and he looked vaguely offended. "Sorry. I just didn't take you for a porridge kind of guy."

"Hey, it's great in winter," he said. "And good for you. Although maybe not this recipe. My grandmother used to make it. I was reminded of it by..." He stopped, shifting from foot to foot.

"Was that what was on the stove?" I remembered throwing the pot at the blight. The idea of injuring it with Grandma's porridge tickled me, but Brad's sombre expression stilled my tongue. I took a sip of my coffee instead. It was good.

He shrugged, his mouth hardening. "Maybe once, before the nightmares came."

"How did you sleep afterwards? Last night, I mean?"

"Dreamless." He tipped his head to the side. "I can't remember the last time I could say that. Will it be like that from now on?"

"No. That was probably because you were exhausted." His shoulders slumped, and I continued quickly. "But your sleep should return to normal service. Dreams and regular nightmares, like anyone else. No more sleepwalking."

"Do lots of people get ... blight infestations?" He pulled a couple of bowls from the cupboard and placed them on the bench. "Is this some super-common thing I've just never heard of before?"

Shaking my head, I eyed the porridge, relieved to see it wasn't the unpleasant grey colour I associated with gruel. Instead it was a warm yellow, dotted with orange flecks. My mouth started to water and my stomach rumbled. "I see maybe one every six months or so." I yawned, covering my mouth with my hand. I ached down to my bones, although the coffee was helping. Or maybe it was the placebo effect. Either way, I wasn't complaining.

"But you said at the hospital you did one the other day. Exorcised it, I mean." Expression thoughtful, he touched the hair above his temple and then winced, his hand dropping to his side.

I nodded. "Hopefully that's my quota for the year."

"And are there other people who go around, treating people for dream possession?"

"I'm the only one I know of," I said, watching as he dished up the food. *At least in the waking world.*

The porridge was good: creamy, sweet, and gentle on my bruised throat. The flecks of orange turned out to be apricot, giving each mouthful an extra burst of flavour. I smiled and Brad grinned back, smug.

The sliding door opened and Jen poked her head in, glasses on. Although she looked dishevelled, her eyes twinkled. "I smell good things. Are they up for grabs?"

"Sure." Brad made to stand, but she waved him back to his seat.

"My arms aren't painted on. I can get my own food. Ooh, porridge. Yum!" Brad looked even smugger, but the expression faded when she continued, "Nice to see you both looking better. And not trying to kill each other."

"I never tried to kill him," I said mildly, scraping the last of the porridge onto my spoon. Would it be too greedy to request a second helping?

"It wasn't my idea," Brad grumbled.

"I know. I'm teasing," Jen said. "How do you feel?"

"Tired," Brad and I said together, and then chuckled.

"I'm looking forward to going home and sleeping for twenty-four hours straight," I added.

"You can't," Jen said around a mouthful of porridge. "Lunch at your uncle's, remember?"

Dammit.

Chapter Ten

I had just enough time for a shower, a change of clothes and some heavily applied foundation to hide the bags under my eyes and tone down the necklace of bruises encircling my throat. I didn't even change my nose stud for the ring my uncle hated. Jen dropped me off at his place on her way to university. She had to research something eye-wateringly boring at the library. I would have traded places with her in a heartbeat.

The house loomed above me, all harsh angles in beige-rendered concrete and glass. Low hedges guarded the front of the property, bulky enough to act as a boundary marker but low enough that passers-by could admire what they didn't have. The hedges looked as if they'd been trimmed by someone using a set square. For all I knew, they had.

The courts had given Uncle Ian and Aunt Lacey custody of me when I was a baby, after it became apparent my late-teens mother wasn't able to care for me. Mum had been admitted to her first home the same day. Mrs Witherspoon, the nanny, had raised me until I was five, after Aunt Lacey had her first child. That was when they'd enrolled me in a very expensive boarding school. I'd only lived with them during school holidays from then on.

But I'd never lived in this house, which they'd only bought a few years ago, after I graduated. It was their dream home. It had formal lounge and dining rooms, as well as family and meals rooms, enough bedrooms to sleep an entire netball team, and a pool, music room, workshop—everything a professional couple and their two children could need, and then some. The children even had their own study. Each.

I'd always preferred their previous home. It had been less grand, but a lot more homely.

Setting my shoulders, I walked up the path, which curved along the front of the building to a wide double door set with slats of frosted glass. When I rang the doorbell, a major chord reverberated deep within the house.

The younger of my cousins, Justin, answered the door with a grin. Not long ago we would have hugged, but he'd hit puberty in the last six months and hugging wasn't done anymore. It made me a little bit sad, actually.

"Hey, Jat." I smiled. Aunt Lacey hadn't taken the Armstrong name when she'd married Uncle Ian, and her two children had been cursed with a double-barrelled surname: Armstrong-Taylor. Hence: JAT.

And yes, my aunt's name was Lacey Taylor, which always made me think of someone who makes lingerie for a living. If I were her, I'd have changed surnames when I married, and professional recognition in the legal community be damned. But Aunt Lacey kept the name

and defied anyone to joke about it.

Very few people tried.

"Hey, Laina."

"Is that *stubble*?" Although I hadn't seen him face-to-face for a while, I occasionally cyberstalked him via social media, so my shock was feigned. I knew he'd lap it up.

"Yep." He lifted his chin so I could examine the trace of fuzz along his jawline. The stubble was a few shades lighter than his dark brown hair. "Like it?"

"I guess. Have you started shaving yet?"

"Yeah, but it's the weekend." He stepped aside so I could enter.

We passed through the entry hall and into the family room, a space two-thirds the size of my apartment. Halogen downlights, on despite the sunlight flooding through the floor-to-ceiling windows, made the timber floors glow warmly. The scarlet suede of the couches, on the other hand, was a visual assault.

We sat at right angles, and I glanced around. The smell of roasting meat wafted in from the kitchen, but there was no sign of movement in there.

"What's for lunch?"

"Lamb," Justin said. But before I had time to contemplate the notion of my first roast lamb in months, he leaned in eagerly. "Dad told us what happened. Show me the bruises!"

"I covered them with makeup," I said, touching the scarf self-consciously. Then I lowered my voice. "I didn't want the others to freak."

"They'll freak anyway." He rolled his eyes, dismissive of the grownups in his life. I apparently didn't count as a grownup because I was cool. "Show me!"

I lowered the scarf slightly. Despite the makeup, I knew the bruises were spectacular. Justin's dark eyes widened. "You can even see where his fingers..." His delight vanished, replaced by outrage as what he was seeing sank in—the imprint of Brad's hands on my throat. "What happened to the guy?"

"Jen hit him on the head. Knocked him out cold."

"Good."

"She broke my lamp, though," I complained, trying to lighten the mood as I readjusted my scarf.

"You can have one of mine. I've got two." He leapt to his feet.

I grabbed his hand, laughing. "Jat, you don't have to—"

"Don't call him that." Justin's older sister, Olivia, breezed into the room. "It's not his name."

"Shut up!" Justin snapped back before I could speak. "I don't care if she does, butthead."

"Real mature." Olivia chose a glossy apple from the bowl on the coffee table. I blinked in surprise; I'd assumed the fruit was plastic. Should have known better.

Olivia was seventeen, but you wouldn't have known it from her appearance: courtesy of well-applied makeup, she looked older than me. Her long, dark hair swung behind her as she walked. Designer jeans hugged her curves and, despite the weather, she wore a babydoll tee. I got goosebumps just looking at her.

"Does Mum know you're here?" she asked me, nibbling the apple.

"I'd have thought so. I didn't sneak in."

"I'll check. She's upstairs getting changed."

As soon as she left the room, I gave Justin a mock-stern

look. "Go easy on your sister about the Jat thing."

"Why?" He crossed his arms and scowled.

"Because her initials are Oat."

We were still laughing when my aunt and uncle came into the room, my cousin trailing behind with the mostly uneaten apple still in her hand. Aunt Lacey gave me an awkward hug—the sort where you try and minimise body contact except for a light pat on the other person's shoulder. She was wearing neat slacks and a blouse that would have made me feel underdressed if her children hadn't also been dressed casually. Besides, with a blue fringe and a nose stud, I could never dress formally enough to please Aunt Lacey.

Uncle Ian was wearing slacks too, but he had a polo shirt on. We didn't hug—like Aunt Lacey, he wasn't a hugger. Unlike her, he didn't bother trying. But he examined me seriously. "Still alive then?"

"Yep," I said.

"Good girl." He thumped me on the shoulder, and I winced. "Let's go talk before lunch. Kids, help your mother get the veggies ready."

"But Dad, I want to hear Laina's story," Justin said.

"You can interrogate her at lunch. This is about other stuff."

"Okay." Justin sighed.

Uncle Ian led me into his study, a huge room dominated by a heavy timber desk. The walls were lined with framed certificates, commendations and a couple of news articles, preserved beneath glass like dead insects. All of them related to his real estate franchise. Given the size of their family home, I guessed business was doing well.

There were no family photos in his study, which always

struck me as odd. But it wasn't that he didn't love them. He just didn't believe in mixing his business with his private life.

He sat behind the desk, leaving me to take one of the chairs in front. The chair was comfortable but I squirmed anyway. This felt like a job interview.

"I gather you're aware of Doctor Willis's wishes to try a new treatment with your mother." He clasped his hands together and studied me. His eyes were the same shade of hazel as Mum's, but where hers reminded me of amber flowers in a field of green, his were more like semi-precious stones: pretty, but also hard and cold.

I nodded, pressing my lips together. Mum must have told him. I had to be careful here, or I could get Ewan fired.

"And you don't approve?" he prompted, leaning forward. His gaze was fixed on mine.

I shook my head.

"Why not?" he said in a voice as smooth as honey. Was this how he got people to buy houses they couldn't afford?

"Because she doesn't want it," I said.

"Doctor Willis told me he thinks her previous medical team was negligent in not attempting to treat her illness before now. Twenty years, it's been, and no one has tried *anything*. Did you know that?"

"No. But is it negligent to respect her wishes?"

He sat back in his chair, frowning. "I believe it is. What sort of quality of life does she have right now? Sleeping the day away, only leaving the home at Christmas, and then sleeping most of that away too. Is that how you'd want to live?"

"No," I said, hating to agree with him, even a little bit.

"But—"

"There you go, then."

I raised my voice. "*But* I'm not her, and she has the right to make that decision for herself. It's not all about me. And no offence, Uncle Ian, but it's not all about you either."

He narrowed his eyes. "You told her not to grant me the additional legal authority over her."

"I told her if she did then her treatment wouldn't be her decision anymore. It's up to her whether she's willing to do that."

"You're splitting hairs."

I shrugged.

"Don't you want your mother back?"

I recognised the attempt at emotional blackmail, and it made me set my jaw. But I managed to keep my voice even. "She's my mother *now*. I've never known her any other way."

"*I* have." He stared at the wall, looking past it to some distant memory. "Davina was charming. Vivacious. One of the most popular girls in her year at school." His voice hardened. "And then that … animal attacked her. He ruined her, and she's never recovered."

I looked down at my hands, curled together on my lap. *Animal*. Uncle Ian was referring to my father. Mum had fallen pregnant at sixteen, and she'd refused to identify her partner, claiming she didn't remember how it had happened. It was a lie—but her family thought she'd been raped and had blocked the trauma from her mind. They believed that was why she had the illness she did now, that it was her mind's defence against a traumatic memory.

Given how implausible the truth was, I couldn't blame them for making assumptions.

"Hey, kiddo." Uncle Ian's voice was gentle, and I glanced up, surprised. "It's not your fault. Don't feel bad about it."

I spluttered. "I never—"

"Your father may be a monster, but you are your own person. The half of you that comes from our family will always triumph over his sickness."

I stared, feeling ill. Was that how my aunt and uncle viewed me? As something inherently compromised? Like a house built with rotten timbers, but on a solid foundation?

Was that why they'd wanted me out of the house once their own children came along? In case I ... infected them somehow?

Their assumption wasn't true. My father hadn't raped Mum. She had gone to him willingly and still loved him, and he loved her. Even if behaviour were hereditary, which I didn't believe for a second, I wouldn't be contaminated by it. Couldn't be.

I took a deep breath, swallowing bile, and nodded mutely. My uncle seemed satisfied.

"Melaina, I want your help in convincing your mother to accept Doctor Willis's treatment program."

"I—"

"She loves you. If you asked her, she'd do it for you. I'm sure of it."

"I don't think she would." Give up Dad? It'd never happen. He'd been with her so long she might go crazy without him, and she'd never given him up for me before. Why would she start now?

"Then persuade her."

I shook my head.

He crossed his arms and stared at me for so long I began to fidget. Finally he sighed. "Melaina, if you won't even try, then your mother is the one who will suffer for it."

My heart skipped a beat. "What do you mean?"

"Convince her. If you don't at least attempt it, I'll stop paying for that nursing home and she can take her chances with the public system." His voice was flat.

I stood. The chair rocked back behind me and almost fell. "Are you serious?" But I knew from the hard lines around his eyes that he was. "You're unbelievable."

"It's for her own good, and if this is the only way I can make you see that..."

"You'd threaten her to make her do what you want?"

"No. I love Davina. I wouldn't do that." He paused, and when he spoke again, his words were a kick in the gut. "I'm threatening *you*."

"What if I try it and she says no?" The question tasted like ashes in my mouth.

"Then I'll leave her where she is and try another approach. But you have to genuinely try."

I narrowed my eyes. "I hate you."

His eyes widened with shock, and then he actually smiled. *Smiled!* I suppressed the urge to punch him in the face by pure force of will. "Olivia tells me she hates me at least once a day," he said. "It means I'm doing something right. So will you do it?"

"Give me some time to think about it."

"No."

I balled my hands into fists and leaned down on the desk, glaring at him. "You're asking me to betray my own mother. And someone tried to kill me yesterday. Give me some bloody time."

He reclined, regarding me through slitted eyes. "Alright," he said finally. "But this is a limited-time offer. You have one week."

Chapter Eleven

Sunday is the one day of the week I usually get to sleep in. But that night I had slept terribly, and all my Oneiroi tricks did nothing to help. Dawn found me glowering at the gap between the curtains, watching a sliver of the world outside as it lightened. A bare branch waved back and forth in the wind, silhouetted against a grey sky. Occasionally the window creaked as a particularly strong blast of air buffeted against it.

Some time between three and four in the morning, I'd decided I needed to talk to my mother.

I was still furious at Uncle Ian. Thinking about him made my fingers curl under the blankets, a subconscious response to the rage in my heart. If he'd just been threatening me I could have lived with it, ignored him and moved on.

No, he'd threatened Mum. His sister. I wondered how my uncle rationalised using her as leverage, even if he honestly believed it was for her own good. He must be certain I would give in, that he wouldn't have to carry out his threat. I wanted to defy him, to prove him wrong and wipe that smug look from his face, but ... Mum. There was no way I could afford to look after her, or to put her into proper care. Since we didn't have internet at home and my phone was the cheap kind that only made calls, on Monday I planned to do some research at the local library to see whether she'd be eligible for disability allowance if Uncle Ian turfed her out onto the street. Just in case.

Finally giving up on the sleep that had deserted me hours before, I rolled over and turned on my bedside lamp. Justin had given it to me, chasing me down the street after I'd stormed out of their house yesterday.

"Where are you going?" He'd caught my arm, turned me to face him.

"Home."

"But we haven't eaten yet." He'd narrowed his eyes. "What did Dad do?"

As much as I'd wanted to scream at the sky right then, I also didn't want to badmouth Uncle Ian to his son. I refused to stoop to his level, using his son against him the way he was using me against Mum. "We had a disagreement. Don't worry about it."

"Here, take this. I want you to have it."

And he'd thrust the lamp at me. Comic book characters strode heroically around the navy blue lampshade. I wasn't surprised he wanted to rehome it—it was a little young for him now he had stubble and everything—but his spontaneous generosity so close on the heels of his father's offensiveness had made my eyes well with tears.

Looking at the lamp now, I reminded myself that not

all of my family were awful people.

A shower and two strong coffees improved my mood. Or at least enabled me to walk in a straight line and talk without slurring, although my eyes were gritty and dry, and my throat ached when I swallowed.

But I was still angry.

As I was putting on my coat Jen emerged from her room, rubbing her eyes, glasses balanced on the end of her nose. "Where are you off to?"

"To see Mum." I yanked my beanie over my ears.

She flicked on the kettle and leaned against the bench, her gaze serious. "Have you decided what to tell her yet?"

I shrugged. I'd told Jen about Uncle Ian's ultimatum the night before. She'd been satisfyingly outraged, so at least I didn't feel like I was overreacting. "It will break her heart to find out what he's doing."

"She has a right to know, Melaina."

Bag over my shoulder and gloves on, I headed for the door. "I know. And I hate it."

I agonised over my decision for the entire bus ride to Wattle Tree Park, fidgeting with the strap on my bag. Jen was right. It was Mum's life and she deserved to have a say in what happened next. But Mum had always seemed so fragile. I'd had the urge to protect her since I was six and really came to understand her situation. That was when she'd told me about Ollie. The irony of our roles being reversed—me being the protector and her the protectee—wasn't lost on me, but I couldn't make that feeling go away.

I found her in the rec hall, which was crowded, people eating breakfast at tables by the windows. The air smelled of toast and good coffee. Better than the stuff Jen and I could afford, anyway.

I'd called Mum on the bus to warn her I was coming and, to my delight, she was even dressed, not still in her nightgown. Sure, she was dressed in a thick, fleecy tracksuit, but still, it was an improvement over my last visit. Being in proper clothes made her seem more real, more solidly rooted in the day-to-day world. Even if it was an illusion.

She smiled and stood, embracing me fiercely. Then she kissed my cheek. "My sweet girl. I'm so glad you're okay."

Okay? Oh, right. The attack. I'd been so preoccupied with Uncle Ian's ultimatum it had actually slipped my mind. I touched my scarf self-consciously. Thinking about it made the bruises seem to ache more. She noticed the gesture but, unlike Justin, didn't ask for a show-and-tell. "We should go for a walk around the grounds," she said instead.

I blinked. "You're kidding, right? It's awful out there."

"It will clear my head. And give us a chance to talk in peace." She indicated the crowded hall with a tip of her head.

"Oh." I looked back out the door and my heart sank into my boots. "Alright."

While Mum went to her room to get a jacket, I approached one of the nurses, Daniel, a quiet guy in his thirties with ash-blond hair and a shy smile. He was dubious about Mum's idea but, after some cajoling, agreed on the condition that I push her in a wheelchair so she wouldn't get fatigued and fall asleep early. He also insisted she take a blanket as well as her jacket. I also grabbed a couple of thermoses of fresh, hot tea.

"She feels the cold more than we do, because she's so

thin," he said as he brought the wheelchair out of a storeroom.

"Are you calling me fat?" I said with a faint frown.

"Uh, no," he spluttered, blushing. "Of course not. You're perfectly … ah, you're…"

I burst out laughing. "I'm only joking. I know she's got no meat on her."

He exhaled, face still ruddy. "Don't do that to me!"

"Are you teasing the staff?" Mum said, walking up the corridor. She'd grabbed a beanie too. Her long hair fell from under it in an inky waterfall down her back. I'd had mine that long when I was a child, but when I hit my teens I'd lost the patience for it.

"A little bit," I said. Daniel raised an eyebrow but said nothing, handing me a thick woollen blanket. "Okay, a lot."

Mum sat carefully in the wheelchair and helped me tuck the blanket around her legs so it wouldn't catch under the wheels.

"Do you want to wear my gloves?" I asked.

"Don't be silly. Your hands will be exposed if you're pushing this thing."

"Tuck your hands under the blanket then," I said as I wheeled her towards the door. It slid open, and a gust of icy wind blew in, even colder now I'd adjusted to the heated air in the home. Mum's hair whipped wildly around my torso.

"The wind certainly has a bite to it." Mum pulled the blanket up to her chin. She looked like a small child huddling in her bed, afraid of the dark.

"No kidding." I shivered.

I didn't think I could manage the wheelchair over the lawn, even as carefully manicured as it was, so we stuck

95

to the winding paths. The closer we got to the wall the more the wind ebbed, although the taller wattles still creaked alarmingly, their top branches rattling together like bones.

"See that park bench?" Mum said, pointing to a timber seat in a garden bed set against the western wall. It was in full sunlight. "Let's sit there."

I helped Mum onto the bench and pushed the wheel-chair to one side. When I sat beside her she arranged the blanket over both our knees. "Now," she said, unscrewing the lid on a thermos and handing it to me. "How did your visit to the hospital go? Did you talk to the young man who attacked you?"

I nodded, relieved not to have to talk about Uncle Ian yet. "Jen and I went over to his place on Friday night to get rid of the blight." Speaking quietly, even though the grounds were deserted, I explained briefly how the blight's eviction had gone, playing down how much it had drained me.

"And when are you seeing him again? Brad, you say his name is?"

I poured some tea into the plastic cup that doubled as the thermos lid and took a sip. Its warmth spread through me. Tucked under the blanket and soaking up the sun, it was almost pleasant out here. "I wasn't ... ah, we hadn't organised anything. Why?"

She pursed her lips. "Something your father told me. Remember how I told you the blights are parasites?"

I nodded. "You said they were spread by eggs."

"Yes. Well, they take a while to infect the host after they are ingested—"

"Ingested?" I'd always assumed the blights were a phenomenon purely of the dream world. That they had

any sort of physical component was a surprise.

"That's what Ollie said. Like tapeworm. You eat the eggs and they develop into larvae."

"Ew." I looked down at my tea with a frown. How would I know if there were blight eggs in it? "Did he say how you recognise them? Whether they are common in certain sorts of food, for example?"

"No." *Of course not.* I didn't say it out loud, though. If I did, Mum would feel guilty for not having asked the right questions. I didn't blame her. Dad, on the other hand... "But he said once a person has been infected once, they are more susceptible to reinfection unless the effects of the infestation are properly dealt with," she continued.

"Did he say what that meant?"

She shook her head.

I put the tea on the bench beside me and considered what I knew. Both Larry's and Brad's dreamscapes had been contaminated by the blights' presence, Brad's more so because his blight had been more developed. I'd cleaned up Larry's, but had been too exhausted by the battle with Brad's blight to do anything about the contamination in his mind. I'd assumed it would heal, but what if it didn't?

I didn't know if that was what Ollie had been talking about, not for sure. But it was the only theory I had. "I'd better call him," I said, digging under layers of clothing to pull my phone out of my jeans pocket.

She nodded, cradling her tea and watching the shivering wattle leaves with a distant expression.

"Hello?" Belinda answered her phone on the first ring.

"Hey, it's Melaina. I was wondering if I could get your

brother's mobile number."

"Oh?" Her voice was laden with meaning. I didn't think I was just imagining the raised eyebrows. "He's in the shower, but I can get him to give you a call in a bit. What shall I tell him it's about?"

"Follow-up from Friday night. Tell him it's important, okay?"

The insinuating tone dropped from her voice. "Is it serious?"

"I don't know," I admitted, then hastened to add, "Probably not. A possible complication, but we should be able to sort it out."

"Alright. I'll let him know." She sighed. "It was more fun when I thought you were ringing to ask him on a date."

"Sorry about that." My cheeks burned with a blush. Brad was seven years older than me, but he was cute. And age meant experience, as Jen would say. "Talk to you later."

"Bye."

I put my phone in my jacket pocket, where it was easier to reach, and turned back to Mum. She was watching a pair of Australian magpies that were eyeing us with interest from the low branches of a nearby tree.

"I think they're hoping we have food," I said, picking up my tea. It had cooled a little, but was still hot enough to be palatable.

"They are." Mum's lips curved in a doting expression. "I feed them sometimes, so whenever I come out here they like to investigate. But I didn't bring anything this time." She raised her voice. "Sorry, birds. Next time, I promise." They ruffled their feathers.

"Brad's going to call me back." I remembered the main

reason I'd come to see her, and my stomach swooped like a magpie defending its nest in spring.

"I heard." She patted my hand. "You'll get him sorted. Don't worry about it."

"I... Mum, that's not what I'm worried about."

She turned to me, hazel eyes wide. "Why? Is something else going on?"

I laughed. It sounded bitter. "You could say that. It's Uncle Ian."

Choosing my words carefully to try and spare her feelings—as if that were even possible—I explained that her brother wanted me to pressure her to agree to a medication regime. And what he'd threatened to do if I didn't.

Mum sat silently for several minutes. Her gaze remained fixed on mine but I had the sense she'd withdrawn into her mind. It was something I'd seen many times before. It was like her eyes were the windows to a great complex of rooms, and she'd stepped beyond them into some secret, internal place.

When I was beginning to wonder if I'd rendered her catatonic and whether I should call a nurse, she stirred. She glanced at the magpies, which had given up on us and were foraging with sharp white beaks in the leaves beneath the tree. Then she looked back at me. To my surprise, she seemed calm. If it were me, I'd be screaming. Come to think of it, I'd done that yesterday.

"What are you going to do?" she said.

I frowned. "What do you mean?"

"Are you going to pressure me to take the medication?"

I shook my head. "But you need to know what's going on."

"He wouldn't actually go through with it," Mum said

with certainty. I had my doubts, but pressed my lips together. She continued, "But it's unfair that he's put you into this situation. So I'll do it."

I nearly dropped my tea. With trembling hands, I put it back on the chair beside me and took her fingers in mine. I could feel how cold they were even through the weave of my gloves. "Mum, I can't let you. What about Ollie?"

"Maybe I'll have slightly less time with him of an evening," she said. "It's not like I'll lose him altogether. I'll talk to Doctor Willis tomorrow, find out exactly what he has planned."

I studied her closely and she lifted her chin, trying to look strong. But her eyes glittered with unshed tears. Spending more time in this world instead of her own: the idea pained her.

"Oh, Mum."

We embraced there on the bench for several minutes before she pulled away from me and stood. "I'd like to go back to my room now," she said, dabbing at her eyes with the corner of the blanket. "I'm tired, and there are some things I need to discuss with your father."

"Okay," I agreed with a heavy heart.

Chapter Twelve

*E*wan was waiting for us at the entry to the nursing home when we got back. Daniel stood behind him, hands behind his back and a chastised expression on his face. Had he gotten in trouble for letting me take Mum outside?

"What on earth are you thinking? Are you both crazy?" Ewan said as soon as the door slid closed behind us. He took in Mum's heavy eyelids and wilted posture, and shooed me away from the wheelchair. "Let me help you to bed, Ms Armstrong."

I hung back until Ewan was well down the corridor. Then I apologised quietly to Daniel. "I hope we didn't get you in trouble."

He shrugged, studying his neat fingernails as though they held the key to some mystery. "Just a difference of opinion. I don't report to Ewan. And his heart's in the right place."

"Even if he does look like a badger with that haircut."

He suppressed a laugh, and I smiled. "Well, she wanted the fresh air. So thank you. And tell Ewan if he wants to chew anyone's arse over it, he can talk to me."

I caught up to Ewan and my mother as they were entering her room. He manoeuvred the wheelchair through the door, which was wider than standard, like the ones in a hospital.

"It wasn't his fault, you know," I said.

Unexpectedly, he smiled at me, eyes crinkling at the corners. "I know. It was yours."

"Actually, it was mine," Mum protested drowsily, climbing onto the bed before we could help her. I pulled her shoes off. "Don't you badger my daughter about it."

I nearly choked on my suppressed laughter.

"Yes, ma'am," Ewan said, pulling a light blanket out of a cupboard and draping it over her legs. "You have a rest and I'll come check on you later."

"I think I will..." Her eyelids fluttered closed and we tiptoed from the room, easing the door shut behind us.

I glanced around. The television blared in the distance, but the corridor was empty, and the nearest rooms all had their doors shut. We wouldn't be overheard here. "Hey, I wanted to thank you for your warning the other day. It was really kind of you. And you were spot on."

He rubbed his forehead. "I was hoping I wasn't. What happened?"

"Family drama." I rolled my eyes. "But Mum's agreed to try the treatment."

"How do *you* feel about that?" Ewan's concern surprised me.

"She's basically been bullied into saying yes. It pisses me off." I scowled at a potted palm so hard I was surprised

it didn't wither under the onslaught, or hold its fronds in front of its stalk to shield itself.

"I can understand that." He hesitated, then said, "Hey, do you want to grab a coffee or something?"

I stared at him, taken aback. His expression was sincere. Was he offering me a sympathetic ear, or asking me on a date? I couldn't tell. If it was the latter, I wasn't interested, his recent friendliness notwithstanding. I couldn't go out with anyone who worked in the nursing home. It would be too weird. Plus I'd promised Jen I would give him her number. "Uh…"

My phone vibrated in my pocket. The accompanying guitar riff ring tone was as wildly inappropriate here as it would have been in a library. Or a chapel. "Dammit. Sorry!" UNKNOWN NUMBER. I punched the answer button awkwardly with my still-gloved finger. "Hello?"

"Hey, it's Brad. You called?"

"Yeah, I did. Can you hang on a sec?"

"Sure." He sounded annoyed, but I muted the phone before he could say anything else.

"Listen, Ewan, I have to take this. But… Okay, this is really awkward, but my housemate Jen is smart, blond, cute and single, and I think you'd like her. And she likes kind men in uniforms. Even nurse's uniforms." He blinked at the onslaught of words, a corner of his mouth twitching. "Are you single? Would you like her number?"

"Uh. Yeah, I guess. Yes, I am." He smiled and it lit up his whole face. "You guys were talking about me?"

"Yeah, yeah. Don't get all egomaniacal about it. Got a pen?" I dictated Jen's number for him, conscious of the call waiting on my phone. "Call her, don't call her: it's up to you. But if you break her heart, I'll come after you.

Got it?"

He nodded. "Got it."

"Good." I took the phone off mute and held it to my ear, hurrying towards the exit. "Sorry about that. I'm just heading outside."

"Okay," Brad said. "What's up?"

"How'd you sleep last night?"

"Better." He sounded relieved. "No bad dreams, no sleepwalking. I didn't even tie myself to the bed. I'll be happy if I never have to do that again, let me tell you."

"Don't rule it out for recreational purposes, though," I drawled. "I hear some girls like it."

Brad laughed, a deep sound that brought a smile to my lips. "Was that why you called? After-sale service?"

"Sort of," I said, "although you never paid me, so it's after-free-sample service, really. Hang on." The glass doors slid open and I darted outside, head lowered, and strode through the grounds towards the gate. I tried to shield the phone with my hand.

"Did you just walk into a wind tunnel?" Brad asked.

"Pretty much. But I needed to get out of the muggles' hearing, if you know what I mean."

"You're a wizard? I knew it!" He was really laughing now. The comedy stylings of Melaina Armstrong, folks.

Unfortunately, I had something serious to discuss with him. "Take a breath, Brad. What are you doing for lunch?"

"Nothing. Why?"

"Don't freak out, but I found out there's a bit of follow-up I need to do."

"What do you mean?" The tightening of his voice was audible even over the wind.

"I told you not to freak out."

Brad raised his voice. "Melaina—"

"Remember how the house in your dream was all broken and covered in, I don't know, blight slime or whatever?"

"Yes...?"

"Well, I've been consulting with my experts and there's a chance that if we don't clean it up you could be more vulnerable to reinfection. So to speak." I took a breath. "Anyway, my office is in the back of Serenity's New Age Gifts, if you want to come past today. Say lunchtime? The shop's closed on a Sunday but I'll let Serenity know. She won't mind."

"Okay. But I don't know where that is."

"That's not really a surprise." I smiled. Poor, sensible Brad. I could feel his discomfort at the name of the shop. He was going to love seeing the wares.

Brad arrived at Serenity's just after midday, tapping on the glass door and then peering into the darkened interior. He jumped when I stepped into view.

The bell tinkled cheerily. I tried to match its enthusiasm. "Hi!"

"You startled me," he mumbled, hurrying inside. Pushed in by the wind, a few stray leaves rattled in after him before I could close the door.

"Sorry." I locked the door behind him. "I didn't want to turn the light on. If people see it, they want to come in."

He put a plastic bag on the counter; the smell of Chinese takeaway filled the room. "But the sign says 'closed'."

I smiled. "I'll let you tell them that, shall I?" I collected the leaves and put them in the bin behind the counter. "Sorry it's cold in here. I've put the heater on in the back room."

"It's better than outside." Brad looked at the shelves with an expression somewhere between curiosity and distaste, peering at labels in the dim light from the high windows. "Do people actually believe in this stuff? Crystals and incense and ... what's this feathery thing?"

"It's a dreamcatcher. And yes, almost everyone who comes in here believes in something. The rest are looking for presents or think they're living dangerously," I said. "By the way, Serenity's rule is 'you break it, you bought it'."

He put the dreamcatcher down hastily and then raised an eyebrow at me. "Do *you* believe in it?"

I shrugged. "I've never seen evidence any of it works. But then, it's not my kind of magic. And who am I to judge, given what I can do?" I matched him eyebrow for eyebrow. "For that matter, who are *you*? You mocked me at the hospital—"

"I did not!"

"—and who was right? Huh?"

"You were," he conceded, peeling off his gloves. "But in my defence, it sounded pretty kooky. Possessed by a dream demon?"

"Kooky's my middle name." I stuck my nose in the plastic bag of food. The steam was pleasantly warm on my cheeks. "What did you get me?"

"Spring rolls, Peking Duck, honey chicken, and rice."

I grinned. "And what are *you* having?"

Brad chuckled.

We fetched clean but mismatched crockery from the shop's tiny kitchen and retreated to my little back room, which by now was toasty and warm. Once we were ensconced in my two armchairs, we ate lunch. I asked him about his job (he was an IT consultant) and family (Belinda was the only one of his close relatives still alive). He answered politely, but his gaze roamed the room the entire time, taking in every threadbare patch of carpet and scratched piece of furniture. He didn't comment, but his keen gaze didn't miss a thing. It made me feel as if I needed to apologise, and that made me cross.

When I was tidying up, he finally said something, in a carefully neutral voice. "This is your office?"

"Yes," I snapped. "I know it's not much, but kooks like me don't get a lot of clients."

"Hey." Brad reached out and caught my hand as I was reaching past him for his bowl. My heart leapt into my throat, and I couldn't have told you which feeling was stronger: excitement or fear. His grip was warm and gentle, and his expression kind, but my mind also flashed back to the first time he'd touched me. Attacked me.

Feeling me stiffen, he released my hand. "I didn't mean anything by it."

My throat tightened with unexpected sadness and I turned away before he could see, putting the takeaway containers and empty bowls in a pile next to the kettle. "I know. Sorry, I'm a grumpy cow today."

"How come?"

Unexpectedly, I found myself giving him an abbreviated

version of events: how Mum could only see my father through her dreams, and my uncle's insistence that Mum get treated for the resultant hypersomnia. He listened quietly, expressing no disbelief, only outrage at Uncle Ian's behaviour.

But when I explained how Mum had decided to give in to my uncle so he'd stop pressuring me, Brad nodded. "That's fair."

I frowned, leaning my elbow on the arm of my chair and resting my head in my hand. "What do you mean?"

"Most people don't have the luxury of spending their entire day with their loved one. They have to live and work. They have responsibilities." He hesitated, reading my expression, then added, "I know this isn't any of my business, but it seems to me your mother has had others look after her for her entire adult life. Including her daughter, which isn't right. She should be looking after you. It's good that she's stepping up and taking some of the burden."

"But..." I wanted to object, but Brad's words struck a chord with me, something I'd thought resentfully in the small hours of the night and then pushed away as uncharitable. Mum's situation was a lifestyle choice, not a medical condition.

Finally, I sighed and sat up straight, resolving to worry about it later. "Let's get this done, shall we?"

Brad pulled his wallet from his back pocket. "Before we do the after-sale support, I should probably pay for the actual sale, don't you think?"

I gaped like a landed fish. "You don't have to..."

"Actually, yes, I do. I know you helped me out of enlightened self-interest—" he grimaced "—but you should

still get paid for it. What's your hourly rate?"

I told him, then added quickly, "But make sure you deduct half the cost of the Chinese from that."

He handed me a hundred dollar note. I couldn't remember the last time I'd seen one. Even when I was working the register out front, the highest denomination I usually saw was a fifty. People didn't tend to carry hundreds around with them. Teller machines didn't issue them, only banks. And who uses a bank anymore?

Brad, apparently.

"Ah, that's too much," I said, stunned.

"You're wrong. That reimburses you from when you arrived on Friday night to when our fevers broke. Belinda told me. Plus I'll pay for this appointment as well."

I wanted to object, badly, but it was enough money to cover this week's rent. Mumbling an embarrassed thank you, I tucked the note into my purse. Then I leaned forward, putting my face close to his.

"Ready?"

He nodded. "How does this work?"

"I breathe on you. Like this."

And I did.

Chapter Thirteen

The kitchen was much as I remembered it from two days before. The fire had burned away the ichor as though it were oil, leaving the actual structure of the house untouched. If I needed any further reminder that this was a dreamscape and not a real house, that was it: a gas explosion like the one I'd triggered would have blown the front off the house, and fire would have gobbled the rest. The only trace of the inferno was a fine layer of soot that dusted everything.

"Well, this could be worse."

I jumped, spinning so quickly I nearly overbalanced. Brad stood beside me, hands in his pockets, surveying the damage.

"I didn't expect to see you here!" I gasped, hand to my chest.

He frowned. "Why not? It's my dream, right?"

"Well, yeah. But usually it's just the dreamscape, maybe some ephemera. I don't see the dreamer."

"Ephemera?"

"Things that seem alive but aren't. Like when you dream of another person."

He bent over and lifted the table back onto its feet. Several holes punctured the surface from when we'd used it as a shield. "Maybe it's because I knew what you were doing. How often does that happen?"

"Almost never," I said. Then I began to laugh.

"What?" he said.

"Your clothes."

"What about them?" He glanced down and then blushed beetroot-red. He was wearing the same high-waisted jeans and *Inspector Gadget* T-shirt he'd been dressed in last time we'd been here. When he was a small boy. At least they'd scaled to fit rather than stretching and tearing over his adult body. "Well, damn. I loved this outfit. I remember, I was so proud of it, walking around with my chest stuck out so everyone would notice…"

"Hey, don't worry about it," I said with a grin. "Gadget's retro. If it'd been Gummi Bears we may have had a problem."

"Well then. That's a relief. Let's get started, shall we?" He looked around. "I wonder where Grandma kept the mop?"

"There probably isn't one, unless it's something you would've been aware of as a child," I said, rolling up my sleeves. "Besides, that's not how this works."

"Then show me, oh wise one."

"Okay." I walked over to the wall near the stair, where the blight's body had crashed through the plasterboard, showering the floor with chips and white dust that crunched underfoot as I walked. Placing my hand on the edge of the hole, I moved it down and across the empty space, visualising the wall healing itself.

The dreamscape complied readily—more readily than I'd been expecting. My shadow flared on the wall before me for a moment, complete with the tantalising hint of wings I'd almost grown used to.

Brad hadn't, though. "Holy... Did you...? Do you...?"

I glanced over my shoulder at him. "Daddy's a moth-man. Give me your hand."

"Why?" But he stepped forward, reaching out.

"I'm testing a theory."

"What's that?" His hand was bigger than mine, but his fingers interlaced with mine as if we'd done it a hundred times before. My heart fluttered, and I swallowed before replying.

"That this is easier with you here. Like you said, it's your dream."

I ran my gaze along the length of the wall—the stripes filled with flaking insulation and bare, dangerous wiring; the curled, charred edges of the torn wallpaper. I imagined it restored, and, with a faint shimmer, it was.

It was as simple as changing my own dream.

"Huh," I said.

"What?" Brad's tone was suspicious, although his eyes were fixed on the new stretch of wall. It was so clean it looked as if it had just been washed.

"Normally changing someone's dream requires effort. Their dreamscape resists. With you here..."

"It's not?" He looked down at me, his lips curving into a smile.

"Good guess." I smiled back.

While I was able to make changes this extensive to

my own dreams, unless Leander was pestering me they were still a solitary experience. But here I had company, and an audience. It was exhilarating. Now I knew how my mother felt, sharing her dreams with my father.

The idea stopped me cold. No wonder she preferred that world to the real one. It would be addictive. I shivered.

"What's wrong?"

"Just thinking." I turned to work on the rest of the house.

When we reached the upstairs hallway, Brad paused to look at the photo I'd rehung on the wall. I looked too: now I knew they were his grandparents, I could see the family resemblance. He had her eyes, his firm jaw.

"I still have that photo," Brad said. "After my grandma died we sold the house, but we've still got the photos."

I mended the whip-like tears in the wallpaper. "This place had to mean a lot to you, for it to play such a strong role in your dreams. It must have been hard to sell it."

"Yeah. But we needed the money." Brad didn't elaborate and, feeling as if I'd put my foot in my mouth about as far as it would go, I didn't probe any further.

We were almost done with the house. The closed doors opened onto two more bedrooms, a bathroom and a separate toilet. The blight damage was minimal in them. In the master bedroom a faint scent of rose and jasmine perfume hung in the air, a miraculous trace of the original dream.

The house wasn't an exact replica of Brad's grandparents' house: I knew that without needing to see the original. It was built from Brad's memories. The pot of porridge on the stove. The iron-framed bed where he'd slept as a child. His grandmother's perfume.

The hissing sound of ... what *was* that sound?

Letting go of Brad's hand, I hurried around the ruffled skirt of the bed to the window, pushing the heavy curtains aside.

The backyard would have been beautiful under other circumstances. A path meandered from the back door to a clothesline, via a small fishpond and orderly rows of camellias. We hadn't cleaned up the blight's contamination out there yet, so the path glistened with slime, the bushes were withered and brown, and fish bobbed in the pond, lifeless orange spots against the dirty water.

But the blight contamination wasn't our problem.

Beyond a cute picket fence like something out of a storybook—except for the coating of ichor—the terrain grew more indistinct, fading to a featureless grey fog.

And in the fog, something moved.

I tried to keep my voice even. "Hey, Brad, come look at this."

He returned a silver-chased hand mirror to the dresser and joined me at the window.

"Can you see that?"

He squinted, then shook his head. "But I can hear a sound. It's..."

"Did your grandparents live on the coast? It sounds a bit like surf." I rubbed a speck of dirt off the window with my thumb, smiling at the thought of a trip to the beach after our work was done.

Then I noticed Brad wasn't moving.

"Hey. Are you okay?"

He shook his head, the movement so faint I could barely see it. "The sound," he whispered. "It's snakes."

As though summoned by his words, a tangle of shapes

in the fog resolved into individual strands. Scales gleamed dully in the omnidirectional light.

I wasn't afraid of snakes. Not exactly. Like anyone growing up in Australia, I treated them with respect, preferably at a distance, because disrespect can get you killed. Australia has a healthy majority of the world's most venomous snakes. The tiger snake. The death adder. The taipan. The innocuously named eastern brown, which is one of the worst. I'd learned to recognise them all in eighth-grade biology.

So I recognised them now, as they slithered through the gaps in the fence. Their eyes, like obsidian flecks, fixed as one on the house. They seemed to be watching us.

They *were* watching us.

Brad made a small sound in the back of his throat. I pulled my gaze away from the mesmerising swarm spearing through the undergrowth towards us to look at him. Sweat beaded Brad's brow, and his lips were pressed together so tightly they were white.

I wasn't scared of snakes, but Brad was. And this was his dreamscape. His nightmare.

Well, I could take care of that.

I snatched his hand up. His fingers dug into my skin. Wincing, I turned to the garden and willed the snakes to vanish.

They didn't. The hiss grew louder, as if they were laughing at me as they slithered closer.

"What the f..."

Brad turned to me, his face whiter than the plaster dust on the hems of my jeans. "Fix it!"

"I'm trying. It's not working!"

The swarm was halfway across the garden now. One

snake paused to snatch up the dead goldfish. They descended down its neck in fat lumps.

"We have to stop them getting in!" He dropped my hand and bolted for the door, thundering along the hall and down the stairs. I ran after him, my heart racing and my palms sweaty. I'd never met a nightmare this stubborn. What was going on? Was it the residual blight ooze?

I found Brad pushing the newly repaired table across to block the kitchen door. He flipped it back onto its side to block the cat flap under the lace-covered window. And just in time, too; several soft thumps sounded from outside. The flap rattled but didn't budge.

Brad scuttled back from the door as though it had grown fangs of its own.

I peered out the kitchen window. The grass outside had vanished, covered in a writhing carpet. The longest tiger snake I'd ever seen reared up and peered back at me. A dark intelligence glittered in its eyes. Malicious glee.

Great. Brad had dreamed up giant, evil, super-intelligent snakes.

As I stared at it, the snake's head darted forward, mouth agape. I recoiled as its fangs rapped the glass. Venom trickled down the windowpane like a tear.

Then it did it again. A chip of glass flew away, rattling into the sink.

Tapping against glass arose from the top of the kitchen door, and from further inside the house. It sounded like a hailstorm, coming from every direction.

"They'll be in soon." Brad's voice cracked with fear. He stood with his back to the wall near the stairs, as far

from the windows as he could get. "You're meant to be a superhero. Like Gandalf or whatever. *Do* something!"

"Gandalf wasn't a superhero, he was a wizard," I mumbled. But his words gave me an idea. "You're not afraid of birds too, are you?"

"What? No!"

Looking up to the fog-wrapped sky, I imagined a flock of eagles, flying in formation like fighter jets. I wasn't holding Brad's hand, and something wrenched in the pit of my stomach as my energy flagged. But that was nothing compared to the triumphant swoop that followed when I sighted the specks in the sky, closing fast. Five giant eagles the colour of strong coffee soared towards us, their tails flared wedges.

Brad ran his hands through his hair. "What did you do?"

"I called the eagles." A smirk tugged at the corner of my lips, but the sound of the python striking the window right by my ear wiped it away. A crack as long as my little finger appeared in the glass.

"What are *they* going to do?"

"Eat the snakes. Do you want some terriers too?" He stared at me, open-mouthed. "Look, it should hold them off for long enough to..."

A new sound began from the next room of the house. It was barely audible over the machinegun rattle of the snakes, but it sounded like ... crying. When Brad started to speak, I hushed him, walking forward, head cocked to the side.

I paused at the door to the lounge room, staring.

The room I'd expected was gone. Instead, I looked into Mum's room at the nursing home. Jen sat by the bed, weeping, face buried in her cupped hands. And even though I knew she was ephemeral, not really there, I rushed to her side. "Jen, sweetie, what's wrong?"

She didn't answer. It was as if she didn't hear me. And then I saw why she was crying, and for a moment my heart stopped.

It wasn't my mother lying in the bed, although the figure had the same long, black hair and pale skin as her.

It was me.

I lay curled on my side, eyes closed and one hand under my cheek. A faint smile curved my lips.

"Wake up!" Jen cried, shaking my—the other Melaina's—shoulder. "Why won't you wake up?" A strand of hair fell across my brow, but I didn't stir.

My mouth went dry and a rushing noise sounded in my ears, as though the tide was coming in. I could barely hear Jen's crying and the *rat-a-tat* of the snakes. My knees felt weak. Why would I choose to be trapped inside a dream? Had I developed my mother's condition, given in to my mother's weakness? Her inability to face the real world?

The sound of smashing glass brought me back to myself. There was a clatter and a heavy thud. Swearing, I turned away from my best friend and my other self, and ran back into the kitchen.

A huge reticulated python was slithering through an uneven hole in the window, ignoring the blood that welled in a jagged line on its belly as it slid over the broken glass. Brad stood against the far wall, holding a kitchen chair like a weapon before him. He bit his lip hard, but his hands shook only slightly.

"It should hold them for long enough to *what*?" he

shouted. Had he even noticed I'd left the room? His gaze was fixed on the python. It ignored me completely, raising itself up in the sink to stare at him.

It wasn't part of my nightmare.

The room behind me was.

And something had us trapped in it.

Like hell.

"Just … hold on! I'll be back!" I yelled. Then, gathering my will like a bludgeon, I battered my way out of the dream, Brad's protest and Jen's grief clamouring in my ears.

Chapter Fourteen

I was half sitting, half lying in my armchair. My head hurt. My neck hurt. Someone straddled my legs, hands pressing firmly onto my cheeks. Warm, dusty-smelling air blew in my face with a sound like the hissing snakes I'd just left behind.

But this time my arms weren't restrained.

I reacted instinctively and violently. The first fist flew even as I opened my eyes. My knuckles connected with a ribcage that gave like putty under my blows. I shoved with both arms, bucking my hips to dislodge my attacker.

She fell to the ground and scrambled to her feet. I stood too, fists raised.

The woman was my height, dressed in rags. Lank hair framed a doughy face. Black, ragged-edged hollows gaped where her eyes and mouth should be. Another creature, with a stockier torso and narrower hips, straddled Brad. It—he—leaned forward, and exhaled into Brad's face with a familiar hiss.

I gasped, stepping back, and almost stumbled over my chair. Was this still the nightmare?

Brad whimpered. His breath whistled from a throat tight with panic. His eyes were scrunched shut, his jaw clenched. The tendons on his neck stood out, and sweat beaded his forehead.

Nightmare or not, there was a real risk Brad's heart might stop.

I glanced at the female. She still hadn't moved. It was hard to read anything from her blank features, but I guessed she was confused. Because I shouldn't have been able to wake up?

Go me.

I reached for the creature straddling Brad, grabbing him by the shoulders and attempting to pull him back. The monster clung on like a limpet, hands and legs tightening around Brad's slumped form. Jerking to life, the female lumbered forward. She grabbed one of my arms, wrenching it free. A faint moan arose, like wind over jagged rocks.

"Hit it!" a voice cried. Leander.

I reached out blindly to my left. My fingers found an empty coffee cup on the side table. Swinging wildly, I smashed it onto the woman's fingers. Blue shards scattered across the carpet, but she let go.

"Aim for the head!" Leander yelled at me from the reflection in the glass lampshade.

Gritting my teeth, I ripped the lamp from the wall socket. Holding the base, I swung the lampshade at her head.

It should have smashed, much like the coffee cup. Instead it passed through her doughy skull as if it were made of air. She exploded into hundreds of small, grey-winged insects. Their carcasses rained to the ground.

I screamed.

Behind me, so did Brad.

I whirled. His skin had flushed scarlet. The dough-man leaned over him, unperturbed by his partner's disintegration.

I raised the lamp again. "Time to wake up," I said and, with a grunt, brought it down on the doughman's head.

He collapsed into a mass of insects too. Dying moths writhed.

I dropped the lamp and reached for Brad, pulling him upright. He gasped and, for the longest moment, didn't exhale. I shook him, trying to remember my ancient first-aid training. Was shaking bad? His eyelids fluttered open.

"Oh, thank god." I hugged him tightly, inhaling his piney scent. "I thought you were dead."

"I'm not," he groaned, moving feebly. "What happened?"

Embarrassed, I released him and stepped back. "Don't move too much. Just sit still."

Ignoring me, he sat up straight. "That was one of the worst nightmares I've ever had. Do you have that effect on all your...?" He trailed off, staring down at his lap. "Why am I covered in dead moths?" He eyed my jumper. "You are too. Are they Bogongs?" He picked one up and studied the pattern on its wings. He seemed to have recovered from the trauma of the doughman's assault, although his eyes had dark circles beneath them, like bruises, and his skin was ashen.

"Can't be." I shuddered, brushing a few dead insects off my jumper. Their legs caught in the knitted weave. Every time I looked at the two piles of dead insects on

my carpet and scattered across the armchair, my skin tried to crawl away and hide in a cupboard. I kept seeing our two attackers collapsing in a shower of chitin and dusty wings. "They don't come out till spring."

"Because Bogong moths out of season is the weirdest thing about this situation." He raised an eyebrow at me.

"Shut up." I picked up my lamp, examining it for damage. I was going through a lot of lamps lately.

"So where did they come from?"

I told him. Nose wrinkling, he dropped the moth back onto the floor and wiped his hand on his jeans.

I wanted to flee the room and never come back. Or maybe set fire to it. But, thinking of Serenity, I set my shoulders and went to get the broom from the cupboard that came off the tiny bathroom.

Leander waited for me in the mirror above the sink, fanning his wings with agitation. I looked at him and then hastily away; his moth wings reminded me too much of other things. *Gaping mouths and hollow eyes.* "Took you long enough!" he said. "I've been waiting."

"Sorry. Thanks for the advice," I said, tucking a dust-pan and brush under my arm and picking up the broom. "You know, before."

"You're welcome." His voice was quiet, and I glanced at him in surprise. His lips were pressed together and his beautiful eyes were full of regret. "I'm just sorry I couldn't help. Physically, I mean."

"You can tell me what those things were. I've never seen anything like them."

"Mara. Spirits of nightmare."

"And the moths?"

"Just moths. The mara use them to gain form. The

moths can't harm you once the mara are gone."

"Their forms didn't look like moths. They had clothes and stuff."

"Illusion. If you look now, you'll find the clothes are gone." He tipped his head to the side. "I'll come to you next time you sleep, if you like. Tell you what I know."

I studied his expression for a long moment, waiting for the catch, but he seemed earnest. I found I wanted to trust him, even as I knew I shouldn't. "Okay."

He smiled faintly. "Glad you're still alive, Melaina." Then he vanished, replaced by my own reflection.

I look as tired as Brad.

"No shit," I muttered to myself, heading back out to my office. It hadn't exactly been a restful nap.

Brad was shaking moth carcasses from the orange throw rug onto the pile on the floor. The armchair itself seemed free of little bodies, although its shabbiness was revealed for all to see.

We cleaned in silence for several minutes before I noticed Brad was deliberately avoiding eye contact with me. At first I thought it was coincidence. But when I handed him the dustpan to sweep up the coffee cup shards and insect bodies that had tumbled under the side table, he kept his eyes firmly fixed on our hands.

"What's wrong?" I scuffed my toe through a drift of moths, and then wished I hadn't as some of them disintegrated with a crunch beneath my foot.

"What do you mean?" he mumbled.

In for a penny... "Are you upset with me?"

"No." He looked up then, blushing faintly. "I'm just ... I'm embarrassed."

"What on earth...?"

"The snakes." He tried to turn away, but I grabbed his arm to stop him. His forehead was creased, and when he turned back to me I let him go. "I'm not proud of the way I handled myself," he said.

"You're not proud of the fact you had a normal reaction to a nightmare? A nightmare deliberately tailored for you by actual *spirits* of nightmare?" I stared at him, one hand on my hip.

"*You* didn't lose it." His tone was faintly accusatory.

"Yes, I did. You just didn't see it." I didn't elaborate. My part of the nightmare had targeted a deeper, more visceral fear than Brad's phobia of snakes. Snakes can usually be avoided. Sleep can't. I cleared my throat and forced a smile. "Anyway, don't worry about it. Even Indiana Jones was scared of snakes."

Brad brushed the fingertips of his free hand across my cheek, and then froze, as though surprised at his reaction. I froze too—but after a moment he dropped his hand and knelt to sweep under the side table.

I exhaled softly and started sweeping again.

"What were they, anyway? The spirits?" he said, his voice muffled. He had, I noticed, a nice backside. Given he had a desk job, he must work out.

"They're called mara. I don't know much, but I'll find out more before we try this again."

"*Again*?" He glanced over his shoulder at me, eyes wide with alarm. I wouldn't have thought it possible for him to pale any further since he was already grey with fatigue. I was wrong.

"We didn't quite finish the job. We don't want another blight to set up shop."

"I almost preferred the blight." He laughed softly.

"I didn't."

His gaze flicked to the scarf around my neck, which I had readjusted while I was in the bathroom. "I guess not. Are they likely to come back?"

"I don't know." He frowned, and I added, "I really don't. I don't know why they were here in the first place. But I'll see what I can find out, and call you tomorrow. I promise."

"Am I going to be ... that is, could they come back tonight?"

I wanted to say no, that I'd killed them, not just disrupted their physical forms, but I didn't know for certain.

My hesitation was answer enough. "Look," Brad said, placing the dustpan and brush on the side table and pulling himself to his feet, "I know you're probably tired and you don't owe me anything. In fact, I still owe you—"

"You already paid me!"

"—for what happened the first night we met, and since. But is there any chance you could come to my place tonight to make sure I don't get possessed again before we can finish cleaning my brain?" He laughed shakily.

I hesitated, then raised an eyebrow. "You have a strange way of hitting on girls."

"I didn't—! I'm not—!"

"Relax." I giggled. "I'm kidding."

"You're terrible," he said, although a smile lit his face. "Did you know that?"

"It's been mentioned before."

Chapter Fifteen

I organised to meet Brad at his place at six that evening. As partial compensation, he offered to cook dinner.

By the time I got home it was mid-afternoon, and I was dragging my feet with exhaustion. I'd almost fallen asleep on the bus and missed my stop.

Jen was sitting on the couch when I entered, heavy books spread out around her, but when she saw my face she stood, taking the bag from my shoulder and putting it on the bench. "Are you okay?"

"Tired," I said. "I'm going to have a nap."

"What happened?"

As I peeled off my outer layer of winter clothing, I explained the afternoon's events to her, including Leander's brief explanation—although I left out the details of my nightmare. I wasn't ready to talk about that with anyone.

Jen pushed her glasses up her nose and then folded

her arms, leaning back against the counter. "Melaina, what's going on? That's the second time you've been attacked in three days. It isn't normal."

"No kidding." I blew on my fingers. My freezing hands tingled in the warm air of the apartment as I piled my beanie, scarf and coat beside my bag. "I've pissed someone off, that's for sure."

"You think it's connected?"

"Has to be. I just don't know how yet." I glanced at my bedroom. "Leander said he's going to drop by, explain what he can. That's part of why I need a nap." I'd realised afterwards that I should've insisted we talk through the reflection in the flat's bathroom mirror rather than inviting him into my dreams. *Too late now.* Besides, I couldn't stop him from showing up if he wanted to. And this way, if he annoyed me, I could smack him in his dream face.

"And the rest is because you're asleep on your feet?" Jen said.

"Yeah." I suppressed a yawn. "Plus Brad wants me to come over tonight." Jen's eyebrows almost disappeared into her hairline. "Not like that. In case the mara come back. But I thought I could try and finish cleaning up the last trace of the blight. I don't know, maybe that's what attracted the mara and it's all a coincidence."

"Alright." But her frown spoke volumes.

I was halfway up the corridor when she called out to me. "Oh, hey. You gave that Ewan guy my number?"

"I told you I would. Did he call?"

She nodded. "We're going out later."

"Gee, he moves fast." I grinned.

"I didn't actually think you'd do it, you know." She blushed faintly, but her eyes sparkled. I was glad to see

her looking so excited.

"You should know me better than that."

"I guess I should. Sweet dreams."

"They'll have Leander in them, so I doubt it." I wrinkled my nose, then disappeared into my room, closing the door behind me.

After setting an alarm on my phone, I pulled my boots off and lay down, fully clothed, on top of the doona. My breath sighed out of me.

Leander appeared as soon as I began to dream. I was in the dining hall of my former boarding school, and he stepped through the double doors, his moth wings spread wide to take advantage of the space. He was a magnificent sight, although I wouldn't have admitted that to him. His long legs were clad in bronze pants that clung like leather. His torso was bare except for a vest of the same material, only several shades darker. The vest hung open, revealing a muscled chest. His bare feet made no noise as he padded across the tiles to my table, but he didn't sit.

"Nice choice," Leander said with faint sarcasm, looking around the hall at the bright school banners, the empty canteen with its bains-marie glittering under the neon lights.

"Not a conscious one. But I'm too tired to bother changing it, so we're stuck with it."

"No, we're not. Allow me." Leander leaned forward, brushing his fingers across the back of my hand where it rested on the metal table. The cafeteria melted away, cool air replaced by sun-soaked grass. We stood on the side of a hill overlooking a rolling valley. A cerulean blue sky stretched overhead and, in a touch that showed me how hard Leander was trying, butterflies danced and wheeled above us.

"Presumptuous much?" I said, but without any real heat to my voice.

He shrugged, dropping down to lounge in the grass, which was far softer than any grass had a right to be. Especially sun-baked Australian grass. He didn't lie perfectly flat but slightly to one side, wings resting together behind him, squashing the grass flat. They were heavier than they looked. "I don't like schools. And you weren't especially fond of that one, as I recall. Do you like it?" He indicated the valley with a wave of one arm. It was dotted with ash trees in their autumn garb: brilliant shades of yellow, orange and purple.

"It's very nice." I settled near him, but not too near, folding my hands behind my head and watching the butterflies' ecstatic swirling for a few moments. My entire body ached with fatigue, even in the dream, but the warmth seeped into my bones, relaxing me almost against my will.

Leander had known me for a long time. He knew I liked the heat, would bask in it like a cat.

Finally I sighed and turned to face him. He was resting his chin in one hand, studying me with those gold-flecked eyes and a slight smile on his lips.

"What?" I scowled.

"Just—"

"If you say you're admiring the view I will hit you," I said.

"I wouldn't dare." Leander chuckled, his wings shifting in the grass behind him. They still reminded me of the hundreds of out-of-season moth carcasses now filling a

garbage bag in the dumpster behind Serenity's, but I was able to look at them without feeling ill. It helped that his wings were a uniform grey, not brown with darker and lighter spots like those of the Bogongs.

"What's with the moth thing?"

He tipped his head to the side. His hair was a warm brown that gleamed in the sun. "What?"

"Your wings. The mara's insects. Moths."

"Coincidence," he said.

"Yeah, right."

"The mara could use anything to give them form. Any insect. They often choose moths, to spite the Oneiroi. They don't like us much."

"Then that's not a coincidence, is it?" My tone was peevish but I didn't care.

He gave me a reproachful look. "Be grateful they didn't use something with a sting."

The mental image of piles of wasps, dying on my office floor, widened my eyes. Would dying wasps attack? The moths hadn't lived more than a few seconds, but... I swallowed. It didn't bear thinking about.

Leander's explanation didn't feel right to me, though, and I wondered if the mara and the Oneiroi were related. It couldn't be a coincidence that my ability to make people sleep by exhaling on their faces—getting them to inhale my breath, along with whatever particles of magic were in it—and theirs worked the same way.

I doubted Leander would admit to having relatives like those, though.

"Can you tell me about them?" I asked.

I'd half-expected him to bargain with me, to haggle for some piece of information about my father, but he didn't. His unexpected generosity surprised me, and I watched him with interest as he spoke.

"They are primarily denizens of Erebus, like us. The world of dreams," Leander began.

I knew that much. Erebus was made up of the interconnected dreams of every sleeping soul, like a giant patchwork quilt whose pieces changed as people entered and left their dreams. The Oneiroi could move between the pieces as freely as I would step over a rivulet of water marking the border between one place and another.

"They have a basic intelligence—say, that of your average dog." Leander plucked several long strands of grass. He began to braid them together, slender fingers moving deftly. "And they feed on strong emotions. Negative emotions, that is. Fear, grief, rage, betrayal... They wander into a dream and twist it, change it to inspire those emotions in the dreamer."

I shuddered at the memory of the snakes and nodded. "The blights do the same thing, don't they?"

"Yes, but they are motivated by wanting to gain control of the dreamer, to influence your world. And unlike us Oneiroi or the blights," Leander continued, "the mara don't have a higher intelligence or capacity to navigate through Erebus to find a particular dream. They sort of just ... bumble around. Like animals."

"I can't do that either," I pointed out. "Find any dream. I need to be physically near the dreamer."

"Yes, but you're tied to a human body," Leander said. "The mara aren't."

"Does that mean they found us by accident?" I asked. Leander shook his head, and his fingers stilled for a moment as he looked at me. "What?" I said, suddenly

cold despite the warm air. "You're freaking me out."

He spoke softly. "Unlike a full-blooded Oneiroi, the mara can sometimes affect the human world. Take form of a sort. It gives them the capacity to find a person sleeping on that side, and then step into their dream."

"Like me. Only without the bugs."

"Yes. The thing is, Melaina, the mara can't take a form on their own. They can only do it if they have been given the power to do so by another. By an Oneiroi."

Goosebumps rippled along my arms. "Someone was targeting Brad?"

"Not Brad."

"Me?" I squeaked.

"It's the only thing that makes sense." He finished weaving the grass, and knotted the two ends together to form a bracelet. "The first time you met Brad, it was because his blight sought you out, remember?"

"Maybe it's a coincidence."

"Yeah, right." He imitated my earlier tone perfectly.

"Okay, so it's not likely. But why—"

"What was his name? The fellow with the glasses?"

"Larry?"

"Yes. Him."

"It can't be."

"Why not? Give me your wrist."

I held my arm out, hand trembling faintly, and he slipped the grass bracelet over my hand. Then he narrowed his eyes, and it transformed from golden grass into actual gold, still imprinted with the woven strands. "Like it?"

"It's pretty," I said. But I was thinking about his question, not about a piece of jewellery that would vanish when I woke up. Why didn't I think Larry was the cause? Because he seemed like such an unlikely source of trouble. But I'd evicted the blight from him, and two days later Brad had attacked me. Maybe I'd pissed someone off. Not Larry, but whomever had infected him. "Is it possible the blights could have sent the mara?"

"No," Leander said, lips pressed together as he glanced at the bracelet on my wrist. "Blights aren't that much brighter than mara. Nor are they powerful enough to direct them. And there's no way the mara would have risked manifesting themselves to help a blight out of the goodness of their own hearts, even if they could do it without aid. It would take an Oneiroi to force them."

"Can you control blights too? Don't Oneiroi drive them out?"

"We do," he said hastily. "The Morpheus, our king, has strict rules about inflicting nightmares on humans. He's what you might describe as an environmentalist. Nightmares make Erebus unpleasant for the Oneiroi, so he doesn't approve..."

He looked away, and I sensed there was something more he was reluctant to say. "But?"

Leander sighed. "But we *can* control blights. It's happened in the past. There have been Oneiroi who have sought to tame the darker creatures of Erebus, to use them for their own purposes. It's a crime punishable by exile and, in grave cases, death. Even the Morpheus's own brother wasn't immune to that rule."

"So I've somehow managed to piss off an unknown Oneiroi?"

Leander nodded.

"Well, that's just great." I sat up. Startled, the butterflies,

which had clustered together on a crop of dandelions, took wing and fled for the trees. "I don't suppose there's any chance they'll give up and stop bothering me?"

"I doubt it."

Dammit.

"What are you going to do about it then?" I poked him on the arm and smiled.

His eyes widened. "What do you mean?"

"Aren't you some sort of Oneiroi enforcer? The police or whatever? You've been hunting my father for pretty much my entire life. The fact you aren't very good at it notwithstanding—"

"No thanks to you!"

"—isn't your job to catch people who are breaking the law?"

"I've got a specific mission." He sniffed. "The Morpheus wouldn't approve."

"He'd probably be grateful to you for showing initiative, catching a bad guy for once."

My teasing had gone too far. He leapt to his feet with a grace I'd never match and strode down the hill, wings stiff with outrage.

"Bugger," I whispered, embarrassed. I didn't know what had gotten into me. Once upon a time, Leander and I had teased each other. We'd had a ready banter. He'd been my cool older friend, someone I hung out with in my dreams. But that was almost ten years ago—before I'd found out he was hunting Ollie, my father. Things had been prickly between us since then, mostly because I'd spent the last decade being furious with him.

I'd forgotten for a moment that I was angry, that I didn't trust him—and when I'd tried to poke fun he'd taken offence. Guilt gnawed at my insides, and I couldn't decide whether it was for making fun of him, or for the longer-term offence of hating him for so long. Part of me still thought he deserved it.

I stood and followed him down the hill, to where it sloped more steeply towards the valley floor.

"Hey," I said. He didn't answer. "I'm sorry. That was unfair of me."

He turned, and his green eyes were wide and sad beneath pinched eyebrows. Even the golden flecks seemed subdued. "Not entirely unfair. You're right; I haven't caught your father. And it's also unfair that I ask for your help to do so. No, unfair is too weak a word. It's a gross injustice, and something you should know I'm ashamed of." He took my hands in his warm grip and gazed down at me.

His acknowledgement thawed a part of me that had turned to ice ten years ago. He seemed sincere, but I had to ask. "You're not going to stop, though, are you?" I said, voice soft.

"No. I can't. But I'm sorry for it."

We stood there together for a time, holding hands and looking out onto the artificial valley, each thinking our own thoughts.

"Leander?" I said finally. "I do like the bracelet. Thank you."

Chapter Sixteen

*J*en dropped me off at Brad's house on her way to meet Ewan. They were having dinner, apparently, then going to see a movie. "Thanks for this," I said as we pulled up alongside the curb.

"No worries. It was on the way." I raised an eyebrow and she added, "Sort of." Engine running, she turned to face me, eyes narrowed. "Call me if there are any problems and I'll come get you."

"Problems like what?"

"Like if, I don't know, those nightmare spirits attack again. Or Brad gets all murderous." Her gaze dropped to her lap as she said the last part. She was serious.

"I thought you liked Brad now?"

"I do. I just... I don't understand your world. I worry something might go wrong. Brad's been possessed before."

"Once we're done tonight, he won't be any more vulnerable than anyone else. Besides, Leander's got my back, and Belinda lives there. They have lots of lamps.

I'll be fine."

I'd tried to sound reassuring, but she snorted. "Leander? Now I'm definitely going to worry. How do you know you can trust *him*?" Jen had heard me rant about Leander's betrayal more times than I could count.

I undid my seatbelt. "Because he wants something from me. Enjoy your date, hon."

"Text me!" she called as I slid out of the car.

"I will."

Brad opened the door as I approached. He looked as tired as I felt, shadows under his eyes and face pale. And I was pretty sure he hadn't dared to have an afternoon nap. But the distinctive smell of smoked salmon greeted me as I hurried inside, making my stomach rumble.

"You cooked?"

"I said I would." He closed the door behind me.

"I thought we might have takeaway again." I followed him through to the kitchen, removing my coat and gloves as I walked.

He shook his head. "Two meals in a row?"

I didn't tell him takeaway was a regular occurrence in our apartment when we could afford it. Somehow I didn't think his objections were financial. "Do you eat seafood?" he asked.

"Yup."

"Phew." He mimed wiping his brow.

I watched for several minutes as he finished dinner preparations, checking a saucepan that boiled on the stove, running a wooden spoon through some cream and basil pesto that simmered beside it, and then getting out two plates. Half a pot of coffee sat to one side, an aromatic explanation of how Brad had kept going this afternoon.

Two plates.

"Belinda's not home?"

"She's working from Sydney this week. She flew out a couple of hours ago."

The thought didn't bother me, but I knew Jen wouldn't approve. She'd wanted to cancel her date when I'd told her where I was going for dinner, but I hadn't let her. I would catch hell from her when she found out.

"It's creamy salmon pasta," Brad said, draining steaming water from the saucepan. "I hope that's okay. I didn't have the energy to go to the supermarket."

"It looks wonderful," I said, watching as he folded the basil, cream and slices of salmon through the penne. He'd had smoked salmon in the house?

We again ate at the breakfast bar rather than the formal dining table in the next room, which I found reassuring. If this were an elaborate pickup routine, I doubted he'd be this informal. *Hey, want to come back to my place and check out my blight infestation?* And they say romance is dead.

The idea made me laugh into my fork. Brad tipped his head to one side. "Something funny?"

"Not really. I'm just tired. At this point I find pretty much everything funny." *Or rage-inducing.* Best not add that part.

"I hear that," he said, washing down his food with a mouthful of coffee.

"I have some good news," I said, changing the subject before I blurted out something embarrassing. "A couple of things, actually. Firstly, the mara that attacked us are unlikely to come after you again."

"How do you figure?"

"Because my sources say they were probably after me."

I said it in an offhand manner, but he stared at me for a long moment. "Even if that's true, how is that *good* news?"

"It means you should be safe."

"And you?"

"Well, that's the thing. It turns out they can only manifest to attack you if they use insects to create a physical form. Live insects." I reached down to my bag, which was leaning against the counter by my feet, and pulled out a large black spray can. "That's why I bought this on the way here."

"Surface spray?" He chuckled. "They really ought to incorporate that into their advertising. 'Protects from flying and crawling insects, and from nightmares made flesh'."

That set me off, laughing till tears trickled down my cheeks. I clutched my stomach with one hand and the edge of the counter with the other, concerned I might topple off the stool. My hysterical, overtired laughter was contagious, and soon both of us were cackling like a pair of kookaburras.

"So we make sure there's no way the little critters can get into the house, just in case?" he said, once he'd finished gasping for breath.

I nodded, dabbing tears away with the corner of my sleeve.

"What's the second bit of good news?"

"I should be able to finish cleaning the blight's contamination tonight." Brad paled, his humour abruptly dying, and I added hastily, "Don't worry. No mara mean no snakes, remember? But I've organised backup, just in case."

"Backup?"

I pushed pasta around my plate. He waited patiently. "When I told you about Mum's condition, what did you think my father was?"

He shrugged. "I didn't know what to think. That he was a ghost, maybe?" The calm way in which he said it surprised me. Most people wouldn't have believed me. But I guess he'd been presented with a lot of evidence in the form of our battle with the blight, and now the dead mara.

"You're sort of right. He's not a ghost. But he's not human." Even though he had to have wondered, his eyes still widened at the words. "Remember how I said earlier today that he was a moth-man?"

"I thought you were trying to be funny."

"Trying?"

"Sorry, *being* funny."

"I was." A smile twitched the corner of my lip. "But it was true too. He's a type of dream spirit called an Oneiroi. They're sort of … guardians and rulers of Erebus. The land of dreams."

"Like the Aboriginal Dreamtime?"

"I think so. Only when Europeans came to Australia, the Dreamtime vanished and Erebus took over." Years before, an elder from the Wiradjuri people had talked to my high school social studies class about the death of the Dreamtime, and I'd been able to read between the lines. Hearing about it had filled me with guilt at the actions of my ancestors. I was half Oneiroi and half European, the latter part a typically Australian mix that in my case involved English, Scottish, Greek and who knew what else. So I felt doubly responsible, even though

141

it had happened almost two centuries before I was born.

Brad chewed his lip and stayed silent for several minutes, enough time for me to finish my food and help myself to a glass of water from the kitchen. Finally he met my gaze across the counter. "So you're half-human?"

I shrugged. "Yeah."

"But how, if your father doesn't have a..." He gestured vaguely down his own body, but I knew what he meant.

"I don't know. Neither does anyone else, not even my mother. Not really. Only my father knows, and he's not telling. That's where Leander comes in." Sitting beside him again, I explained about my childhood imaginary friend, who'd turned out to be a very real Oneiroi on the lookout for my wanted father. Brad listened, food forgotten in front of him.

"Say something," I said when his silence had gone on too long.

"I'm still stuck on the part where you're only half-human," he said. I scowled and he immediately realised his mistake. "Not 'only' as in 'just'," he spluttered, cheeks flaming. "I just, I mean... You look *normal*."

"I *am* normal. No doctor has ever noticed something different about me. I broke my arm when I was eight, and the X-rays showed normal bones. And I seem to have the regular number of hearts, lungs and other organs. I've never had a brain scan, so I can't confirm whether that's different, but medications work normally. As far as I can tell." I pursed my lips at the sour taste in my mouth. "Of course, for all I know I'm like a mule and the money I'm spending on contraception is a waste, but there's no way to know till I try to have kids."

He sat back a little, eyes widening at my tirade. "Sorry."

"Yeah, well. You touched a nerve," I muttered, fidgeting with my glass.

"You've bottled that up for a long time, haven't you?"

I glanced at him, but there was no trace of mockery in his expression. "I guess," I said, sighing. "There aren't many people who know."

"How many?"

"Mum. Jen. You. And you're the first one I've…" I trailed off.

"Mentioned your concerns about infertility to?" Brad said delicately.

"How did you know?"

"You're blushing pretty hard."

I buried my face in my hands. My ears burned as if they were on fire; I half expected the smoke detector in the ceiling to start up a shrill protest. "I could die right now."

"I'd rather you didn't," he said, reaching over the counter to put his plate in the kitchen without leaving his stool. "The police would never believe I didn't have anything to do with it."

I looked up, an angry retort on my lips. But he was smiling, chocolate eyes twinkling. After a few moments, I smiled too.

"I've never met anyone like you," Brad said.

"Because I'm abnormal?"

"No," he said, voice low with conviction … and something more. He turned to face me, leaning closer. My breath caught. "Because you're extraordinary."

And then he leaned over and kissed me.

My heart leapt as his soft lips brushed mine. The kiss was tentative, as he waited to see whether I would pull away. I waited too. My memories of Brad weren't all exactly positive. I should have run for the door. Anyone else would have.

Instead I hopped off the stool and stepped into his embrace, kissing him back. It was gentle at first—but soon I found my hands wrapping around his neck and my lips parting. Taking the invitation, his tongue slid into my mouth, tasting of our dinner and his coffee. Heat blossomed in my belly and I shivered. His fingers curled in my hair, tugging gently, and I moaned. The sensation was delicious; even the faint rasping of his stubble against my cheek was exhilarating to my heightened senses. Still seated on the stool, he was the same height as me; his legs were on either side of me, his knees brushing against my thighs in a way that made me crave more contact, more sensation. When he slid off the seat to press against me, I shivered.

I don't know how long we stood there, enjoying the touch and the taste of one another. I know what made me break away, though. I caught sight of our reflection in the small window above the sink. Or, rather, of Leander, watching us.

Flustered, I dropped my arms and would have retreated, but my back was against my stool. Brad felt the change in my body language and stepped back too—although he kept one hand resting loosely on my shoulder, running a lock of hair through his fingers. He was smiling.

"I've wanted to do that for ages."

I laughed breathlessly. "We've known each other four days, and the first day doesn't count."

He laughed, his thumb running down the side of my throat. "Okay, since yesterday morning. When I woke up after my nightmare and found you asleep in my bed."

"I'm glad you didn't try it then," I said. "I don't think I'd have taken it well."

"I figured."

I glanced again at the window, embarrassment warring with irritation. Leander was gone, but I slipped out of Brad's embrace and walked into the kitchen. "You shouldn't leave these open at night. It lets all the heat out."

And I closed the blinds.

Chapter Seventeen

"*D*o you mind if I listen to the footie, love?" The taxi driver glanced at me as he pulled out onto the street.

"Nope," I said, blowing on my fingers through my gloves. "Not so long as you turn up the heater."

"Rightio." He laughed, twisting several dials on the dashboard. The heater's *woosh* was barely audible beneath the excited call of a commentator who sounded as if he'd been drinking too much coffee. No one should be that animated at this time of night.

I'd finished cleansing the blight contamination from Brad's mind a half hour earlier and, although he'd asked me to stay in case the mara returned, I was positive he wasn't their target. I'd told him I was too tired, and called a cab. But I'd left him the surface spray, just in case.

The truth was, I wasn't sure I could trust myself to sleep under the same roof as Brad, let alone in the same bed. There'd been some more heated kissing, both before

and after working on his dreams. I found my sudden lack of self-control around him disturbing. I'd had partners before, a couple of them, but I wasn't a girl who jumped into bed with a guy right at the start of a relationship.

I didn't even know if Brad and I had a relationship.

A car swept past in the other direction, its headlights briefly flooding the cabin with light. A reflection loomed in the side window and then vanished, like a ghost.

Only it wasn't my reflection. The next time a car passed us, I looked harder. Leander stood there, arms folded tightly across his chest. He said nothing, for which I was grateful. Although the cabbie wouldn't hear him, I was hardly in a position to answer. But it was clear the Oneiroi wasn't happy.

The brief glimpses of his shadowed eyes made me uncomfortable, embarrassed. I averted my gaze, watching the taxi's meter ticking over as though my life depended on it.

If it weren't for the money Brad had paid me, I wouldn't have been able to afford a taxi home. He'd offered to drive me, but he'd been so exhausted he was swaying on his feet. And I'd been tired enough that the idea of the long bus ride home had made me want to weep. So: taxi.

When we arrived at the front of our apartment block, I paid the driver and stepped out of the superheated cab into the frozen night air. Frost was already settling on the pavement and clinging to blades of grass like a cold-fingered lover. Fog wisped along the street, torn to shreds by my boots as I hurried through the glass door into the tiny foyer of our building. The shut doors of the downstairs apartments loomed on either side, guarding silent interiors. It was late.

I'd only placed a single boot on the concrete stair up to our floor when Leander spoke from behind me. "Aren't you going to talk to me?"

I turned to face his reflection in the door. He was still wearing the leather pants and vest from my dream earlier in the day, and the bare flesh of his arms and stomach made the tiny stairwell seem colder. Or maybe that was due to his frosty expression. Irritation surged for a moment—what right did he have to look so disapproving? But I took a deep breath and suppressed the feeling. The peace between us was fragile. I didn't want to break it if I could avoid it.

"You're right," I whispered, hoping not to rouse the neighbours. "I owe you thanks for looking out for Brad and me while I cleansed the blight taint. So thank you." He hadn't shown himself directly in Brad's dream, but his presence had been there, like static-charged air.

"I wasn't looking out for Brad," he said, voice sullen.

"Well, I appreciate it." I smiled stiffly. "Now, if you don't mind, I'm freezing here." Again I began to turn, and his voice called me back.

"You do owe me, and not just thanks."

I narrowed my eyes. "And what do you think I owe you?"

"You know what."

All my anger at him returned, like acid at the back of my throat. "For the love of... Leander, *I don't know where he is*!" My voice echoed sharply off the brick and concrete, and I winced. To my left came the click of paws on vinyl and the snuffling of a nose against the bottom of the door. The neighbour's miniature dachshund, Ruben. I willed the dog to stay quiet, not to wake up the entire apartment block.

"But you suspect it, don't you?" Leander's voice was as cold as the pane of glass in which he'd appeared. I didn't answer. But he was right. There was only one place it made sense for my father to be.

My mother's dreams, hidden behind that impenetrable wall around her mind.

Leander knew as well as I did that Dad visited Mum's dreams. He'd spent years trying to find a way in, the secret door my father was using to get in and out. It had never occurred to him that an Oneiroi might give up the freedom to walk in others' dreams to hide in one mind, one dream. Forever.

I was pretty sure that was what my father had done. It would have been romantic if it hadn't incapacitated her.

Leander's gaze ran over my face, taking in my narrowed eyes and compressed lips. I wasn't going to answer. If Leander took my theory to the Morpheus, the Oneiroi king, he might send an army to smash into Mum's mind, to ferret my father out like a rabbit from a burrow. I had no idea what damage that would do to her. And I didn't think they'd care.

"Goodnight, Leander," I murmured. Behind the door, Ruben wuffed softly.

"You're wrong to trust him," Leander called after me as I started up the stairs.

"I don't." I kept walking.

"Not your father." I glanced back. Leander's arms were folded again, and his expression was dark. "Brad."

"What? Can we talk about this later?" Again my voice was too loud. Ruben's answering bark was louder, and I swore under my breath.

Leander nodded curtly and vanished. I hurried upstairs

to our apartment before the dachshund woke the dead.

I'd texted Jen to tell her I was coming home, but her reply had given no indication she'd already done the same, so I was surprised to see the flickering light of the television under our door.

She muted the sound when I let myself in. "You're home sooner than I expected."

"I caught a cab." I shed my bag and coat with a grateful sigh.

"Wow."

"I know, right? This is how the other half live!" I tipped my head to one side, taking in her pyjamas and furry blanket. "You weren't waiting up for me, were you?"

"A little bit," she said, shuffling to one side on the couch so I could sit next to her. "How'd it go?"

"Good." I must have blushed, because she narrowed her eyes suspiciously. "Uh, he kissed me," I added.

Jen's eyes widened and her mouth fell open for a moment. Then she asked, "And did you kiss him back?"

"A little bit." I grinned.

"Did you guys...?" She made an obscene gesture with her hands. I batted them away.

"No! I cleaned his dreams and then decided it was safer to head home. I didn't want to have buyer's regret tomorrow." I leaned forward to unlace my boots, murmuring, "But I *really* wanted to."

"That's hardly a surprise." Jen's tone was so matter-of-fact that I stared at her. "Oh, don't act all shocked. You always did like bad boys."

"That's not it at all!"

"Isn't it?"

"No! And he's hardly a bad boy, anyway. He's pretty

much an IT geek!"

"A hot IT geek who tried to strangle you that one time."

"That wasn't his fault!" I yanked my boot off with unnecessary force, nearly flinging it across the room.

She held up her hands as if to ward me off. "I know, I know. I'm just saying, you like bad boys and it's got to help."

I caught my hand stroking the scarf I still wore to hide my bruises, and scowled as I realised how it must look. "You make me sound like a deviant."

"I'm not saying that."

"What *are* you saying?"

She sighed. "That I'm glad you came home. Just take it easy with this guy, okay?"

"I was planning on it." I realised how angry I sounded and took a deep breath. "I'm sorry. I had an argument with Leander and it's making me pissy."

She gave me a quick hug. "What's his problem?"

"The usual. He helped me with Brad's dream, watched my back, then tried to say I owed him."

"Your dad?"

"Yeah. And here I thought he was helping out of the goodness of his heart."

We watched the silent television without talking for several minutes. The late news had come on, the camera panning past images of shattered buildings. A warzone or a disaster zone; I couldn't tell. Was there a difference? War was usually a disaster.

Jen sighed. Shame filled me, deepening my sudden melancholy. I hadn't asked about her evening. "So how did the date go? I was half-hoping you'd be the one staying out all night."

"Not that great," she said, watching her hands as they fidgeted with the edge of her blanket.

"What did he do?" I turned to face her, putting one hand over hers to stop her picking the blanket to pieces.

"It doesn't matter."

"I'll clobber him the next time I see him."

Her mouth fell open. "Oh, you can't!"

"Why shouldn't I?"

"Because he didn't do anything wrong. He just—"

"What?"

"He spent the whole evening talking about you!" Her cheeks flushed pink, but I couldn't see her eyes through the reflection of the television on her glasses.

I stared. "Pardon?"

She started to fidget again. Stunned, I didn't stop her. "I think he only agreed to come on a date with me to find out about you. He asked lots of questions, raved about how amazing you are. Which I agree with, of course, but..." She shrugged.

"I'm so sorry," I said, mortified. "I had no... I didn't... I'm sorry, Jen!"

"Not your fault. If he had such a thing for you he should have asked you out."

Guilt chewed at my insides as I remembered how he'd asked me for coffee and I'd given him Jen's number instead. Had that been a sign? I pulled a face. "If he tries it, I'll say no and crush his heart under my boots."

Jen laughed, and I relaxed a little. She wasn't angry with me. I, on the other hand, was furious at Ewan for taking advantage of my friend. I wasn't flattered; I was offended. In my mind I demoted him from badger to skunk again, despite his warning about Mum's doctor.

That one act of kindness only got him so much credit.

"They are great boots for breaking hearts," Jen said. "Steel caps and all."

"Damn straight."

Chapter Eighteen

*I*t had started raining by the time I finished work that Tuesday. Serenity beamed as I held the door open for my departing client, a heavily pregnant woman named Maria who'd worried her nightmares about her baby were a premonition. I'd been able to reassure her it was a combination of hormones and anxiety, and sent her home with a program of restful dreams that should last at least a week.

"How is she?" Serenity asked when the door jingled closed. The store was empty, so she wasn't worried about appearing to be a stickybeak—and she'd referred Maria to me, the same way she had Larry, so I guessed she felt invested.

I didn't complain. Most of my clients came via word of mouth. And Serenity had a very big mouth.

"She's fine. Hopefully she'll be able to sleep through for a while, get some rest before the baby comes."

Serenity snorted a laugh. "Unlikely. She'll be up to

pee at least three times a night!" She would know; she'd had several babies of her own.

I shrugged. "Not much I can do about that."

"But the baby is fine?"

"As far as I can tell." I'd tried to brush its dreams while its mother was sleeping, but it had been wide awake and apparently engaging in some enthusiastic kickboxing—vigorously enough that Maria would have woken if her sleep hadn't been magical. Another reason Serenity was right about Maria not sleeping, I supposed.

"Good." Serenity brushed an imaginary speck of dirt from the counter. "You're off then?"

"Yeah." I wrinkled my nose at the rain dimpling puddles on the pavement outside. "I promised Mum I'd drop by and see her after work. There's a bus in five minutes." It had only been two days since my last visit to the home, but so much had happened it seemed like longer.

"You're a good girl," Serenity said.

"Not that good." I shrugged into my coat. "Under other circumstances I'd probably make excuses, given the weather. But..."

"She started the new treatment yesterday, didn't she?"

I nodded.

"And you want to go check on her."

"Yeah."

"You're a good girl," she repeated, with more authority this time. "Do you need to borrow my umbrella?"

"Then what will you use?" I hadn't heard the forecast before I left the flat that morning.

"I have a car. You don't."

The rain was growing heavier. "Uh. Yes, please."

I darted out to the bus stop barely thirty seconds

before the bus rumbled along the street. Normally I wouldn't be impressed that it was running early, given the odds I'd miss it, but this time it saved me from standing in the rain longer than I had to, so I was grateful. I hurried aboard and sat under one of the heating vents with a sigh, resting the dripping umbrella on the floor beside me.

Serenity was right, I did want to check on Mum. Doctor Willis had started her on the new drug regime first thing Monday morning. She'd only given permission on Sunday afternoon, but Uncle Ian didn't waste time. Mum had called at lunchtime and, although she'd said everything was okay, I knew better. She was trying not to worry me.

I trudged into the home, folding Serenity's umbrella and shaking the rain out the door. The first sight to greet me was Ewan, flicking through some papers at the reception desk.

Dammit.

"Hi, Melaina." He greeted me with a cheery smile as I signed in.

"Hey. Where's Mum?" My tone was curt, but I gave myself points for not coming across as surly. Or dour.

His smile wilted. "In her room."

Okay, maybe a little bit surly.

"Thanks."

I left the umbrella in the brass stand by the door and set out for Mum's room at a brisk walk. To my irritation, Ewan fell in beside me. "I don't remember if I thanked you for giving me your friend's number. I had a great evening with her."

"Seriously?" I blurted, stopping to stare at him.

He took several steps past me before realising I wasn't with him anymore. "Yeah." He frowned. "Why, didn't she have a good time? Did she say something?"

Awkward. I wished I'd bitten my tongue. "She, ah, got the impression your heart wasn't in it. So to speak."

"Well, we'd only just met. Did she expect cards and flowers?"

"That's not what I mean."

"What do you mean?"

"Look, it isn't my place to say." A blush heated my cheeks. Flustered, I resumed walking.

Ewan hesitated. "Should I call her again?"

I thought that would go down like a lead balloon, but I'd meddled enough, so I decided on non-committal. "That's up to you."

"I would have called already," he said quickly, hands clenching and unclenching in an anxious gesture, "but I was trying to play it cool. I didn't want to come across as too needy."

Was he nervous because he wanted to make sure I gave a good report to Jen, or because he was trying to make a good impression with me, personally, so I didn't think he was a scumbag? Had Jen misread his choice of conversation topics on Sunday night? Maybe he was so socially awkward he couldn't think of anything else to talk about except the one thing he and Jen had in common: me.

His conversation also reminded me that I hadn't heard from Brad since our make-out session on Sunday, which made me cranky. I squared my shoulders. "How's Mum been since the treatment?"

"Good," he said. "She's been awake more. Doctor Willis

is very happy."

"And her? Is *she* happy?"

He lowered his voice. There was no one else in the corridor but several doors were open, including Mum's. "She seems subdued. You'd be a better judge of what that means than me."

"Right." I stopped outside her door. "Thanks."

He took the hint and turned, heading back down the corridor.

"Mum?"

She sat by the window beside the table, gazing out at the miserable afternoon. She didn't turn when I entered, and I hurried to her side, taking her hands. They were icy. "Are you okay?"

Raindrops trickling down the window cast faint, moving shadows onto her cheeks, the ghosts of tears she wouldn't shed. "One of the wattle trees out there is dying. Do you think I should tell someone?"

I shrugged. "How are you feeling?"

"I'm as you'd expect, sweetheart. Awake."

There was only one chair in the room, so I knelt beside her, chafing her fingers between mine in an attempt to warm them. "And Ollie?"

"He's not always there when I sleep now." she said, a knot of pain in her voice. "Or maybe he is, and I can't recall. I don't always remember my dreams anymore. I remember them when I first wake up, but then they slip through my fingers like sand."

"That's how most people are with their dreams."

Her hands clutched at mine and panic widened her eyes. "I'm not most people. My husband is an Oneiroi, and I'm losing him, one pill at a time."

"We'll tell Willis to stop," I said, trying to reassure her.

"We can't. Your uncle—"

"Screw him." I scowled, standing, but she clutched my fingers tightly to hold me still.

"Ollie said we should give it a week, that he'd find a way around the chemicals."

I tipped my head to the side. "Is there any way you could, you know, not take the pills? Flush them down the toilet? Throw them in the trash?"

"They'd notice."

I narrowed my eyes. "Are they forcing you to take them?"

"Oh no, nothing like that," she hastened to reassure me. "But if I started sleeping more..."

"So don't," I said, my voice sharper than I intended. She winced, and I felt as though I'd kicked a puppy. I took a breath and tried again. "What I mean is that you and Ollie *choose* for you to spend most of your day sleeping. Can't you moderate the amount, so it approaches something more normal? Then the doctor would be happy, Uncle Ian would be happy—and they'd never know you weren't taking their pills. You'd have less time with Ollie, but at least you'd be able to remember it."

I tried not to hold my breath as she considered the answer.

"I suppose we could. I'll have to talk to Ollie. If I can find him." Her voice broke on the last sentence, and I ruthlessly suppressed a surge of self-pity. Knowing Mum could have chosen to be awake more at any time during my childhood hurt. But she was in pain. I would wallow later.

I considered asking her to talk to Dad about Leander's theory—that I'd earned the wrath of an Oneiroi who was sending blights and mara after me. But she was so preoccupied with her problems I decided not to mention it. I'd wait till she'd regained her equilibrium, and then put the idea to her. I could hold off the spirits till then.

Besides, if I told her about my problems and then she couldn't find Dad, she'd be even more distraught.

I stayed for the rest of the afternoon. We lay together on her bed like a couple of teenage girls. It was a king single, not a narrow hospital cot: another sign of how much this home cost. I kept her distracted from her brooding with gossip from the shop. She listened with more interest, more focus, than I could ever recall from her. It caused such a welter of mixed feelings in me that I had to talk around a lump of emotion in my throat.

I'd never really had the full attention of a mother before. Not my mother, at any rate. And her new attentiveness was because of the drugs she hated, the drugs I was going to help her circumvent.

Babbling on, preoccupied with my thoughts, I was surprised to hear myself telling her about recent developments with Brad, and Jen's theory that I liked him because he was a bad boy. I stumbled to a halt, embarrassed. My relationship with my mother wasn't normal, but I still didn't talk to her about boys.

"Do you think Jen is right?" she asked me with a smile when I remained silent, my cheeks burning.

"I don't think so. No. But I'd never normally be attracted to someone like him, either."

"What do you mean when you say someone like him?"

"A..." I stopped, really thinking about it. I usually liked musicians and artists, people with something to give back to the world. Strong personalities, bright minds.

I didn't know about art, but Brad certainly ticked the other boxes.

And he was hot.

"Okay, maybe he is my type. But it's not the trying-to-kill-me thing that makes him my type," I said.

"There you go then. Have you spoken to him since all the kissing?"

The burning feeling in my cheeks grew stronger. "Uh. No, he hasn't called."

"So call *him*!" She threw her hands up in the air. "Honestly, this is the twenty-first century, Melaina. You don't have to wait for the guy to make the first move."

"I know." I bit my lip to stop myself from smiling, but it didn't work.

"What are you grinning about?" she said. "Can't you see I'm scolding you?"

"I just can't remember ever seeing you this animated," I confessed.

Her expression sobered, and I mentally kicked myself. But then, to my surprise, she leaned over and kissed me on the forehead. "My poor baby girl. It isn't easy for you, having the parents you do, is it?"

"Not especially easy, no," I said, and her face fell. I hurriedly added, "But it could be worse. You could be drug dealers or have left me in a dumpster or something."

"I considered it, but your father would have never let me hear the end of it."

I knew she was teasing, though. My father had never given me any indication he cared one way or the other.

When dinner arrived I glanced at my watch, surprised. It was only half past five, too early for me to be hungry, but still. I hadn't noticed it was getting so late.

An orderly brought in the tray, which barely fit on the table. The smell of hot lasagne filled the air, making my mouth water. He helped Mum over to her chair, handing her a tall glass of iced water and a little plastic cup filled with coloured tablets.

Locking eyes with me where I sat on the edge of her bed, Mum put the tablets in her mouth and sipped the water dutifully. My heart sank.

"Enjoy your meal," the orderly said, ticking something on a chart and leaving the room.

Mum leapt to her feet, knocking her chair over in her haste, and seized a tissue from the box. Then she spat the half-dissolved tablets into the tissue and folded it into a tight ball. "I'll flush it later," she whispered, her grin the gleeful expression of a teenager pulling a prank. "Don't tell anyone."

"I don't know what you're talking about," I said with a wink, sliding off the bed. "I'd better get home before it gets dark."

"Call that boy, won't you?"

I nodded. "Have a good night's sleep."

She smiled slowly, a twinkle in her eyes. "Oh, I will."

"Ew, Mum!"

Chapter Nineteen

"Would you like to come up for coffee?"

"Sure," Brad replied, turning the steering wheel. The indicator clicked loudly in the quiet interior of his car as it nosed in to the small car park at the back of our apartment block. We pulled into the visitors' parking space, then scurried through the downpour to the building's back entry. Jen's car was gone; she had a late lecture on Wednesdays.

My stomach did backflips, and I wasn't sure whether it was because of the idea Brad and I might have a little privacy or the delicious beef *massaman* I'd stuffed myself with at dinner.

I'd called Brad after leaving Wattle Tree Park the day before, figuring there was no excuse since I had nothing better to do on the bus ride home. He'd seemed happy to hear from me and apologised for not calling sooner. He said he'd been busy at work and, to apologise, he'd offered to take me out to his favourite Thai restaurant the next night.

Tonight.

Our apartment was dark and chilly when I let us in, so I bustled around, flicking on the heater and lights, and closing the curtains across the door to the balcony. Brad tried to help me in the kitchen but I shooed him out. Our kitchen was really a one-person affair.

"You're in luck," I said as I pulled a fresh bag of ground coffee from the fridge, handling it as if it were precious metal. "I bought this yesterday. Usually we only have instant."

"I don't mind instant," he protested.

"Cheap instant." He wrinkled his nose, and I laughed. "Tell me about it. The life of a uni student and her kooky flatmate."

"You're not kooky."

I raised an eyebrow but said nothing. In a way he was right. Aside from the blue streak in my fringe, I didn't dress that differently from others my age—and even the hair streak wasn't totally unheard of. People regularly came into Serenity's shop looking much less mainstream than I did. Even Serenity, with her voluminous floral coats and tie-dyed jeans, looked kookier than me.

All of my strangeness was on the inside. I was willing to bet that there, I'd beat pretty much anyone in this city hands down.

I put on the radio for background noise and, coffees cradled in our hands, Brad and I sat on the couch. I inhaled the steam coming from my mug, enjoying the aroma of real coffee and the warmth that seeped into my cold fingers.

Brad's observant gaze took in the apartment. At first I thought he was cataloguing its faults, the same way

he'd taken in my office at the shop. But a frown marred his features and tension knotted his shoulder blades.

It was when he got up to pull back the curtain screening the balcony, peering out into the rain-soaked darkness, that I realised what he was doing.

He was trying to remember.

"Any of it coming back to you?" I tried to keep my tone light, watching the lines of his back. The light spilling from the lounge room illuminated the balcony itself, but little else. Drops of rain flashed by, exploding in a continuous flurry on the concrete and hammering against the door. We were on the top floor and, unlike those below us, we didn't have a roof over our little slice of the outdoors. The storm had nothing to stop it from drenching our view.

At least the landlord had replaced the latch on the door. Maybe he was afraid I'd sue.

Brad shook his head and let the curtain fall back into place. When he turned, his eyes were shadowed. "The police told me I broke in through the balcony door." There was a question in his voice.

I nodded, sipping my coffee so I didn't say anything stupid.

He laughed, but there was an edge to it. "I wouldn't trust myself on a ladder in the dark. But I scaled two storeys via balconies? At night? I…" He shook his head.

"You were even wearing boots when you did it, not gym shoes," I teased. "Jealous of blight-you?"

"A little." He chuckled sheepishly. "I just… I don't want to remember what happened, but part of me wishes I could, you know? To reclaim the part of me that was stolen."

I put my coffee on the side table and stood, taking his

hand. "Want to see where you, um, did the deed?"

"I..." He hesitated but didn't say no, so I led him up the short corridor, past Jen's closed bedroom door, to my own.

"Is this just an excuse to get me into your bedroom?" he joked. But his voice was hoarse with tension, and not the good kind. I barely managed a half-smile.

"Ready?" I opened the door before he could answer.

He gazed around my bedroom for far longer than such a small space warranted. I only had side tables piled with books, a built-in wardrobe—mercifully closed to hide my mess of shoes and unfolded washing—and a bed. Oh, and the Afremov print on the wall. I resisted the urge to straighten the doona: I'd only made a perfunctory effort to make the bed this morning, and it showed.

I did tuck the leg of my pyjamas under the pillow when he was looking the other way, though.

His hand was still in mine, and now his grip tightened, setting my heart to racing. Had I been incredibly stupid, bringing Brad here? What if it triggered some sort of flashback?

But his eyes, when he turned to face me, weren't the glassy, blank stare of a blight-possessed puppet. They were his own, and they were dull with anguish. "I still don't remember anything. But god, Melaina, I'm so sorry."

"You've said that before."

"I know. But, standing here, I'm starting to get a sense for how I must have terrified you. It's such a small room. You had nowhere to go..."

Remembering made goosebumps shiver along my arms. "You got mud on my sheets too," I said, forcing a smile.

It startled a laugh from him. "You weren't afraid?"

"I thought I was going to die," I whispered. My knees

turned to water as the memories came back. I sat on the edge of the bed before I could fall, and looked at the floor. "But it wasn't you."

"Are you trying to reassure me, or yourself?" Brad's voice was gentle. He sat beside me and turned my face to his with the tip of a warm finger. My heart skipped a beat as he trapped me in his gaze.

"Both," I breathed. His hand was still on the side of my face, caressing my cheek, running down and along my jawline.

"Are you afraid of me?"

"No."

"I'd never hurt you. Not deliberately."

"Good to know." My voice was barely a whisper. My heart raced, but it wasn't with fear. I was suddenly even gladder there were no reflective surfaces in my room.

His fingers ran down the side of my neck and hesitated, recoiling from the scarf. He flinched. "Sorry."

"Don't be," I said, unwinding the scarf and putting it on my pillow.

Brad's gaze lingered at my throat, his lips tight.

"It's pretty horrid, I know," I said. The bruises had started to turn a sickly greenish colour. At least Brad's bruise from where Jen had hit him was hidden beneath his hair.

"Does it ... still hurt?"

"A little bit. If you touch it lightly it's okay." I took his hand, which hovered indecisively beside my neck, and placed it back on my throat. Then I ran it gently down over the surface of the bruise. "Like this."

"Like this?" His fingers brushed lower, against my collarbone. I bit my lip to suppress a gasp. His eyes had grown dark and heavy-lidded with desire. I could have drowned in them. "I really want to kiss you right now." He ran his thumb along the collar of my shirt, lips parted.

"Then why haven't you?"

"I didn't want to frighten you off. This is where—"

"I'm not that easily frightened."

We leaned into each other. One of Brad's hands entwined itself in my hair, making me tremble with delight, and then our lips were locked together. These weren't the gentle kisses we'd shared on Sunday, building a slow fire of desire. The heat was instantaneous, racing through my body as his tongue caressed mine. I wrapped my hands around his broad back, enjoying the smoothness of the shirt fabric, the taut muscles underneath it. His other hand was still poised at my shirt, but after several moments it inched lower, lightly caressing my breast through the layers of fabric. I moaned into his lips.

"Is this okay?" he whispered, kissing from the corner of my mouth to my ear. I arched my neck and nodded, enjoying the butterfly-light touches of his lips and tongue. He took my earring in his teeth, tugging it lightly, tasting my earlobe.

It shouldn't have been arousing. Common sense told me I shouldn't enjoy this, not with this man. Not here. I should have been afraid of anything but the gentlest touch. But his mouth lit me afire, and I wanted more.

I gasped when he kissed his way down my throat, his lips gentle on the bruises but nibbling and tasting along my jawline and the hollow of my throat, away from the injured area. His other hand ran lower, to my waistline, and slipped under the bottom of my shirt to touch my stomach. It quivered with tension.

"Lie down," he whispered, and, after a moment's hesitation, I did, lying sideways across the bed. He started to lean in over me, and I shook my head.

"Beside me, please." I wasn't sure I could handle his full weight on top of me. Not yet. What if I freaked out?

"Okay." He reclined next to me, resting his head on one hand, the other returning to my waist.

I wiggled onto my side and undid one of his shirt buttons, slipping my hand inside it. He flinched slightly, and then laughed, a throaty chuckle. "Your fingers are cold."

"Sorry." I smirked, unrepentant. His chest was warm, lightly dusted with hair. I ran my fingers through it, enjoying its curl and tug, and the way his lips parted as he watched my face. Then he leaned in and kissed me again. His hand ran gently along my spine and up to my bra clasp, rucking my shirt up in its wake.

He paused there and murmured into my lips. "Is this okay? Tell me if you want me to stop."

"Have I said stop yet?"

His only reply was to undo the clasp, clever fingers managing it with a minimum of fuss and then pulling the bra up. Cool air brushed the base of my breast, followed by the gentle, exploring touch of his hands.

"You couldn't have worn a shirt with buttons?" he said, and I laughed softly. "No, of course, that'd be too easy."

"Never let it be said that I'm easy," I replied, tweaking one of his nipples between my fingers.

"Hey!" he gasped, gripping my breast more firmly, his hand fitting around it in a way that stoked the heat in my belly to an inferno. I moaned. Responding to my reaction, he rolled my nipple gently between his thumb and forefinger. When I didn't object, he caught it between his lips, grazing the tip of it with his teeth. I gasped in surprise. His mouth was warm and wet on my breast and I shuddered beneath him.

I wanted him, badly. More, maybe, than I'd wanted any other man. My mind was awhirl with desire, overwhelmed with the sensory feedback from his touch and with the urge to wrap myself around him—all of him—and not let him go until I was sated. I opened my mouth to tell him so, and—

Jen's keys jingled in the stairwell outside our front door. I cursed under my breath, sitting up abruptly and running my hands through my hair. Brad lay still a moment longer. "Damn. Talk about timing."

We hadn't closed my bedroom door. "Tell me about it." I laughed shakily, reaching around to do up my bra. "I'm going to need a cold shower."

"You could come to my place?" he suggested tentatively.

I thought about it. I really did. But as the heat faded, my doubts about whether I wanted to sleep with someone on the second date returned. "Uh. Maybe next time, okay?"

"Okay. How about tomorrow?" The twinkle in his eye told me he was teasing.

"I'll call you."

"Sure." He sat up. I quickly did up his shirt button and then stood as the front door swung open, squeaking.

"Hi Jen," I called as she rustled in the door.

"Hi," she called back.

"Is that the lamp you hit me with?" Brad stood too, trying to look casual, and eyed the comic book characters with a faint smile.

"No. That's the replacement. My kid cousin gave it to me." I emphasised the word "kid" slightly, to explain the

décor decision. "Besides, it was Jen who hit you, not me."

"Damn straight," she said, coming up the corridor. "Hi Brad. Are you staying over?" When she poked her head around the doorframe, her expression was carefully neutral. Uh oh. I would cop an earful later.

"No, I just dropped Melaina home. I was about to head off."

"Rightio then. Have a good night." She disappeared into her bedroom.

"I'll walk you to your car," I said, grabbing my jacket and beanie.

"It's still raining."

Now he mentioned it, the hissing sound of the rain hadn't decreased at all. I'd forgotten about it for a while there. Awkward. "Oh, so it is. I'll walk you to the door then."

When we reached the bottom of the stairs, he leaned in to give me a gentle kiss on the cheek. "Thanks for the date."

"I should thank you. You paid."

"Then thanks for calling. I didn't know if you would."

I rolled my eyes. "Despite what Jen thinks, you're not a bad boy." Then I covered my hand with my mouth, mortified. Why had I said that?

"Jen thinks that?"

I nodded, wondering if I'd offended him. "She thinks I go for bad boys." He tipped his head to the side, eyes on my face. Then he burst out laughing, loudly at first and then quietly when I shushed him. "Don't wake the neighbours!"

"Sorry. It's just … that's pretty funny."

"Why?" I didn't get the joke, and didn't know whether to be offended or not. But Brad hadn't been offended by what I'd said, so I settled for suspicious.

"Because Belinda suggested maybe the reason I liked you was because I like bad girls."

"Me? Why would she...? I'm so not a bad girl!" I said. "I've never even smoked a cigarette!"

He ran his fingers through the cobalt streak in my hair, his gesture so tender I wanted to throw myself at him again. "Maybe 'bad girl' isn't quite the right term. But since I met you, I've been in rather a lot of dangerous situations."

"That was hardly my fault!" I protested, my voice loud.

He put a finger on my lips. "I know," he whispered, and kissed me again, silencing my objections. "Are you sure you don't want to come with me tonight?"

I took a trembling breath and then nodded. "Not tonight. But I'll call you tomorrow, okay?"

"Okay." His breath trembled too. "Make sure you do."

"Drive safely." *Oh lord.* "To get home, I mean. Not anything else." *Like into me.* I clamped my lips together before I said anything even more embarrassing.

"I always do." He slipped out the door into the rain, laughing.

I walked up the stairs slowly, Brad filling my thoughts. I was going to need that cold shower.

Chapter Twenty

A guitar riff repeated itself at annoyingly short inter-vals, jolting me from a very nice dream. I fumbled for my phone, homing in on the glowing screen through bleary, sleep-gummed eyes.

"'Lo?"

"Melaina?" I could barely hear the voice on the other end. What sounded like a large engine rumbled in the background, almost drowning the person out.

"Yes? Who's this?" I focused on the clock. Three in the morning. Ugh.

"Serenity." Her voice was tight with emotion.

I sat up, a sick feeling creeping over me as my mind woke up enough to realise no one ever calls after midnight with good news. "What's wrong? Where are you?"

"There's a fire. At the shop."

"Oh god."

"Well said," she replied, although her voice hitched on the second word. "Can you come down?"

I frowned, biting my lip. "I'm not sure. The buses..."

"They won't be running. Of course. I'm sorry." She sounded dazed.

"Are you okay? Is anyone hurt?"

"Yes. No. Look, I should have known. I shouldn't have called."

"Don't worry about it," I said. "I'll catch a cab. Don't worry. I'll be there soon."

I dressed quickly, throwing on heavy jeans, and a thick jumper over a camisole and a long-sleeve tee. Then I grabbed two pairs of socks and my boots, and crept out to the lounge room to put them on. I didn't want to clomp around more than I had to.

My caution was unrewarded, though, because Jen poked her sleep-tousled head out of her bedroom door just as I was sitting down to pull on the first pair of socks. Her glasses were slightly askew on her nose. "Did I hear your phone?"

"Yeah. Serenity called. There's been a fire at the shop."

She swore. "Do they know what caused it?"

"No idea. I'm heading down now."

"Hang on." She disappeared into her room for a couple of minutes and appeared, fully dressed, running a brush through her hair. "Have I got time to brush my teeth?"

I'd just finished lacing my boots. I loved them, but they weren't quick to put on. "You're coming?"

She rolled her eyes. "Duh."

On consideration, the teeth thing seemed like a good idea. My mouth was dry and Serenity had enough problems without me knocking her out with morning breath. But I also didn't want to take a huge amount of time. When Jen emerged I compromised by quickly gargling

some mouthwash, with a silent apology to my dentist. I could brush properly later. Maybe I'd even floss to make up for it.

Leander was in the mirror when I looked up from spitting. He opened his mouth to speak, and I cut him off. "I don't have time, Leander. There's a fire at the shop."

"Be careful," he called after me as I left the room, flicking the overhead light off to leave him in darkness.

"Let's go."

Once we were in the car, Jen tuned the radio in to the local radio station, hoping to catch the news. A song was playing, a guy with a sultry voice singing about making love in a way that reminded me uncomfortably of my dream. Mercifully, Jen turned it down to a murmur. "Poor Serenity."

"I know."

"Should we get coffee?"

"At this time of night?" I stared out the window at the deserted street. At least it had stopped raining. The streetlights' reflections shone in puddles on the road. Curls of fog wisped here and there—by dawn, it would be thick enough we couldn't see our hands in front of our faces.

"The Macca's in the city will be open. The drive-through."

I wrinkled my nose at the detour. "I'd rather go straight there."

"It'll only add five or ten minutes."

"But—"

She glanced at me, eyebrows raised. "What are you expecting to do when we get there? Put out the fire with your own two hands?"

"Serenity sounded really upset."

Jen's expression softened, but she persisted. "A hot cup of coffee is a great comfort on a cold night. Plus, I'm tired."

"True. Okay." I stretched, relaxing into the seat. I'd had about four hours sleep, and my brain was shrouded in the same fog I expected to see for real later. "Hey, you haven't lectured me about Brad."

"Was I supposed to?" It was hard to tell in the poor light, but she looked as if she was smiling.

"I thought you would."

"You know what I'd say, though, right?"

"That I should be careful?" It was a guess, but an educated one.

"Right. So I don't need to say it." She sighed dramatically. "I do so hate to be predictable."

We bought three coffees and drove the rest of the way to Serenity's shop in silence, except for a string of annoyingly jaunty pop songs on the radio, played back to back with no interruptions from a DJ. "Maybe they put their music collection on shuffle and go home for eight hours." I glared at the radio display as if it were its fault.

"Maybe." Jen stifled a yawn. "Are the coffees cool enough to drink yet?"

I took a cautious sip of mine and scalded my tongue. "Ow!"

"So that's a no?"

I would have thrown something at her if she hadn't been driving. Also, the only things I was holding were hot enough to cause third-degree burns.

Even if we hadn't known there was something going on at the shop, we would have been able to see there was

trouble from quite a distance away. The strobing lights of the police car blocking the end of the street cut through the night in red and blue flashes. We parked in the first vacant space on the corner, and then got out, taking the coffees with us.

The police car was empty, so we hurried past it along the shopfronts. The twenty-four hour bottle shop was the only thing still open. The eighteen-year-old who worked the night shift stood on the street, staring gape-mouthed at the hulking yellow fire trucks parked askew across the road. His phone was idle in one hand. Had he already uploaded the photos to Facebook?

Two powerful jets of water sprayed into the air and through the shattered window of Serenity's shop. I couldn't tell from here whether the heat had blown the window out, or the firemen had smashed it in.

"You can't get any closer." A police officer hurried over to us. She was in her thirties, with an angry frown that sat so comfortably on her face it may have been her normal expression.

"I work for Serenity," I said quickly, before she marched us back to our car. "She asked us to come down. Where is she?"

"The shop owner? She's over there." She pointed across the wide street. Opposite the store, a cluster of people watched the blaze. Serenity towered over most of them, even the men, her purple coat making her stand out, an amethyst in a sea of obsidian.

"Thanks," I said, flashing a grateful smile that didn't thaw the officer's demeanour one whit. I strode over to the group, Jen beside me. Fortunately my flatmate had the presence of mind to grab the tray of coffees from me just before Serenity enveloped me in a huge hug that reeked of smoke.

"Thank you for coming," she said when she released me. "I wasn't sure who else to call. Your office... Well, everything should be covered by insurance, but—"

"I'm not worried about that," I said, waving her words off. Jen handed out the coffees. Serenity's grateful expression made the detour worth it. "Do they know how it started yet?"

Several of the gawkers, probably nearby residents, inched closer to hear Serenity's response, but their faces fell with disappointment when she replied, "No. They said it was too early to tell."

"You!" An angry voice cut across the rumble of the idling trucks. We turned in unison to look. A small, balding man with eyes like hard grey pebbles hurried along the path towards us, shoes slapping on the wet cement with the force of his stomping stride. The frowning policewoman intercepted him and he sidestepped her as though she wasn't there, bearing down on Serenity. The crowd withdrew slightly in the face of his wrath. Or maybe it was to get a better view. "What. Have. You. Done?" He bit off each word as if it were a piece of overcooked steak.

Despite towering over the man, Serenity seemed to sink into herself. "Melaina, let me introduce you to Graham Ross. Mr Ross, this is—"

He cut her off with a sharp gesture, his face flushed with fury. "One of your beatnik customers, no doubt. I don't care." His breath fogged in the air, making him look like a dragon with a comb-over and a thick moustache.

The policewoman, frowning even more now, laid a

hand on his shoulder. "Excuse me, sir." The words were polite but her tone was so cold it could have put out the fire blazing behind her.

Ross turned to stare at her fingers, and then up to her face. Oil dripped from his next words. "I apologise, officer. I am the owner of this shopping complex and this, this *woman* here—" he cast a scathing look at Serenity "—is my tenant. I came over to ask her what stupid-arse candle she left burning, or incense or bong, to start this fire?"

The policewoman's eyebrows rose at the word "bong". She looked at Serenity.

"Nothing! I locked up like I always do. All the heaters were off—everything!"

"She's very thorough," I added.

"And who are you?" Ross glared at me.

"If you'd let Serenity finish introducing me before, you'd know the answer to that, wouldn't you?" I retorted. His eyes narrowed to slits, but I didn't care. "My name is Melaina, and I work with Serenity, and I can promise you she didn't leave anything burning."

"We don't allow lit candles, incense or oil burners in the shop. Nothing with an open flame," Serenity said, her tone apologetic. Then she glanced at the policewoman and added, "And definitely not drugs."

"A likely story," Ross said through clenched teeth.

"It's true."

"Well, I guess we'll see once the investigation is done. And if it turns out your negligence caused this fire..." The unspoken threat hung in the air long after the condensation of his breath had dissipated.

The policewoman gave us a sympathetic look. "Excuse

me, sir. Could you come with me? We'll go sit in the car where it's warmer and you can give me a statement."

I was smart enough to wait till they were out of hearing distance before observing, "What an angry little troll." Behind us, someone sniggered, but when I glanced at the crowd they were all watching the shop again. I had to respect the level of curiosity that would have people out on such a cold night. We weren't close enough to the fire to feel any warmth from it, especially as a breeze was blowing perpendicular to the storefront, driving the chill into our bones and the smoke away from us.

"He is," Serenity agreed. "Although I can understand why he'd be angry."

"But it's not your fault!"

"I wonder," she murmured. Her gaze was fixed on the fire too, the orange glow of the flames reflecting in her eyes as she watched her livelihood turn to ashes. The possessions I'd lost in the fire were worthless compared to the value of all the stock going up in sandalwood-scented flames. At least the takings were kept in a fireproof safe. "Maybe I missed something."

"I'd bet you all the money in my pocket that you didn't." I sighed. "Look, there's no point worrying about it now. Why don't you head home?"

"I caught a cab here. My hands were shaking too much to drive." Serenity sounded almost embarrassed at that.

"And fair enough too," I said.

"We'll drive you," Jen added, and I shot her a thankful look. "Do the police need you for anything right now?"

"I'm not sure," Serenity said.

"I'll go check." I glanced at Jen and she nodded, her lips pressed together. She'd stay with Serenity.

Coffee cup cradled in my hands, I approached a small cluster of police officers who stood talking with a fireman in yellow protective overalls and a red helmet. If my stomach hadn't been knotted with worry, I would have been appreciative of all the men in uniform. As it was, I just wanted to go. My toes were starting to go numb inside my boots. "Excuse me?"

"Yes?" One of the officers turned, and then blinked with surprise. "We've met, right?"

My memory of those who'd been in our apartment the night of the assault was pretty blurry, but I remembered David Nelson. He was the one I'd thought was making a pass at Jen. He had neat, dark hair speckled with grey the colour of iron filings. A smile dimpled his cheek.

"Yeah," I said, extending my hand to shake his. His thick leather gloves squeaked faintly in my grip. "Melaina Armstrong."

"That's right!" Nelson's gaze dropped to my scarf-wrapped throat, but only for a second. He was good. "What can I do for you?"

"I work for Serenity, the owner of the shop. We—that is, Jen and I—were wondering if we could take her home. Do you need to interview her or anything?"

Nelson checked his notebook, but I had the feeling he already knew the answer. "We've got her details, so we can get in touch tomorrow. No need for you all to stay."

"Great. Thanks."

I turned to go, and he fell in beside me. "How have you recovered from the incident last week?"

"Good," I said, glancing at him. "The bruises are starting to fade."

"Have you decided whether you're going to make a

statement about what happened?"

"Yes. I mean, no. I'm not going to."

"May I ask why not?" There was an odd note in Nelson's voice that made me stop and look at him. His eyes were narrowed.

I thought quickly. "Because I don't believe sending someone who's mentally ill to jail is the best thing for them."

"A commendable sentiment ... as far as it goes." He tipped his head to the side like a hound catching a scent. "I'm trying to remember. Did you know the man who attacked you?"

Trying to remember, my fabulous leather boots. "No, I didn't." I was on dangerous ground here. I didn't want to lie to the police, but I could hardly explain my real reasons for believing Brad was innocent of the crime he'd committed. Before Nelson could push any further, we reached Serenity. "Good news!" I said to her. "We can take you home."

"Thank goodness," she said, exhaling with relief.

But I felt Nelson's stare on my back as we hurried away.

Chapter Twenty-One

Fuelled by caffeine and adrenaline, Jen and I stayed up talking until the sun peeked over the horizon. The remaining clouds had disappeared, driven east by a determined wind that had made our building creak even as it scoured the sky. When the sun rose the world glittered, bedazzled by drops of water that clung to every surface like tiny balls of glass.

Not long after, Jen left for her morning lecture, refusing to skip it despite my urgings. As the door closed behind her, all the weariness from the evening before settled into my bones. I'd had a shower when I got home and my hair no longer reeked of smoke, but the miasma of the fire still clung to me like a dark, invisible cloud.

Maybe it was just fatigue.

I lay down for a nap on the couch, too tired to relocate to my bedroom. The winter sun slanted in the balcony window and onto one half of the couch, warming my legs through my black jeans. I stretched, enjoying the heat, and closed my eyes.

Had Serenity managed to get any rest? Maybe we should have stayed at her house long enough for me to help her nod off. Had she sat up all night, alone?

That vague sense of guilt followed me into my dreams, and was still there when a pounding on the front door startled me awake. I managed to catch myself before I fell off the couch, but it was a near thing.

"Hang on a sec," I called as the person knocked again. Maybe they hadn't pounded the first time, after all. I untangled myself and stood, running my hands through my hair and glancing at the clock on the DVD player. Half an hour. I'd only slept half an hour.

When I opened the door to Senior Constable Nelson, looking far more awake than he had any right to be, that guilty feeling sharpened. I'd never had the police come knocking on my door before. "Ah. Can I help you?"

"I hope so. May I come in?"

"Sure, I guess." I stood aside and he entered. He was alone. "Sorry. You woke me up," I added, to explain my vagueness and rumpled appearance.

"My apologies." His gaze swept the apartment. "Is your flatmate here?"

"Why? You want to ask her out?" I bit my tongue as soon as the words escaped. Apparently my tact and good sense were still asleep on the couch. Lazy things.

Fortunately, he laughed. "No, I was just wondering. It's you I want to talk to."

"Right." My stomach fluttered with anxiety. To buy myself time to think, I went into the kitchen. "Want a hot drink? Or some water?"

"Only if you're making something."

"I am."

We exchanged pleasantries as I made coffee. He roamed up and down our only corridor as we talked, and I had no doubt he was checking whether there was anyone else in the apartment. Anxiety knotted my stomach. If he intended me harm, there were no witnesses here—and who'd believe my word over a police officer's? Then I chided myself for being paranoid. I had no reason to believe he wanted to hurt me. Although I seemed to have an unknown enemy in the supernatural community, Nelson showed no signs of the zombie-like behaviour Brad had exhibited when he was being controlled by the blight. If anything, the constable was the opposite: hyper-alert and moving briskly. The sort of person you'd want on your side in a zombie apocalypse. And he definitely didn't look like the insect-riding mara that had attacked Brad and me at the shop four days before.

A thought occurred to me with the suddenness of a lightning strike. What if the mara had lit the fire at Serenity's shop? I already knew they were able to get access to the building even if the shop was locked up, sending their insects in through the air vents. That was how they'd accessed the shop the previous Sunday, and, although I'd applied surface spray at our apartment and Brad's home, I hadn't done the same at the shop.

Mentally cursing my foolishness, I fumbled the plastic container of sugar as I twisted the lid off … then swore as it spilled across the bench.

"Are you okay?" Constable Nelson reappeared, his set jaw and narrowed eyes easing when he saw the mess I'd made. "Here, let me help you."

"I've got it," I said, retrieving the dustpan and brush

from under the sink and sweeping the mounds of glittering sugar crystals off the bench, dumping them in the bin. "At least I didn't spill all of it, or I wouldn't be able to ask whether you'd like sugar. Would you?"

"Yes, please." His polite smile didn't reach his steely eyes as he stood with the thumb of one hand hooked in his thick leather utility belt. The only thing hanging off it was a gun in its holster. I tried not to stare at the weapon, but I wasn't used to being so close to firearms.

When I handed him the coffee, he sipped it once and then put it down on the bench. "Before we go any further, I need to ask—you're aware it's an offence to lie to a police officer in the course of investigating a crime, aren't you?"

I nearly dropped my coffee. We were jumping straight in, then. "Uh. Yes. Why?"

"Just checking." His smile was so thin now that it didn't even dimple his cheek. He flicked open one of the many pockets on his vest and retrieved a notebook and pen. "I wanted to ask you again what the nature of your relationship is with Bradley Peterson. Your attacker from a week ago."

"I told you last night. I'd never met him before that evening."

"And have you seen him since?" Something about the way his eyes narrowed told me he already knew the answer, although I couldn't imagine how ... unless he'd spoken to Serenity already this morning? She knew Brad had come by the shop the previous Sunday—I'd let her know I'd be using my office while the shop was closed, in case someone contacted her to say they'd seen movement inside. I wouldn't want people to think I was up to no good.

So I nodded, reluctantly. "I gave him a therapy session last weekend."

He wrote something on his pad. "What kind of therapy session?"

"Dream therapy." He stared. I lifted my chin, defiant. I could read his disbelief as plainly as the writing on the side of my coffee mug—which said *Keep calm and drink coffee*. I did as advised, taking a large gulp.

Nelson frowned. "Someone breaks into your apartment and assaults you, and you invite him over for ... dream therapy?"

I nodded, clenching my jaw so I didn't say anything confrontational. I got this sort of response all the time. People might be quick to judge Serenity's customers, but at least those same customers didn't judge me.

When I didn't continue, Nelson said, "And was that here, or...?"

"The shop."

"He knows where you work then." Another note on the page; maybe he'd written "AHA!"

The feeling I was being led around by the nose irritated me. "Yes, he does. What's all this about?"

"Our initial investigations lead us to believe the fire at Serenity's New Age Gifts may have been deliberately lit."

It was my turn to stare, and I put my coffee cup down on the bench before it gave away the tremble in my fingers. I didn't believe for a second that Brad had lit the fire. For a start, he'd been at our apartment for at least part of the evening, not breaking and entering. It was more likely that my speculation about the mara was correct. My heart sank into my stomach. Was this my fault?

Nelson studied my face as intently as Jen studied her

textbooks, and as effectively. I tried to still my expression. "Why do you think that?" I asked, trying to sound casual.

"Someone broke in the rear door," he said. "Smashed an adjacent window and unlocked the handle."

I took a wavering breath. "Oh." My thoughts raced. If the arsonist had smashed his or her way in, then the mara probably weren't involved. They had no reason to break in when they could crawl through the ducting. But it still could have been someone blight-ridden.

"Oh?" Nelson prompted. The intensity of his gaze made me shift uncomfortably. I started stacking dirty dishes by the sink, wiping down the benchtop—anything so I didn't have to meet his gaze.

As I tidied, I spoke quickly, "Why would someone target Serenity? I mean, her landlord clearly doesn't like her, but I doubt he'd set fire to his own building. Was it a robbery? A teenage prank?"

He moved around the other side of the tiny breakfast bar so he could see my face in profile. "We haven't ruled those out yet. But we're also not sure Serenity was the target."

I dropped a dessert spoon into the sink. It clattered loudly. "Me?" My voice squeaked.

"It seems logical. That you should be attacked twice in the space of a week is an odd coincidence, don't you think?"

I *did* think. In fact, I agreed with him. I just couldn't tell him my theory. So I said nothing.

"I'll ask you one more time, Miss Armstrong: what is your relationship to Bradley Peterson? An ex-boyfriend with a grudge, maybe?" Nelson's tone changed from confrontational to softly sympathetic. "I won't hold the fact you concealed it from us against you. I understand

why you wouldn't want to admit you dated someone who would attack you—"

"I've dated douchebags before," I snapped, turning to face him with my hands on my hips. "And I'm not ashamed to admit it. I've made mistakes. But Brad Peterson isn't one of them. I swear to you, I'd never met him before last Thursday!"

"And what's your relationship with him now?" he probed. "Is he just a client?"

My cheeks burned in response to his eyes on me, judging me. "We also went out to dinner once."

Something in his posture changed: a lessening of suspicion, perhaps, as though I'd admitted something he suspected. Maybe it was the blushes that lent my declaration credence. "He's your boyfriend?" he asked.

"I don't know. We haven't had that conversation." My cheeks burned hotter.

He flipped his notepad closed. "We have a partial print on the rock used to shatter the back window. If it turns out it was Peterson, we'll know soon enough. Thank you for answering my questions."

"No worries." I followed him to the door, overwhelmed with relief that he was leaving.

He paused in the doorway to gaze down at me with genuine concern. "You might want to reconsider your latest choice of douchebag," he said, the smile gone. "He's already tried to hurt you once. Even if he didn't light the fire, why risk it? If he's mentally ill, as you believe, dream therapy isn't what he needs. And if he's not … well, all the dream therapy in the world won't turn a thug into a nice guy."

"Thanks for the advice." I tried to smile but it came

out as a grimace. He sighed and nodded, and then turned to walk down the stairs, his shoulders slumped.

I closed the door and leaned my head against it. "He's not a thug," I whispered to the cool surface. But my words rung hollow in my ears. Brad had left my apartment at around eleven the night before. The fire had been lit several hours later.

The doubt Senior Constable Nelson had seeded wormed into my mind and refused to budge.

Chapter Twenty-Two

*T*oo shaken up by Nelson's visit to continue tidying the kitchen, I sat on the couch, staring at the wall. What was it they said on crime shows? Motive, means and opportunity? Brad had the means to have lit the fire, and the opportunity. With Belinda out of town, he would have no alibi for where he'd been when the fire was lit.

What I didn't believe was that he had the motive.

The blights and mara had a motive, even though I didn't know what it was. They were too organised for their behaviour to be random. Was it possible Brad had already been reinfested by a blight? That he'd gone back to the shop last night, after he'd left our apartment, and set the fire? I didn't think so. The blight I'd evicted from his mind the previous weekend had taken at least a week to establish its hold, like slow-growing ivy working its tendrils into his mind until it choked him. There was no way a new blight could have established such control over him so quickly.

I chewed my lip, self-doubt making me queasy. Was it possible I'd missed something? Left some shard, some fragment of the creature in Brad's mind that had allowed it to regrow at an accelerated rate? No. The last time I'd been in there, Leander had been with me. I was good with dreams, but Leander wasn't just good. He was Oneiroi. The dream realm was his native plane; dreams were putty in his hands. Leander would have known. To believe Brad was still infected was to believe Leander had betrayed me. And, despite my regular fallings out with my childhood friend, I trusted him ... at least when my father wasn't involved.

By the time I'd reached that conclusion, my coffee was cold. I tipped it—and Constable Nelson's, which he'd barely touched—down the sink and grabbed my mobile phone, finding Brad's number. After a moment's hesitation, I dialled it.

It went straight to voice mail. Crap. I left a message and then rang Serenity to make sure she was okay. She seemed tired but otherwise as if she was coping—her oldest daughter had come down from Yass to look after her. When I asked if the police had come by, she said they had. They'd had all sorts of questions.

No surprise there.

I attempted to read a book, but couldn't focus on the words. So I sat on the couch and stared blankly at the television, trying not to worry. It was a Thursday morning. Brad was at work. Of course he hadn't answered; he was probably in a meeting.

When he eventually called back at lunchtime, I snatched the phone off the arm of the couch so hastily I almost

dropped it on the floor. "Hello?" My voice sounded breathless to my ears, and I took a deep breath, trying to still my anxiety.

"Hi," he said, and there was an odd note to his voice. My stomach felt as if it had sunk into my socks. "You'll never guess where I've been."

I had a pretty good idea. I leaned my head back on the couch and closed my eyes, rubbing them with my free hand. They were gritty from lack of sleep. "The police station?"

There was a long pause. "How did you know?"

"They came here too," I said. "Well, one of them did."

"Did they fingerprint you too?"

My heart sank to join my stomach. My socks were getting crowded. "No..."

"They fingerprinted me. And asked all sorts of questions. About you. About Serenity." His voice trembled with outrage. "They told me Serenity's shop caught fire—"

"It did."

"—and I'm pretty sure I'm their number one suspect."

"I know."

There was another pause, and when he spoke again his voice no longer shook. In fact, it was dead calm. "How? What did you tell them?"

"Nothing. I mean, I said I'd given you a therapy session at the shop—"

"That's just great." Sarcasm dripped from the words.

"I'm sorry! But they knew before I said anything. Serenity told them. And if I'd lied about it, it would've looked like we were hiding something." He didn't say anything, and I took a long, slow breath through my nose, counting to five. "Are you pissed at me?"

"No." But I heard the hesitation in his voice. Tears prickled my eyes and I curled my free hand into a fist as anger rushed through me.

"You know what, Brad? I'm the one whose workplace got burned down last night, so how about you remember that, huh?"

"I'm sorry," he said, his tone contrite. "It's just ... they came to my office. They asked me to come down to the station in front of my boss. Like a criminal."

I could imagine it too easily—the humiliation he must be feeling. The worry about being fired. "Oh, god. I'm sorry too. For dragging you into this."

"What makes you think you dragged me into this? It might be the other way round."

"Remember how I told you I thought the mara were trying to attack me?"

"Yeah?"

"Well, this is just more evidence I'm the target. You were a..." I trailed off. There was no nice way to say it.

Brad said it for me. "A tool?"

"Um. Yes."

"Boy, today is a good day to be me." His voice was dry, but at least he didn't sound angry anymore.

"To them, I mean," I said hastily. "Whoever's behind it. Not to me. Obviously."

"Relax, Melaina. I get what you meant." There was another silence. When he spoke again, his voice was quiet. "What do you think the fingerprint results will say?"

"That you didn't break into the shop."

"You're sure?" There was hope in his tone, and I realised the true source of his anxiety and anger: the idea he might actually be guilty of the crime they suspected

him of. That he might go to jail for committing a crime he didn't remember.

Another crime he didn't remember.

"Yes." *Pretty sure.* "There's no way you could've been controlled so quickly, even if you were exposed to another blight egg. Which would be an odd coincidence."

"I just…" He sounded as if he wanted to believe me, but was unable to.

"Okay, look at it this way. Did you have any strange dreams last night?"

"Not strange ones, no."

I wondered if his dreams had been as steamy as mine, and felt my cheeks redden. *Focus, girl.* "No nightmares? No sleepwalking?"

"No."

"And when the blight controlled you before, did you have nightmares, as well as sleepwalking?"

"Yes!" There was dawning comprehension in his voice. "Horrible ones."

"Well, there you go then."

He heaved a sigh of relief. "Thank Christ. Melaina, I…"

"I know. Don't worry about it."

"Is your boss alright?" he asked. "Was she there when it started?"

"She's pretty shaken up, but no. She was at home. The fire was in the middle of the night."

"And you?"

"I wasn't there either."

"That's not what I meant. Are you okay?"

"I'm fine. Tired." I fought back a yawn.

"Melaina, if someone's targeting you—"

"I'll be fine, Brad."

"Let me finish," he said, sounding annoyed that I wasn't taking him seriously. "They could just as easily have broken into your apartment and set a fire there. Sure, the mara know where you work, but if the same person controlled the mara that controlled my blight, they also know where you *live*. Think about that for a second."

I did, with dawning horror.

"Come to my place," he said abruptly. "Stay with us till this blows over."

"Then they could set fire to your place instead," I protested. "The blight knows your address as well as mine. Better, probably."

"I'd like to see them try," he said, voice dark with intent.

"I wouldn't."

"Melaina..."

"I don't want to put you in danger any more than I want to endanger Jen. Staying with you isn't a solution." My thoughts whirled. I held the phone with both hands to stop it shaking. What should I do?

"What about a hotel then? Somewhere you've never stayed? If you don't advertise where you are, it should be safe."

I couldn't believe we were having this conversation. "Don't you think that's a little extreme?"

"No. I don't."

Hesitation softened my resolve. But... "I can't afford it," I sighed.

"I can."

"No!"

"I really can." I heard the smile in his voice.

"That's not what I meant."

"I know." There was a brief pause, and when he spoke again the words were tight with emotion. "Let me do this for you. You're an amazing woman, and if I wasn't responsible for putting you in danger then I was at least part of the problem. Let me help you."

"Running isn't going to make my attacker go away."

"I know," Brad said. "But it will keep you alive long enough that we can figure this out. You and me, and that moth friend of yours. Leander. There's got to be some reason you're being targeted."

He sounded so confident. I hadn't told him about my conversation with Leander, and his belief an Oneiroi was hunting me. I also hadn't told him about Leander's and my most recent falling out. I wasn't sure Leander would help me.

But my father might.

I wondered how Mum was faring now she'd decided not to take the drugs anymore. I hadn't called her since my visit two days before. At first I'd been preoccupied with my date with Brad, and then, after the fire, I hadn't wanted to worry her. But maybe Ollie knew something that could help explain the mess my life was becoming. Given how little interaction I had with most of the Oneiroi, the only explanation I could think of for one having a grudge with me was that it was an old enemy of my father's who'd tracked me down. He might be able to give me a clue as to who that might be. Then I could see what Leander could—or would—tell me.

"Melaina?" Brad was waiting patiently on the other end of the line for an answer. "Let me pay for a hotel for you."

"Okay," I agreed reluctantly.

"Great! Shall I pick you up at dinnertime?"

"Um. I want to visit Mum this afternoon. Maybe I can catch a bus into the city and meet you afterwards?"

"If you like. But Melaina?"

"Yes?"

"Pack an overnight bag." His voice was husky with meaning, warming me all the way through.

Chapter Twenty-Three

I didn't recognise the girl on reception when I arrived at the nursing home, but she recognised me. "She's in her room," she said as soon as I walked through the door. Then she chewed on a nail while I signed in.

I wasn't that intimidating, was I?

When I approached my mother's room, I realised the cause of the girl's nerves had little to do with me. Mum's door was ajar, and raised, angry voices carried out into the corridor. A few curious residents stood in the doorways to their rooms, trying to eavesdrop. They withdrew like hermit crabs into their shells when I increased my pace, boots thudding on the carpet.

Glowering, I entered the room. Everyone fell silent and almost all of them turned as the door clicked shut behind me.

Uncle Ian loomed closest. His hands were on his hips, his posture stiff with outrage and his expression thunderous. He glared at me, eyes narrowed to slits. I knew with the certainty of long experience that he'd find a way to blame the cause of his ire on me. Whatever it was.

Beside him was someone I'd never seen before, an older gentleman with glasses, steel-grey hair and a perfectly groomed goatee. He wore an expensive-looking navy suit and held a clipboard.

Beyond them both, near the window, stood Ewan. His hands were shoved in the pockets of his pale blue nurse's uniform and he slouched like an uncomfortable twelve-year-old witnessing a fight between his parents.

The only one who didn't look at me was Mum. She lay on the bed, asleep despite the racket they'd been making—like Snow White after she'd been poisoned. When she was in the glass coffin.

My heart sank.

"This is Melaina," Uncle Ian said, indicating me with a flick of his fingers. I stiffened. "She's Davina's daughter. Melaina, this is Doctor Willis."

I glanced at Ewan and he nodded, lips pressed together.

"Pleased to meet you, Doctor," I said. It wasn't entirely honest, but politeness seemed in order given the emotions crackling in the air like static electricity. I offered my hand. Willis shook it, his grip firm but not aggressive. That put him one up on my uncle.

"And you," the doctor replied. "A shame it's under such trying circumstances."

"Oh?" I raised my eyebrows.

"Davina didn't wake up this morning," Uncle Ian said in a measured voice that did little to conceal the fury beneath the surface. He turned back to the doctor, his hands balled into fists. "Doctor Willis here was just explaining how that could be."

"She was showing signs of responding to the medication until last night," the doctor said, meeting my uncle stare for stare. "Her somnipathy was normalising. She was sleeping around—" he consulted a chart in his hand "—nine hours of an evening and having an hour-long nap in the middle of the day. I think you must agree that this is much improved from—"

"Except now she won't wake up!" Uncle Ian jabbed a finger at Willis. "I'm not agreeing to anything until you tell me what went wrong. Is she still being given the medication?

Willis glanced at Ewan, who shook his head and shuffled from foot to foot, clearly wishing he could sink into the floor.

"Not today. If she doesn't wake by tomorrow we'll put her on a drip and then we can look at intravenous alternatives," Willis said. I gritted my teeth at that, but a tiny part of me admired the way he kept his voice neutral despite Uncle Ian's provocation. I guess he had a lot of practice at dealing with angry patients and their families. "Did your mother say anything to you this week about the medication? Anything to indicate an adverse reaction?" He peered at me, grey eyes bright with intelligence. My stomach was suddenly full of lead, plummeting into my boots, and I understood Ewan's desire to vanish.

Stalling, I looked at Ewan, and he shook his head. "Not to me," he said. Doctor Willis frowned, clearly unimpressed with the staff.

My thoughts chased themselves in circles. Was Mum's sleep because she'd stopped taking the drugs on Tuesday? But that was two days ago. Surely it wouldn't have taken so long to have this effect?

Would it?

I grew conscious of three pairs of eyes fixed on me. Ewan looked sympathetic, Willis patient, and Uncle Ian... He looked suspicious. I swallowed hard before speaking, and decided to be honest. Well, as honest as I could be. "She did mention it," I said. "She wasn't happy. Her dreams were affected by the medication."

Willis tipped his head to the side, like a bird. "How so?"

I considered how to explain it without revealing too much. "Less real." The doctor raised his eyebrows, and I added, "Mum has pretty active dreams. Vivid, I guess. She felt like the drugs were cutting her off from that. It distressed her."

"Given how much time she spends asleep, the dreams may be her brain's way of dealing with the lack of conscious input," the doctor said to himself, making a note on the chart. "Interesting."

But Uncle Ian didn't seem interested. He stepped closer to me. I stiffened, but refused to retreat. If I did, my back would be against the door. When he spoke, his voice was silken, but I could hear the steel beneath it. "Did the drugs distress her enough that she might have stopped taking them?"

Doctor Willis looked up again. Even Ewan seemed interested in my reply.

"I don't know," I lied, narrowing my eyes. Time to go on the offensive. "But she didn't much like being bullied."

"Bullied?" Willis's mouth fell open. Didn't he know about Uncle Ian's tactics? I'd assumed given what my uncle had told me that the doctor had been all for treating Mum, no matter what. That didn't seem to be the case.

Could the doctor actually be an ally?

"Melaina—" Uncle Ian began, in a loud voice.

His reaction decided me. I raised my voice to be heard over him, meeting Willis's gaze. "My uncle threatened to kick Mum out of the home if she didn't do what you said." The doctor paled. "You didn't know she was being black-mailed into accepting your treatment?"

"I most certainly did not!" He stared at my uncle, aghast. His reaction seemed genuine. "Mr Armstrong, how could you?"

Uncle Ian could have denied it. It would have been his word versus mine, and I was a disreputable-looking twenty-something university dropout. He was a pillar of the business community. With Mum unable to speak, the doctor might have believed him.

But lying would be admitting he'd done the wrong thing, if only to himself, and my uncle could never do that. Instead he scowled at the doctor. "Don't give me that, you quack. You were the one who suggested I persuade her to say yes to the treatment. You were the one who said her previous medical team had been negligent."

"Persuade, yes. Not force. Good god, man." Willis's thoughts were written across his face, as plain as if he'd scrawled them on Mum's chart, part of her medical record. He could be sued. He could lose his licence. He turned to me, putting the chart down on the edge of Mum's bed and reaching for one of my hands. "I had no part in this!"

"I believe you." I extracted my hand from his clammy grip.

The pure fury in my uncle's gaze was frightening. Blotchy patches stained his cheeks, while his lips com-pressed so hard they turned white. He clenched his fists again, and for a moment I thought he might hit me. But he looked through me as if I wasn't there, turning his gaze on the doctor. "I'm paying you," he snarled. "Will you treat my sister?"

Out of the corner of my eye I glimpsed Ewan edging towards the phone on Mum's table. I hoped he was going to call security.

"Until I receive contradictory instructions from her, I will." Willis's expression was stern. "But once she awakens, I will be speaking to her about her true wishes, and then following them. And I don't want to hear any more talk of blackmail. Are we clear?"

"Crystal." Uncle Ian took a trembling breath and then shoved past me, throwing the door open and stalking out.

"Well," Doctor Willis said, eyeing the door as it bounced off the wall and slowly swung closed. "This is regrettable."

"Yeah." I stepped past him to Mum's bedside, taking her cool fingers in mine. "Can I ask something?"

"Of course."

"Before the drugs, Mum used to sleep up to eighteen hours a day. Why are you and Uncle Ian so freaked out that she's still asleep now?"

He raised an eyebrow, maybe at my choice of words, but answered. "Part of the concern is obviously that we need to identify why the drugs have stopped working. But the other is that while your mother did sleep a lot before this week, during daylight hours she tended to catnap. Such a block of unbroken sleep is, I understand, unprecedented for her. That is why I phoned your uncle, to advise him of the change in her condition."

"Is it a reaction to the medication?"

"We'll be conducting some tests to figure that out."

He looked at Ewan, who nodded vigorously. For a moment I'd forgotten the nurse was there. He'd done a pretty good impression of sinking through the floor for someone who, well, couldn't.

I sighed, rubbing a temple with one hand. I had a headache coming on. "Can I have some time alone with my mother please?"

"Of course." Doctor Willis reached into the breast pocket of his shirt and pulled out a business card. "I will finish my rounds. Please, if you have any concerns in the future, call me at my practice. Or if your mother does after she awakens."

"Sure."

Ewan hesitated by the door after the doctor had left, holding it open with one hand. He was still slouching, his other hand in his pocket, like he wished he was elsewhere. "Did she?" he asked softly.

"Did she what?" I didn't really have the energy for Ewan and his mixed messages. I wished he'd go away.

"Stop taking the drugs."

"I told them I didn't know."

A smile twitched at the corner of his mouth. "You did, didn't you?"

I didn't say anything. With a conspiratorial wink he walked out, closing the door softly behind him.

Sighing with relief, I sat on the edge of the bed. It was hard to imagine that two days ago, Mum and I had lain there together, gossiping like Jen and I would do after one of us had been on a date. She'd been so optimistic about not taking the medicine, at the idea of seeing Dad again. Was that what this was? They'd been apart for forty-eight hours and were having a spectacular reunion?

I didn't want to think about that too hard.

The idea of being so dependent on someone else that I couldn't function without them made queasiness roil in my stomach. Mum's teary paralysis on Tuesday wasn't romantic. It was unhealthy.

"Are you in there, Mum?" I whispered, brushing her hair back from her face. She'd braided it before sleep the night before, but strands had come loose and wisped around her head like dark cobwebs. I found a hairbrush in the top drawer of the bedside table, and rolled her head to one side so I could unwind the braid. Then I ran the brush through it till it gleamed.

A single strand of silver hair lay among the ebony locks, a glimmer of precious metal on a bed of satin. Mum had spent her entire adult life locked in this strange relationship with my father. As I touched the silver hair with my fingertips, I wondered if she'd die the same way. What would Dad do when she did? Leander had shown no signs of aging. Would my father outlive Mum? Would he find another bride, another woman in whose head he could nest like a parasite?

I hated him then. As much as Uncle Ian hated me for standing in the way of his sister's recovery. I understood how he felt, even if his anger was directed at the wrong person.

My hand had curled in Mum's hair until it would have hurt, if she'd been awake. I took a deep breath and gently disentangled myself, brushing her hair until it flowed smoothly again. Then I carefully re-braided it, and sat by her bed in silence until it was time to leave for the bus.

She didn't even stir.

Chapter Twenty-Four

I met Brad at the merry-go-round in Civic as darkness rolled across the city, stealing what little heat there'd been in the day. The merry-go-round was closed, but I peered through the security grill as I waited, looking at the wooden horses frozen mid-stride. In the poor light they looked shadowy and sinister, teeth bared in grimaces.

"I love this thing," Brad said, stepping up beside me and hooking an arm around my waist. "My grandad used to take me for rides on it when I was a kid."

"I've only been on it once," I said. My voice was gloomy, but I couldn't seem to shake it. "When I was a teenager, for a lark."

"What's wrong?" He turned me to face him.

"I was thinking it must suck to be a carousel horse, riding around the same boring route every day. Trapped."

He blinked. "Whoa. It's not that bad. What about all the joy they bring little kids?"

I leaned into his arm and sighed. "Sorry. It's been a

rough afternoon."

"Let me buy you dinner."

"You're already paying for my accommodation tonight. Don't you think that's enough?"

"Not really. The place where I work didn't burn down today, so I guess I'm feeling generous." He shrugged.

A particularly strong gust of wind rattled dead leaves along the pavement, and I shouldered my overnight bag. "Well, wherever we're going, let's do it fast."

He led me to a restaurant on Garema Place. We managed to nab a table at the back, as far from the open door as possible. Once we'd ordered soft drinks, I tried again to express my concern.

"I'm grateful for your generosity, believe me. It's just that I have no idea how long it will be before I can resolve my ... situation." I glanced at the next table and spoke softly. "It could be days. Weeks, even. That's not going to be an option."

"If it gets to weeks we'll reassess. But days is fine. I want you safe." He ran his fingers across the back of my hand. Despite my mood, something inside me warmed and tightened at the gentle touch, and my gaze fell on the cuff of his shirt, before running up to encompass his whole look. He was wearing business attire—slacks and a faintly striped shirt. The formal look suited him. "Have you got any leads?"

"Leads?" I suppressed a smile. "You make me sound like a PI or something."

"Aren't you?"

"Ah, no." A waiter brought over our drinks and laid napkins and cutlery on the table with flamboyant precision. I stopped talking until he'd sashayed away to get

menus. Then I spoke softly. "I went to talk to Mum this afternoon."

"What did she say?"

"She didn't. Her condition ... well, she's worse." I cursed the catch in my voice. Despite the ambient noise, Brad heard it too, and squeezed my hand. I continued quickly, "She'll be no help."

"What about your, ah, friend? Leander?"

"I'll try, but he's pretty pissed at me."

"Why?"

"He wants me to do something for him and I can't."

The waiter returned, saving me from having to elaborate. I was already in a bad enough mood without dwelling on Leander's persistent requests that I betray the father I didn't like, which would devastate the mother I loved. We ordered—steak for Brad, pasta for me—and then I changed the subject, asking how his day had been.

I'd always assumed when he'd said he worked in IT that he built computers or was a programmer. It wasn't that I wasn't computer savvy, exactly; I'd just never considered all the other things required when you network more than a couple of computers together. Listening to Brad I discovered it was a lot more complicated than I'd first guessed. That was why Brad was able to pay for a hotel room for a few nights without blinking an eyelid. Apparently some IT consultants were quite well paid.

Brad chattered until our food arrived, only falling silent as we ate. After a few mouthfuls he gave me a sheepish look. "Sorry."

I smiled. "Don't be. It's nice to hear about normal stuff. Even if I didn't understand most of it."

He laughed. "Have you got any idea what you're going

to do now?"

"Serenity's trying to find a new space to rent. Once the insurance money comes through, she can get new stock."

He raised an eyebrow, his fork paused halfway to his mouth. I eyed the piece of steak with a little bit of food envy. "That could take months to sort out. What are you going to do in the meantime? You're not actually tied to Serenity's business, are you?"

I shook my head. "No. But it would be weird working somewhere else. She sends me a lot of my clients."

"I don't think she'd blame you if you found somewhere else to work temporarily, though."

He was right. My requirements weren't complex: all I needed was a comfortable space for people to sit. I could even work out of someone's lounge room, if it came to that. Not mine, unless I got desperate. Or I could do house calls, although I wasn't wild about that idea, especially at the moment. I twirled spaghetti on my fork. "There are a few people I could hit up. The local community hall, maybe. I know there's a yoga class that runs there. I'll make some calls tomorrow."

After dessert we rugged up and scurried back to Brad's car. We were only a few blocks from the hotel, but, as Brad pointed out, if we drove there now he wouldn't have to come back for his car later.

I'd assumed he would rent me a cheap hotel room, which was the only sort I'd ever been inside, so I was pleasantly surprised when he led me into the foyer of a ten-storey apartment hotel. "I figured since you might be living here for a few days you'd want a kitchen and laundry. They don't do room service, but the hotel does have free wi-fi, a gym and a pool. I hope that's okay."

"Okay?" I squeaked.

The room was better than okay: by my student accommodation standards it was luxurious. The wood panelling in the kitchen was laminate rather than timber, and the "granite" bench top was a convincing plastic replica, but there was a dishwasher, and the television in the little lounge room was bigger than the one Jen and I had at home. When I checked the bathroom, I was impressed to see they'd squeezed a washing machine and dryer into the space, as well as the toilet and the obligatory combined bath and shower.

I'd had friends at uni whose student accommodation had been smaller than this.

"Wow," I said, turning to Brad. "This is amazing. Thank you."

He leaned against the kitchen bench, grinning. "I'm pretty proud of myself."

I pulled out my phone. "I'd better call Jen and tell her where I am."

"Is that a good idea? The plan was to keep where you are quiet. I even booked the accommodation in my name."

"I'm not, like, posting it on Facebook or anything," I said, putting the ringing phone to my ear. "But I have to tell Jen I won't be home or she'll—"

"Hey, mate," Jen answered.

"Hi." I poked my tongue at Brad.

"What's up? I'm about to drive home." In the background, a car door clicked unlocked.

"I won't be home tonight."

"Oh?" The word contained a world of questions. "Are you at Brad's?"

"We're at a hotel in the city." I found myself reluctant

to explain why. It was ridiculous, paranoid. "His treat."

"Ooh, nice." If there was any disapproval in her tone it didn't show. "I was going to pick up Chinese on the way home, but I guess I won't now."

"You could get it and have the leftovers tomorrow."

"True." Her car started. Music blasted briefly in my ear before she switched it off. "Sorry. Hey, Melaina?"

"Yeah?"

"You'll be careful, won't you?"

"I'm always careful." My cheeks burned and I turned away from Brad to look out the window. Cool air radiated off the glass from inches away.

"I'm not talking about sex, dumbarse. I'm talking about everything else."

"I know." I chided myself for being an idiot. I had to tell Jen about Brad's theory. Of course I did. "That's sort of why we're doing this, actually. Brad thought it'd be safer for me to stay somewhere else for a while, till I figure out what's going on. Serenity's store, the attacks on me and him..."

"It does seem like an odd set of coincidences," she said.

"Yeah. But ... Jen, if it's not a coincidence, if I'm being targeted, it's not safe for me to stay there right now."

"You think they might try something here again?"

"Not now I'm gone. But keep the doors locked, okay? And don't let anyone in. Just in case."

She laughed. "I'll sleep with a lamp in my hand too."

"Good."

I couldn't help but wonder, after we'd hung up, whether I should have invited Jen to come stay at the hotel with me. But ... I looked at Brad and my heart fluttered. I wasn't sure I wanted a chaperone tonight.

Chapter Twenty-Five

"*D*id you want me to go after this?" Brad sipped the coffee I'd made in the little kitchen—it was instant but, despite that, not bad. At least it didn't taste like it'd been scraped off a floor in a coffee factory someplace. "You must be exhausted."

I gave a lopsided shrug. We sat together on the tiny two-seater couch. I was conscious of his thigh pressing against mine, warm even through the thick fabric of my jeans. "I had a nap earlier." I tried to keep my voice neutral, but my thoughts kept straying to our date the previous evening, to Brad's hands gliding over my stomach. His mouth on my breast. I hadn't been sure whether I'd wanted to sleep with him then, but there was one thing I'd learned in the last twenty-four hours: life could change in an instant. Why wait to do something I really wanted to do? Or some*one*? The thought made me grin.

"Even so, it's been a hard day," Brad said, clearly not catching my look.

I put my cup down on the coffee table and turned in my seat to face him, trying to read his expression. Was he looking for an excuse to leave, or just being a gentleman?

His brown eyes, usually the colour of hot chocolate, had darkened with the intensity of his gaze. But still, his free hand remained politely in his lap.

"It *has* been a hard day," I said with a theatrical sigh.

Turning from me, he finished his coffee in one long gulp and stood to put it in the dishwasher. My eyes strayed down the length of his back to watch his butt, appreciating the way his slacks hugged his narrow hips. "Brad?" My voice was husky.

"Yes?" He turned to face me.

I met his gaze fearlessly. "Since I'm your kept woman for the next few days, are you going to take advantage of me?"

"I ... uh..." He swallowed. I smiled slowly and the tension flowed out of him. His lips parted with sudden desire. "Would you like me to?"

"I need something to take my mind off today," I said, peering at him through my eyelashes as he closed the distance between us. He knelt on the floor in front of me. "As you said, it's been a *very* hard day."

He spread my legs, positioning his hips between them so he could lean forward, locking his lips to mine. His coffee-flavoured kiss was gentle. Too gentle. I locked my fingers in his hair and kissed him back fiercely, my tongue twining with his, my teeth nibbling his bottom lip. He moaned, and I felt him swelling against me, even through our clothing.

"Brad..." There was urgency in my tone.

"I don't want to rush this." He silenced me with a kiss.

I squirmed as he pressed against me, his hands slowly running along my sides, taking in the shape of my hips and thighs. I grabbed the bottom of his shirt and worked it free of his pants, then let my fingers explore the length of his spine, nails lightly scratching his skin.

When he sat up to undo the buttons on my top, I took a trembling breath. "Shall we relocate to the bedroom?"

He pulled me to my feet and, stumbling, we found the bed. Brad kicked off his shoes and then bent to unlace my boots. I tried to brush him away, to do it myself, but he shook his head. "Don't. This is like opening a Christmas present."

"Are you one of those people who unpick the sticky tape and take ages?"

His smile was brilliant. "Maybe. But only with the special presents."

I lay back on the bed and let him finish removing my boots, wishing I'd worn flats. But soon enough the mattress shifted as he lay down beside me, his shirt gone to reveal the finely muscled chest I'd explored through the fabric. He ran one hand through my hair, the other undoing the buttons of my top as he kissed me. When the fabric fell open he paused, running his gaze over my stomach, over the curve of my breasts where they peeked above my bra. I would have felt self-conscious but for his smile.

He met my gaze again, his hand going still in my hair. "Are you sure about this?"

I answered by sliding out of my top and reaching one hand behind my back to unclasp my bra. Together we removed it, but when I moved to unbutton my jeans he caught my hand in his. "Not yet." And he kissed me again, starting at my bruised throat. The faint pressure of his lips on the tender skin sent a thrill through me. He continued on to my collarbone and down to my breasts. I moaned when he kissed one nipple and then the other, giving each equal attention, his palms warm on my skin. When his hand ran down between my legs, gentle against the denim of my pants, I pressed against him.

"Brad, if you don't do something soon…" I moaned.

"You'll what?" The words had a teasing note, but he unbuttoned my jeans.

"I don't know, but … oh!"

He'd slid his hand inside my underwear. When he felt how ready I was for him, he growled low in his throat, an unthinking expression of desire. I trembled as he pulled my jeans off in one swift action, shed his pants in the next, and stood before me. His eyes were black now, heavy-lidded with want as he produced a little foil packet. Smiling, I sat up and took it from him, tearing it open and discarding the wrapper. His shaft was long and firm, and I took my time sliding the condom down over it, enjoying the way his hips shifted in response to my slow movements.

As soon as I was done, I grabbed his hand and pulled him on top of me. He caught himself on strong arms and gazed down into my face for a long moment. I exalted in the feel of his hot skin against mine, down the full length of my body. Goosebumps rippled along my arms. "I didn't think you wanted me on top," he whispered.

"I don't care anymore," I said with fervour, kissing his cheeks, his chin. "I want you. Now."

We both cried out as he slid inside me, an involuntary sound arising from the satisfaction of realising a desire

withheld. Slowly he filled me to bursting before pausing, his eyes closed as he savoured the sensation. Then he began to rock his hips gently, in time with mine, gazing down at my face.

"You are amazing," he breathed.

"So are you." Unlike his hands, mine were free to explore, and I ran them across his chest and down his sides, getting to know the shape of him the way he'd done with me. I ran my tongue along the stubble of his jaw and he moaned, thrusting harder inside me. I nibbled at his neck, enjoying the reaction, trying not to leave a love bite ... even though the temptation was nearly impossible to resist.

He lifted himself higher, out of reach of my kisses. "My turn." He sat up, kneeling between my legs and holding my hips up with one hand so we stayed joined together where it mattered most. My legs curled around his back, holding him to me. Still moving inside me, resuming that slow, delicious, infuriating pace, he ran the fingers of his other hand down over my stomach and to the private place below, finding the centre of my pleasure. His fingertips stroked me in time with the movement of his hips. I whimpered, closing my eyes and giving myself up to the sensation as it built and built.

"You're so beautiful," he whispered, increasing his pace.

My climax smashed through me like a tsunami through a sandcastle. I quivered around him, and Brad grasped my hips with both hands, pounding into me, driving the sensation of pleasure higher than I'd known was possible. I gasped as he came too, moaning as we writhed together. He panted in my ear as he collapsed on top of me.

I didn't feel even a hint of fear. I loved the feeling of being trapped beneath him.

After taking a moment to catch his breath, Brad rolled to the side and lay there, one leg sprawled across mine. For a minute or so all I could hear was the racing of my own heart. Then I laughed, shakily, running a hand through my hair. "Damn, boy."

He blinked slowly and stretched, languorous as a cat. "What? Did I do something?" I punched him lightly in the arm. "Ow," he said, but without feeling. If anything, he sounded smug.

"I'm going to have a quick shower, and then I'm going to bed." He smiled slyly and I added, "To sleep."

He raised an eyebrow. "It's only eight!"

I poked my tongue out at him, rolling out of bed. "It's been a trying day, remember?"

"Want someone to wash your back?" He grinned.

"Okay. But don't get any ideas."

"Too late."

As soon as I walked into the bathroom and stared at my naked reflection in the mirror, I realised I should've said no to company. Leander wasn't there, mercifully, but I could never shake the feeling he might be watching. I whipped a towel off the stainless steel rack and, standing on my toes, wedged the corners behind the top of the mirror. The arrangement was precarious, but the towel stayed put.

"What are you doing?" Brad's hands slid around my waist, but when I glanced over my shoulder at him, he was frowning. "You're not self-conscious about your reflection, are you? Because, let me tell you—"

I cut him off before he could launch into a compliment

that would make me blush. "No, it's not that. Um. When I mentioned the Oneiroi, did I tell you they can see out of reflections?" His hands dropped to his sides and his mouth fell open in a perfect expression of surprise. "I don't know if they can do it everywhere, or only when I'm near. But I don't like to risk it."

"No. Of course not."

I stepped past him to reach for the taps in the shower, fiddling with them till I figured out how to make the water come out of the showerheads instead of the bath faucet. When I stepped over the rim of the tub and turned to face him, Brad was still standing there, looking bemused.

"Are you okay?" I asked, brushing his shoulder with my fingertips.

"Yeah, it's just ... every time I think I get a handle on this thing, your world, something else happens to knock me for six." He stepped into the bathtub and I shuffled to one side to make room for him. The tub was narrow, but dual showerheads meant we could both stand under the spray. "I mean, I think I took the news of my possession reasonably well—"

"You threw me out of your hospital room."

"—but then there's attacking bugs and peeping moth-men in mirrors..." He sighed. "It makes my head spin."

I ran a hand down the taut muscles of his stomach, admiring the way they glistened in the hot water. "Are you sure that's what's making it spin?"

He looked at me and smiled. "No. Maybe it's not."

219

A sound like a chirping bird pulled me from a sleep so deep I couldn't remember dreaming. For a few moments I wondered what the noise was, and why my pillow felt different. Then Brad stirred beside me and my memories of the previous night came back in a happy rush.

"What time is it?" I brushed the hair from my eyes and frowned at Brad as he swung his legs over the side of the bed, turning off the alarm on his phone. The bird chirp fell silent. The window to my left was covered by heavy drapes, but I should've been able to see light around the edges if the sun was up yet.

"Just after six." It wasn't.

"God," I groaned, dragging my pillow over my head.

"Sorry, but I've got work." The bed moved as he stood. I peeked out to see him stretching.

"Can't you blow it off? Stay with me?" I pouted. The expression was futile, given he couldn't see more than a single eye peeking out. "I'll be lonely."

He shook his head, giving me a longing look. "I have an important meeting today. And I have to get home and get fresh clothes. Hence the early alarm."

"Well, poop," I said, retreating completely under the covers like a reluctant turtle.

I tried to fall asleep again, but it evaded me. After the shower turned on I sighed heavily and threw the covers off, scrambling out of bed and wrapping myself in a terry towelling dressing gown. It was huge, a one-size-fits-all affair that swam on me, and I hugged it around myself with satisfaction. Since someone else was paying the electricity bill I'd left the heater running all night, and the apartment was warm as I padded across to the window with bare feet rather than scrounging around in my

overnight bag for clean socks.

I pulled the drapes to one side and gazed out.

Fog wreathed the city. We were several storeys up and, when I pressed my forehead to the chilly glass and peered down, I could barely see the sidewalk below. The traffic lights at the corner glimmered like luminous emeralds and rubies, taking turns as a lone car drove through the intersection. At this time of the morning there wasn't a lot of traffic, but what there was stood out because there was nothing else to look at except the gleam of headlights.

"The sun won't even be out of bed for another hour," I grumbled to myself, peering at the trees masking the horizon. But I was facing west, I realised, so I wouldn't be able to see the sunrise anyway.

As I moved, I caught a glimpse of my own pale reflection in the window. The bruises on my neck were like the shadow of a nightmare, starting to fade. The sight of them still made me wince, but part of me couldn't regret what had happened. Otherwise I wouldn't have met Brad.

Staring at my reflection reminded me that I'd been hoping Leander would make an appearance in my dreams last night. He hadn't, and I cursed his timing. Why did he always disappear when I wanted to talk to him?

"Leander, are you there?" I said, my breath steaming up the window in front of me. He didn't appear.

Sighing, I let the drapes drop back into place.

I jumped when my phone rang, vibrating its way across the bedside table. At least Brad hadn't seen me acting like a frightened schoolgirl.

The display read Uncle Ian (H). Why was he calling at six-thirty in the morning? My stomach sank as I pressed the answer button.

"Hello?"

There was silence on the other end of the line. No, not silence. I could hear quiet voices. And ... was that someone crying?

"Uncle Ian? Is that you?"

"No." The voice was harsh, rough with emotion. So much so that I barely recognised it.

"Aunt Lacey?"

"Yes."

"Is everything alright?"

"He's dead."

My knees went weak. I half sat, half fell onto the bed. "Who?"

"Ian."

"Oh my god. What happened?"

"He died!" I flinched at her sudden shout.

There was a brief commotion on the other end of the phone, and then I heard it change hands. Following another brief pause and the sound of a closing door, my cousin Justin spoke. "Hey, Laina." He sounded as if he had a cold, his nose stuffed.

"Oh, Jat, I'm so sorry."

"Thanks." His voice quivered and he took a deep, trembling breath. "Sorry about Mum. She's losing her shit."

"Understandably. Are you okay?"

"Yeah, I'll be alright. It's just crazy. He was fine when he went to bed last night, and then Mum woke us up screaming at, like, four. He'd died in bed. She didn't even wake up when it happened, you know? He was already cold."

Nausea dried my mouth. I couldn't even imagine waking

up next to your life partner and finding them dead beside you. I hadn't liked Uncle Ian, and I still didn't like his wife, but I wouldn't wish that on anyone. Not ever.

Justin was still talking. Something he said caught my attention, dragging it back to him. "Say that again?"

"I know it sounds crazy, but there were, like, bugs everywhere. All through the sheets. Even in his h ... hair." He began to cry softly on the other end of the phone, a hiccupping sob.

I heard my voice say something soothing and meaningless, but my mind ran in circles, gibbering and screaming. Bugs. They'd found bugs.

Uncle Ian had been killed by a mara.

Chapter Twenty-Six

The fog burned off early on the morning of the funeral. The sun glared down like an overbright fluorescent light, casting the stark shadows of trees onto the frigid ground.

Five days. That was how long it had been since Uncle Ian had been murdered. Not that the doctors called it that, of course. They said it was a massive heart attack, probably brought on by stress and too much red meat.

They were half right: he'd had a heart attack. But I was sure the cause was the mara ... possibly even the same ones that had attacked Brad and me. I didn't know if my driving them off that day had killed them or only disrupted their physical forms. I hadn't thought to ask Leander at the time, and I hadn't seen him since.

The guilt was crushing.

I'd been hiding out in the hotel. Jen packed me a suitcase full of clothes and came to visit every other day, but no one else knew where I was staying except Brad.

He hadn't said anything about ending my stay in the apartment and, as much as being dependent on him embarrassed me, I hadn't asked him to. I did venture out, meeting a couple of clients at their homes for appointments. But I did that in the evenings, and Brad or Jen came with me, driving me to and from each one.

I was afraid. The fear gnawed at my heart like a rat at a carcass. I couldn't shake the notion the attack on Uncle Ian had been meant for me. When I'd made myself unavailable as a target, they'd killed him—perhaps as a warning, a shot across the metaphorical bow. Fear for my own safety ranked only slightly below the terror Olivia or Justin would be next.

Or Jen.

Or my mother.

I couldn't protect them all. I was utterly helpless. Leander was still nowhere to be found. And Mum hadn't woken from her sleep.

Walking up the curved path to the crematorium, I thought that, when she did wake, she would be devastated by the news of her brother's death. And she might never forgive herself for sleeping through the funeral. I'd been to the home and told her, but there was no indication she could hear me. Tears prickled my eyes at the memory.

The crematorium was set in the centre of an expanse of lawn kept green despite the nightly frost. Neatly trimmed bushes and small trees lined the paths and dotted ornamental garden beds. In spring they'd be awash with flowers but at this time of year they were a subdued green. There were no deciduous trees on the grounds, no bare branches to jar mourners with their starkness. The building itself was a low, squat structure made of yellow brick.

The doors were open wide despite the weather, and people milled near the entrance, talking in soft voices. I only knew a handful of faces.

Brad walked with me, one arm around my waist. As we approached the crowd, Jen came towards us, sweeping me into a tight embrace. She didn't say anything as she stepped back, just gave me a little smile.

"Are you okay?" Brad asked. "Do you need anything?"

I'd spied my aunt in the throng, talking to a tall, fair man about her age. I didn't recognise him. "There are a lot of people here."

"Is that a surprise?"

"I don't know. Uncle Ian was a businessman and a ... what's the word ... a schmoozer? He knew a lot of people. But when they told me it was a memorial service, I thought it might be smaller."

"Let's go inside and find a seat," Jen said, hugging her arms to her stomach.

"I'd better find my cousins first. You guys can go in if you like."

Brad shook his head. Jen rolled her eyes.

We found Olivia standing at the far left of the gathering, enveloped in the arms of a guy about my age. My first instinct was to raise my eyebrows at the age gap, but Brad was seven years older than me so I wasn't in a position to judge. Her face was buried against his chest, hiding from the world. The guy had tried to dress for the occasion, wearing black jeans and a woollen overcoat buttoned to his throat, but he'd forgotten to shave the stubble from his chin. Or maybe it was a deliberate facial hair choice.

He met my gaze and whispered something to my

cousin. She looked at me with puffy, red-rimmed eyes and nodded slightly before returning to the shelter of her boyfriend's embrace.

The crowd parted with a quiet murmur. Justin walked through the gap, ignoring the sympathetic looks from those around him. "Hi, Laina," he said, his voice rasping.

"I'm so sorry," I said, hugging my younger cousin tightly. He stood stiffly in my arms for a few heartbeats before melting against me. He trembled and there was a quiet sob by my ear, but when he stood back his face was dry. He was trying to be strong for his mother and sister. It was easy for me to spot, since I'd spent so long doing the same for Mum.

"Brad, this is Jat. Justin, I mean."

"Laina's boyfriend?" Justin asked as they shook hands.

I bit my lip, but Brad agreed without hesitation. Warmth flooded through me.

Jen kissed my cousin on the cheek. He stood a little taller, appreciating the adult treatment.

"Any news?" I don't know what I was hoping to hear. Something to show that the mara hadn't killed his father, I suppose.

But he shook his head. "You?"

"Serenity called this morning. The police have confirmed an accelerant was used at the shop."

"That blows," he said, but without conviction. "We're about to go in. Let's go."

We followed him to the entrance, entering a simple antechamber. A table to one side bore a couple of books for people to write their names in. As I joined the back of the short queue, I wondered if it was there so Aunt Lacey could check to see who had bothered to show up.

But everyone was filing past, signing in as though it was perfectly normal, so I did too. A man stood behind the desk, a member of staff dressed in a black suit with a subdued grey shirt and matching tie, murmuring condolences to each person as they signed.

Inside, the chapel wasn't what I had expected. There was no religious iconography on the walls, although maybe it was hidden behind the heavy curtains hanging along the entire front of the room. The two side walls were made of glass, which let sunlight in to mix with the warm, diffuse glow of the downlights glittering overhead. A central aisle passed between rows of chairs to the coffin.

It was raised on a marble bier that sat on a small platform running the length of the room, a discrete stage. The coffin looked expensive, to my untrained eye: timber had been polished until it glowed, and brass fixtures glittered in the light. An armload of roses covered the closed lid.

Justin led me to the front row. Jen and Brad hesitated, but I beckoned for them to follow. We sat together on the outside edge of the row, leaving plenty of room towards the centre for the rest of the family. Justin sat beside me.

As his mother and sister approached, his hand slipped into mine.

Olivia sat beside her brother. Her boyfriend sat in the row behind us. I was wondering whether I should have asked Brad and Jen to do the same when Aunt Lacey stopped in front of me.

"Melaina," she said, and gave me a tight smile. It didn't reach her red-rimmed eyes.

"Aunt Lacey." I stood and kissed her lightly on the cheek. She smelled of lavender. "I'm sorry for your loss."

She raised her eyebrows, radiating a scepticism I didn't understand but found highly offensive. But I didn't want to argue with the widow at her husband's funeral and, before I could figure out what to say, Olivia took her mother's hand and led her back to her seat.

"What was that all about?" Jen whispered into my ear. She was between Brad and me.

I shrugged but didn't answer as a small, round woman in clerical robes entered the room, ascending the two stairs to the stage and standing behind a lectern that reminded me uncomfortably of high school assemblies.

But when the woman spoke, I was surprised at the warm timbre of her voice as she welcomed us to the service. She was all soft edges and soft smiles and softly spoken words. It was like listening to a hug.

The service was non-denominational Christian. The woman spoke of Jesus and how he'd learned about human comforts during his time on Earth—food, wine, and the comfort of a pillow—and how she was confident he'd used that knowledge to make Heaven a comfortable place for those who followed after. I wasn't particularly religious, but I liked the idea of a Heaven full of pillows where you could lounge around, drinking conjured wine and playing your harp. I wondered how Jesus's father would feel about the change of décor. And whether, if Uncle Ian had made it to Heaven, which I didn't think was guaranteed, he'd be allowed to set up his billiard table.

Several people gave brief eulogies—a colleague of Uncle Ian's from work, followed by Aunt Lacey's brother, speaking on behalf of her and her children. Then the tall man I'd seen talking to my aunt spoke. He introduced himself as Thomas, a childhood friend of my uncle's. He talked about their adventures in a way that gave me a glimpse of what Uncle Ian was like before he became a real estate tycoon: getting chased by the neighbour after stealing a bucket-load of plums from his fruit tree; trying to sneak up on dozing kangaroos; hiding under a blanket that smelled like dog in the back of a station wagon overstuffed with teenagers. The stories were mundane but he told them in a jocular way that had even Aunt Lacey smiling. And then he talked about how Uncle Ian had felt when he'd met his future wife, and at the birth of each of his children: how he'd talked on the phone to Thomas of bursting with pride as he counted their tiny fingers and toes, adored their rosebud lips. The audience murmured its appreciation. Beside me Justin blushed and stared intently at his lap.

Thomas looked at me then, blue eyes sympathetic, and added, "And Ian also spoke to me of his niece, Melaina, who was like a daughter to him."

My mouth fell open. To my left, Jen made a faint sound of disbelief. Even Justin looked surprised.

I couldn't see Aunt Lacey's face without craning forward, but I'd wager she wasn't impressed.

The rest of the service passed quickly after that. There were a couple of prayers, and family were invited to come forward and place long-stemmed roses bound with ribbon onto the already brimming pile of flowers. I followed my cousins to the stage and placed my flower as quickly as I could, avoiding looking at the coffin.

The idea that my uncle lay behind that thin sheet of wood, eyes closed forever, reminded me of my guilt. And my fear.

Chapter Twenty-Seven

*A*fter the service, everyone retired to my aunt's house for the wake. I wasn't sure I'd have wanted a hundred people to come to my home if I'd just buried my husband of twenty years, but Aunt Lacey was made of hardier stuff than I.

I did feel bad for Justin and Olivia, though. Judging by their downturned faces and grim expressions, they both wished they could retreat to their rooms and stay there. But their mother would have none of it, insisting they mingle with their guests. At least she'd hired a caterer, so they didn't have to carry trays of appetisers through the crowd.

Jen had offered to ditch her lecture to come to the wake, but I'd told her not to worry. So Brad and I stood alone together in a corner of the family room. My aunt held court in the neighbouring lounge room, near the fireplace. I didn't know which was hotter, the smouldering logs or her narrow-eyed gaze, so I stayed away from her.

I'd have liked to be able to keep a low profile, but people kept stopping to offer me their sympathies. Since Thomas had bumped me up from "rogue niece" to "like a daughter" of the deceased, I was drawing a lot more attention.

"Tuna and watermelon ceviche?" A server stopped in front of us, proffering a silver tray of finely diced fruit cradled in what looked like curled crisp bread. I shook my head, but Brad took one, thanking her politely before popping it into his mouth.

His face turned red. He swallowed and then croaked, "Whoa. Chilli."

"Would you like something to drink, sir?" The server managed not to smile, although her eyes crinkled at the corners with suppressed mirth.

"Yes. Please," he gasped, eyes watering. "They really ought to warn a guy," Brad said as she disappeared into the crowd. Then he tipped his head to the side, licking his lips. "Once the burning subsides, it's actually pretty good. Watermelon and lime. You should try it."

"I'm not hungry."

He lowered his voice. "Too sad?"

I leaned in so no one else could hear me. "Worried." I really meant scared, but my remaining shreds of pride wouldn't let me admit it out loud. "As soon as we can manage it without being totally rude, let's get out of here, okay?"

"Sure." He slipped an arm around me, hugging me tightly against his side. "Nothing's going to happen, though. I won't let it."

"Thanks..." The back of my neck prickled, and I glanced up. Thomas had entered the room and was talking to several other men I didn't know. Our eyes met and he

hastily looked away.

I knew why I felt guilty. But what was he worried about?

I turned my head towards Brad's chest, letting the tail of my fringe fall over my eyes, and then peeked sideways. Within seconds Thomas was watching me again.

I stiffened. Brad kissed the top of my head. "What's the matter?"

"Thomas."

He glanced over. "What about him?"

"He's looking at me."

"You're an attractive girl."

"Ew. No. He's just … I don't know, it feels weird."

Brad looked between me and the tall man across the room several times. A frown formed. Abruptly he released me, taking a step away. "Let me go talk to him."

"What? No!" The idea of Brad causing a scene on my behalf made my cheeks burn. "I'm probably being paranoid."

"Probably." He smiled. "Don't worry, I'm not going to start a fight or anything."

I tried to look cool as Brad weaved his way across the room, pausing to get the glass of water from the returning server. Then he wandered over to where Thomas stood, leaning against the back of the scarlet couch. They shook hands politely, but I couldn't hear what they were saying over the background murmur and the classical music coming from the next room.

"My sincerest condolences." An older woman wearing an impressive amount of foundation moved between Brad and me, her herringbone print-clad shoulders blocking my line-of-sight. She leaned in, giving me a powdery kiss on the cheek.

I tried not to let my annoyance show, wishing she'd go away. "Uh. Thanks."

"Ian was a truly great man. Kind to his friends, generous even with his extended family. He sent you to boarding school, didn't he?"

I nodded, craning my neck to look over her shoulder. No good.

Her eyes narrowed slightly. She didn't seem to like that I wasn't giving her my full attention. "And what are you doing with that stellar education, I wonder?"

That brought my focus back onto her, although not in a way she appreciated—she retreated a step at my black look. "Living my life," I said.

"Well." The woman glanced around for reinforcements and an older woman waved to her from across the room. "Excuse me." She scurried away.

"Rude old bat," I said under my breath, wondering if she was one of Aunt Lacey's friends. Probably.

At least now I could see Brad again. He and Thomas were still talking, their postures intense: Brad had his legs spread and his hands on his hips, while Thomas frowned, blue eyes glittering with displeasure. His arms were folded, but his hands had curled into fists beneath his elbows.

"Dammit, Brad, you said you weren't going to start a fight," I muttered, heading towards them. But before I could get more than a few steps Brad's phone trilled. Several people scowled at him as he fished it from his pocket. He ignored them, waggling the phone at me, and then pointing towards the glass door behind Thomas as

he put the device to his ear.

That left me alone in a room with twenty other people who eyed me with either curiosity or contempt—Herringbone Woman wasn't my biggest fan—and a man who kept staring at me.

Putting my hands in my pockets, I wandered towards the bathroom, trying to look casual. But as soon as I was out of sight of Thomas, I scurried up the stairs to the first floor.

Relief made me sigh out loud. It was quieter up here. But then I realised why. The top floor of the house was my aunt and uncle's private space: a huge master bedroom and a retreat Aunt Lacey called her study—although most studies weren't equipped with a treadmill, rowing machine, and private balcony. I'd never been up here before, and stared into the room with wonder. It was as big as the combined lounge and dining space in my hotel apartment.

I turned, and my gaze fell on the king-size bed, visible through the open double doors of the bedroom. The hair stood up on the back of my neck.

That was where Uncle Ian had died.

As though in a trance, I walked towards the bed, conscious of my boots' heavy tread on the glossy timber floorboards. I felt as if I was trespassing, not on Aunt Lacey's privacy so much as my uncle's resting place. Which was silly, because he was being cremated elsewhere, probably as I walked across his bedroom floor.

I didn't believe in ghosts. Of course, I didn't *not* believe in them either, but I'd never seen any proof, one way or the other. And this brightly lit bedroom, which was an exercise in minimalist luxury, seemed like an unlikely place for a haunting. But still, a chill crept over me as I stared at the neatly made bed.

Did Aunt Lacey even sleep in here anymore? I wasn't sure I'd be able to, after finding someone the way she had Uncle Ian: wide-eyed and cold, covered in the carcasses of insects.

Insects...

I hurried to the bed and lifted the corner of the bedspread, looking underneath for any leftover evidence of the mara, something to definitely prove they had been involved in his death.

But there was nothing, not even dust. Aunt Lacey's cleaners were too efficient.

A soft footstep thudded on the stair behind me. I jumped back, whirling.

"What are you doing up here?" Olivia stared at me from the head of the stairs.

"I wanted to get away from the crowd for a minute."

She nodded, her jaw unclenching. "It's suffocating down there." Then she glanced at the bed and back to me. "You know that's where he died." It wasn't a question.

"Yeah." I straightened the bedspread, trying to look sad. But my ears burned with guilt.

"I hate coming up here," she said, her tone soft.

"I never had a chance to say. I'm sorry, Liv." I crossed the room and hugged her. She returned my embrace briefly, arms tight around my ribs.

"We'd better go back. Mum's looking for you."

We turned to head down the stairs. "Am I in trouble for something?"

"Who knows, with her?" she said with a teenager's finely honed sense of persecution.

"Go easy on your mum."

She glanced over her shoulder, eyes glittering. "I will if you do."

"Deal."

Aunt Lacey waited for us at the bottom of the stairs, arms folded. A bearded man stood behind her. With his weather-beaten face, he would have looked at home on a fishing trawler, but his suit fit his huge frame neatly. It had to be tailor-made.

"What were you doing up there?" My aunt glared past her daughter and straight at me.

"I had to use the bathroom, and the downstairs one was taken," I said, hoping Olivia wouldn't call me out for the lie.

She didn't, but Aunt Lacey's lips puckered as if she'd tasted something sour. "Both of them?"

I nodded, feeling foolish. Of course they had two downstairs toilets. I'd never used the one beside Uncle Ian's study, so I'd forgotten it was there.

"Next time, use Olivia's en suite. Upstairs is out of bounds."

I glanced in surprise at my cousin. "You have an en suite?" I'd never been inside her room. Unlike Justin, she was fierce about protecting her privacy.

"Don't you?" she replied, raising an eyebrow.

"Not so much." I turned back to my aunt. "I'm sorry, Aunt Lacey, it won't—"

"Call me Lacey," she said. From anyone else it might have sounded like an acknowledgement of my maturity, but not from her. To make sure there was no doubt, she continued in a soft, angry voice, "Now your uncle is no longer with us, there's no familial tie between you and me."

"Except for Olivia and Justin, of course," I murmured.

Her cheeks reddened but, before she could muster a retort, the man behind her cleared his throat. He reached a huge hand past her smaller frame and seized my fingers in his grip, shaking vigorously. "I'm Phillip. Phillip Barbato."

"Phillip is the family lawyer," Aunt Lacey—no, Lacey—said. She clearly didn't like losing control of the conversation.

"I thought *you* were the family lawyer," I said. Olivia elbowed me in the ribs.

Lacey's eyes narrowed. "The Armstrong family lawyer. His firm was retained by Ian's father prior to his death, to manage the family trust."

"Oh."

"He has matters to discuss with you." She extended a hand to her daughter. "Olivia, it's rude to leave our guests unattended. Let's return."

Before they could walk away, Phillip placed a hand on Lacey's shoulder. "Is there somewhere private I could speak to your niece?"

"You can use Ian's study," Lacey said, face pinched. "She knows where it is."

As we walked up the corridor to my uncle's study, Phillip spoke ruefully. "I'm afraid I'm the cause of your aunt's current irritation with you."

I glanced back at him as I opened the study door. "How?"

"She knows the news I bear, and she's not thrilled about it. Let's sit, and I'll explain."

The study had been tidied since the last time I was there. Then, manila folders stuffed with paper were piled on the desk amidst a scattering of pens. Now, the desk

was bare except for a penholder. I wondered whether Uncle Ian had tidied at some point or, as seemed more likely, someone had been through and straightened everything up after his death, returning the files to his agency's office. Every surface gleamed, as if dust didn't dare enter the room.

Phillip took one of the chairs on the side of the desk closest to the door, his huge frame filling it to capacity. After a brief hesitation I took the other. I couldn't bear the thought of sitting in my uncle's chair. The idea made my skin crawl as much as the notion of sleeping in the bed where he'd died.

Phillip leaned back and the chair creaked. "As your aunt said, my firm manages the Armstrong family trust on behalf of your uncle."

"I didn't even know there was a trust," I said.

His eyebrows twitched, a subtle expression of surprise. "When your grandfather Jonathan passed away, half his estate went to his son, Ian. The other half was put into a trust for the care of his daughter, Davina. Your mother."

I stared at him. "I never knew that." All this time Uncle Ian had let me think he was paying for Mum's expenses out of his own pocket. If he'd been alive, I would have hit him. Or at least thought about hitting him.

Phillip nodded. "Jonathan's instructions were that the trust would be executed by your uncle on your mother's behalf unless she recovered sufficiently to manage her own affairs, in which case the trust would be dissolved and she would inherit the balance. In the event of Ian's death, the management of the trust would pass to Ian's wife, Lacey, unless Davina's daughter had reached the age of twenty-one."

"Oh." I'd turned twenty-one at the start of the year. "That explains why Aunt Lacey is so angry at me. She wanted the money."

"She wouldn't have been able to access it for personal gain, if that's your concern. And I don't think she'd have tried. I've worked with Lacey before and she has a strong sense of right and wrong." He hesitated. "But she also has specific ideas about the direction Davina's care should take."

"I can imagine." Uncle Ian had been frustrated by my mother's continued refusal of medical treatment, but Lacey had been scathing. She thought it was weakness, pure and simple, and that my uncle coddled Mum. I'd heard those rants many times over the years. I was sure her first order if she'd had control of the trust would have been to move Mum into accommodation designed to make her want to get better. Something awful. I shuddered. "What now? What do I need to do?"

"Unless you give me any instructions to the contrary, I'll be continuing with business as usual. I'll have some documents prepared before the end of the week, detailing the trust's current financial position. Did you have any concerns you wanted to raise?"

I glanced down, biting the corner of my lip in thought. Mum was well cared for at Wattle Tree Park; she knew the staff and seemed happy there. The only problem had been my uncle's insistence she accept treatment. I'd thought Doctor Willis was to blame, but after our conversation the previous week I didn't think so anymore. "No, but can you let her doctor know about the change in circumstances? I want to talk to him about her current treatment, and I'm not sure he'll discuss details with me

without permission first."

"I can do that. How is Davina doing? I thought she'd be here today."

"She's ... not well."

"I'm sorry," he said. "Is there anything we can do?"

I shook my head.

"Well, we'd best return to the wake." He stood, offering me his hand. I wasn't short, but he towered over me by almost a foot. "I'm sorry for the loss of your uncle, by the way."

"Thanks." My eyes drifted past his huge form to one of the pictures on the wall. It was a framed newspaper clipping, showing Uncle Ian shaking hands with the Chief Minister as they announced some property deal or other. My uncle beamed at the camera. "Let's get out of here."

Chapter Twenty-Eight

*T*wenty minutes later, as Brad walked me to the car, I told him about the change in the trust fund. "So that's why Lacey hates me even more than usual at the moment."

"People do funny things when they're grieving," he said, pulling his keys from his pocket. "When my grandma died, my grandfather went completely off the rails. He ended up driving himself into a tree."

I stared at him. "God!"

"I'm not saying that's what your aunt is going to do," he added hastily. "But she might be lashing out over the whole trust fund thing because she needs to blame someone for something right now."

We didn't speak again until we were in the car. My thoughts spun with visions of Lacey doing something crazy. She'd always seemed so calm and in control. Even when she was furious she didn't shout—she just got more intense. She was the last person in the world I'd have thought would

act out due to grief, or anything else for that matter. But if her hating me gave her something to focus on, maybe that was a good thing. I squared my shoulders, telling myself I was doing a public service. Still, I was grateful for the change of subject when Brad offered it.

"I have some good news." He started the car and the engine rumbled to life. Cold air blasted from the heater vents, but he turned the air off before my nose could go numb. "That phone call I got was from the senior constable investigating the fire."

"Nelson? What did he want?"

"The fingerprint analysis came through. For the shop fire." Brad grinned at me before turning his attention to the road. "I'm pleased to say I'm innocent."

"Told you so," I said, poking my tongue at him.

"Well, it's nice that the police agree. I'm not sure they would've taken your word for it."

"I know." I stared at him for a couple of minutes, twisting sideways in my seat, watching as he drove. His posture was relaxed, a subtle tension gone that I hadn't realised was there until now. Finally giving in to temptation, I ran a hand up the outside of his arm. "You're not *that* innocent, though. Do you have to go back to work this afternoon?"

He glanced at his watch. "It hardly seems worth it. Shall I take you back to your hotel, my lady?"

"Yes please. And then you can take me … somewhere else."

He laughed, low and sexy.

Brad and I spent the rest of the afternoon in bed, enjoying each other's company. I felt guilty, making love in the afternoon after a funeral in the morning. When I commented on it as we lay sprawled across the bed in a tangle of limbs, he told me it was a natural reaction: that humans crave physical contact when presented with a reminder of mortality, as a way of defying the inevitable.

"That's deep," I murmured, tracing circles around his nipple.

"I read it in a book somewhere. That tickles. Stop it."

"Make me!"

Later he dressed and went out for food, which we ate in bed, watching trashy shows on the television in the corner of the room. I was avoiding thinking about the funeral; my uncle's death; my probable, albeit unwitting, involvement. I'd worried so much about those things in the last five days that the thoughts were like a mouse running on a wheel—covering the same ground over and over, never getting anywhere, wearing me out for no appreciable gain.

I fell asleep early, nestled under the covers, the sound of a cheesy laugh track following me into my dreams.

My subconscious, keen to direct my mind to the very things I'd been avoiding, dropped me into the middle of a nightmare about the shop fire. I sprawled across my battered chair in the back office, struggling to rise, as a thick layer of smoke inched down the walls, closer and closer to my face, like water filling the room in reverse. The bottom of the descending smoke roiled as hot air moved. Things popped and tinkled, exploding in the heat, and around me the fire roared, although I couldn't see flames, just a flickering orange glow that came from everywhere.

With sheer force of will, I struggled to my feet, only to be knocked back into the chair again. A mara loomed over me, its doughy face radiating pleasure despite the lack of eyes and mouth. Bugs crawled inside the hollows in its skull.

The mara was dressed in a polo shirt and slacks. My uncle's clothes.

Melaina. It's a dream.

Closing my eyes, I willed the nightmare away. The shop faded, its details running like the ink on a newspaper left in the rain, blurring until there was nothing left but an indistinct grey world. Heavy, dry fog surrounded me. It was as though I stood in a room that had been blasted with a smoke machine, only without that irritating, sweet smell.

"Melaina."

I turned around, expecting to see Leander. I'd even opened my mouth to ask him where the hell he'd been when I needed his advice so badly, but … it wasn't him.

The Oneiroi stood a couple of inches taller than me. He had warm, dark hair the colour of polished timber, and skin like milky coffee. His eyes were a brown so deep it was almost black, and his wings were a mottled tan. He wasn't dressed in the ostentatious finery Leander usually mustered for his visits to my dreams. Instead, he wore clothes much like mine: comfortable jeans and a T-shirt. The only difference was that I wore my boots while his feet, when I caught glimpses of them through the fog, were bare.

"Err. Hi?" I'd never met another Oneiroi before. I was a little alarmed at how easily he'd slipped into my dreams. Would I have even been aware of his presence if he hadn't revealed himself to me?

"Melaina." He moved forward, arms outstretched, and I stepped back, almost tripping over my feet in my haste.

He stopped, crestfallen. I realised with growing shock that he'd meant to embrace me.

Other than Leander, there was only one Oneiroi I could think of who might be so presumptuous.

"Ollie?" I whispered, incredulous. "*Father*?"

He nodded. "I'm so pleased to finally see you with my own eyes." Resentful thoughts scrambled for attention in my mind, like unruly children: that the delay had been his decision, not mine; that he was a selfish insect who had taken my mother from me. But he continued before I could speak, and a chill filled me at his words. "Even under such circumstances."

"You're not talking about Uncle Ian's death, are you?"

"He died?" He blinked slowly. "I didn't know. Davina will be devastated."

"Make sure you tell her."

"I can't."

I narrowed my eyes. "Why? I sure as hell can't right now." How typical of him. Or rather, how typical of how I'd imagined he'd be: all fun and no responsibility. Leaving me to deliver the bad news.

"Neither can I."

That brought my internal ranting up short. "What do you mean?"

"I haven't been able to enter your mother's dreams in several days."

"How many days, exactly?" My stomach churned. "Five?"

"Yes. How did you...?"

"We haven't been able to wake her since then. And

that's the same day Uncle Ian died too." My thoughts whirled again, but in a new, alarming direction. What if the events of the past few days hadn't been aimed at me? My mother's apparent coma, my uncle's death: what if they hadn't been about me but her? What if Uncle Ian's murder wasn't a warning to me, but was to get him out of the way? What if the medication Mum had been receiving had actually been preventing something else?

Preventing whatever was happening now that Ollie was here and not with her?

I could see the beginnings of a pattern forming, but I didn't have all the pieces yet.

I focused on Ollie with a scowl and he fluttered his wings in agitation. "Tell me everything," I said.

"What do you want to know?"

"You've been holed up inside Mum's brain for years, right? Hiding from the Oneiroi police?" I asked. He nodded, eyes widening. "So what happened? Did you leave and couldn't get back in, or...?"

"I was forced out. We were together, Davina and I, having something of a reunion after she stopped taking the medicine—"

I held up a hand. "I don't need details about that!"

"—when suddenly it was ... well, everything went black. The ground shook, and a terrible force knocked me, knocked all the breath out of me. Everything spun, and I woke up in a different part of Erebus. A child's dream halfway across the country. It took me three days to get back, and then I spent two trying to find a way back in." He stopped, and took a trembling breath. "I'm sure you've noticed how I turned her mind into something of a fortress, so no other Oneiroi could get in."

"Yes. So you could hide."

"It was as much for her protection as mine, you understand," he continued hastily. "The fact she was able to bear you, my miraculous daughter—well, that would be of great interest to other Oneiroi. Not all of them are law-abiding creatures. The Morpheus wouldn't be able to stop them from taking advantage of her."

My anger softened. I told myself it was because of his obvious concern for my mother, not the fact he'd called me miraculous. "But you couldn't get back in?"

"No. I left the tiniest of holes, a way for me to enter and exit her dreams if I had to, and it has been closed. Someone else is in there, and they've locked me out."

I shuddered, folding my arms across my chest. "Who?"

"I don't know."

"And you think I can help?"

He hesitated, and then settled on brutal honesty. "I don't know that either. Not for certain. But you're strong … and who else could I ask?"

"The Morpheus's police? Leander? They'd throw your butt in jail afterwards, but they'd help, right?"

"Maybe. I can't be sure. And if they didn't, Davina would be helpless." He twisted his hands together, shuffled his feet. "I swear to you, Melaina, I'd give myself up to them if it would help." Tears stood in his eyes, making them glitter like pools of ebony.

A voice emerged from the fog. "*Done.*" Leander strode out of the mist. For once he was dressed in a subdued grey. It blended perfectly into the fog, as did his ashen wings. The only spots of colour were the honey skin of his bare hands and face, and his emerald eyes, which gleamed like a cat's. He swept forward, the mist swirling around

him, and brushed his fingertips against Ollie's elbow. As quickly as that, my father was trapped, heavy silver rope binding his arms to his sides and his wings flat against his back. He struggled, but his efforts were futile.

Leander was more powerful than I'd thought.

"Help me," Ollie begged, tears streaming down his cheeks.

I raised a hand to Leander and, before he could do more than turn towards me, he too was bound with silver rope. His eyes flashed with outrage.

"My dream. My rules."

Leander swallowed his anger and drew a breath. "Melaina..." he began in a voice as slippery as silk.

I stomped my foot with exasperation, cutting him off. The gesture made me feel as if I were twelve, but I didn't care. "We were talking. You can't just barge into my dreams and ... and arrest people!"

"Sorry," Leander said, chin raised and not looking the least bit repentant. "But I've been tracking Ollie for days, since I got word he was moving around Erebus. It was too good an opportunity to pass up."

"Whatever. Shut up and let us finish talking," I said, putting my hands on my hips. "Or I'll gag you too."

He shut up.

"Right. Ollie." I narrowed my eyes, shooting my father a venomous look. "This wouldn't have happened if you'd ever taught me to screen my dreams. Why didn't you ever explain, oh, *anything*? I've had to learn it all on my own or from Leander, and you can imagine he hasn't been particularly forthcoming on matters concerning my privacy."

Leander had the good grace to look ashamed, his

shoulders slumping and head hanging so his hair fell in front of his face.

"Because it wasn't safe," Ollie said.

"You could have made it safe if you'd taught me."

"The risk was too great. And you were developing brilliantly without my help, growing into a strong and intelligent woman. Powerful too." He glanced at Leander's bindings.

"There's no way you could have known that," I said, hearing the bitterness in my voice. But I didn't care. "You've never even met me before—"

"No..."

"—and you don't know me."

"That's where you're wrong." His voice trembled. "Your mother has shared every one of her memories of you. I remember you losing your first tooth, and your first boy band crush, and your high school graduation. I know you as well as she does. I'm proud of the woman you've grown into. I love you like, well, a daughter. My daughter."

"Oh." My response was stupid and inadequate, but words failed me. I wanted to believe him, but I still didn't know if I could. Trust had to be earned, and he hadn't put in the man-hours. Oneiroi-hours. Whatever.

Leander snorted, his expression sceptical. It drew my ire. "And *you*," I growled. "Spying on me, using me to capture my father! I've half a mind to trap you in *my* mind forever, just to punish you. Clip your wings, moth-boy."

"You wouldn't do that." His honey skin paled.

"Are you so sure? You haven't exactly won me over recently."

"That's because I've been looking out for you, with Brad—"

Ollie's gaze flicked to Leander. "What about him? Davina thought he sounded like a good match for her."

"He's been blight-infested. I don't trust him."

"But she evicted the blight, didn't she?"

"Yes. He's definitely clean," Leander said. "But here's my concern: how did he get infected in the first place? Blight eggs aren't exactly commonplace. He could become compromised again."

"Do you two mind?" I said, cutting into the conversation. I couldn't believe they had the gall to discuss my private life together like meddling aunts. In front of me. Inside my head.

Although…

How *did* he get infected?

"You two stay here. And play nice." I tried to smile, but it came out in a grimace. "I'll be back."

Their raised voices followed me as I pulled myself out of my dream.

Chapter Twenty-Nine

*B*rad sprawled naked on the bed beside me, his breathing slow and even. The sight made me smile.

Don't get distracted, girl.

"Sorry," I muttered to Brad, then grabbed his shoulder and shook him, hard. "Wake up!"

He woke abruptly, sitting up straight and brushing my arm off. "Wahh? Mara?"

"No, it's me. I need to ask you a question."

He rubbed his eyes and glanced at the clock on the bedside table. It was just after ten in the evening. "What? I was having a very ... interesting dream." His gaze caressed my half-exposed body. Unlike in my dream, where I had mercifully been dressed, in the real world I was also naked.

Thank god my father hadn't shown up during the sort of dream Brad was talking about. I'd had a few of those lately.

I pulled the blanket up under my armpits and Brad

pouted. "Focus. I need to ask you something," I said. "I was having an interesting dream too—not like *that*—and it got me thinking this whole thing might be about Mum, not me. Maybe she's the key. Have you ever met her? Davina Armstrong?"

He shook his head, the cheeky smile dropping away. "I don't think so."

"She doesn't get out much, so it's not likely. Unless..." I stared at him through wide eyes. "Have you ever been out to Wattle Tree Park? That's her nursing home."

He stiffened, eyes widening. "That's my grandfather's home."

"Your grandfather? The one who..." *Drove into a tree?* I stopped myself before I said it aloud. "I thought he was dead."

Brad shook his head, his jaw tight with anger. "No. He might as well be, though. He knocked his stupid self into a coma. They resuscitated him after the accident, but he's never actually regained consciousness. He's been in that home for three years." He ran a hand through his hair. "That's why we sold their house, to pay for the care. He wouldn't want to be in a hospital."

"He's the sleeper," I whispered, remembering Ewan telling me about a patient at the home who was worse off than Mum: one who never woke up.

Brad grimaced. "I guess, yeah."

"It's weird I've never seen you out there."

"Not that weird," he said, his gaze sliding away from mine. A blush turned his ears pink. "I only go out there once a month or so. When Belinda makes me. That place gives me the heebie jeebies."

I snatched my phone off the bedside table and scrolled

through my contacts. It had been two weeks since I'd treated him, so his number had dropped quite a way down the received calls list.

"Who are you calling?" Brad asked as I put the phone to my ear.

"Shh."

"Hello?" The voice on the other end of the phone sounded cross.

"Larry. I'm so sorry to call so late, but it's important."

"Who is this?"

"It's Melaina. Melaina Armstrong. You saw me two weeks ago?"

"I did," he said, his voice softening. "I owe you big thanks for that, by the way. I've been sleeping much better. No more nightmares. It's fantastic. I don't know what your secret is, but I've been recommending you to all my friends."

"That's very kind of you," I said, trying to sound grateful when I wanted to scream at him to shut up and listen. "Now, this is a bit of a weird question, but please bear with me. Do you have any connection to Wattle Tree Park? The nursing home?"

"My Aunt Mim volunteers there," he said, sounding surprised. "She and her poodle do pets-as-therapy work with the patients. Why?"

I lay back against the pillow, my head spinning. "And had you been out there yourself? Before your appointment with me, I mean?"

"A few times. I live with Aunt Mim, and sometimes I pick her up." He sounded embarrassed.

"Okay, well, thanks very much for your help, Larry. Sorry again for the late call." I hung up on him before

he could say anything else.

"Who was that?" Brad asked, eyes wide.

"Larry. The guy I booted the blight from just before I met you. I think you both got infected at Wattle Tree Park. Blights spread via eggs. You have to swallow them in food or drink."

Brad cursed.

"No kidding," I agreed.

"My grandad's out there."

"And my mum." I threw the covers off and strode around the bed to the bathroom. Brad scrambled after me.

"What are you doing?"

"I'm going over to the home. Something's going down there. Something big."

"Now?" He gestured to the clock radio through the open bathroom door. "There's no way they'll let you in."

"I'll cross that bridge when I come to it."

He hesitated, but then shook his head and disappeared back into the bedroom.

I had a quick shower. When I stepped out Brad was waiting for me, already fully dressed. He held my towel out.

"Thanks. You're coming?"

"Of course. I'm not letting you go alone." Gratitude warmed me to my toes. "Besides," he added, "my grandad's out there, and you'll need a ride."

I'd been planning to call a taxi, but was relieved I didn't have to wait. Pecking Brad on the cheek, I scrambled into my clothes, telling him as I did about my dream. I could feel Leander and Ollie as a twin presence in the back of my mind, still trapped. I hadn't been sure whether the bindings would hold once I woke up, and knowing they had filled me with satisfaction. Let both Oneiroi stew for a while. Who knew? Maybe they'd bond over their newfound dislike for me.

Brad's brow furrowed as I finished talking, but he didn't say anything.

"What?" I prompted, tugging a heavy jumper over my head.

"I was wondering what your dad's like."

"An Oneiroi. Winged and annoying. Much like Leander."

"Does he look much like you?"

"He's bipedal." I sat on the bed to lace up my boots. "That's about it. I guess I got my fabulous good looks from Mum. That's definitely where I got the lack of wings."

"That makes sense," he said, not reacting to my joking tone. I didn't think he was talking about wings.

"Huh?"

He shifted from foot to foot. "It's just a theory."

A noise from the hall cut our conversation short: a faint rattling noise, as though someone was trying the handle. We listened carefully, but I couldn't hear anything much over my suddenly racing pulse.

There was a pause, and then a tap on the door. Frowning, Brad walked out to the lounge and peered through the peephole. Then he relaxed. "It's Jen," he said, unlatching the door.

She leapt on him like a crazed animal.

Brad stumbled back into the room. Jen followed him in, nails extended to rake his cheeks, leaving lines of red in their wake. He swore, holding one hand up to shield his face, and shoved her with the other. She reeled.

I tackled her from the side, knocking her backwards onto the tiny couch. Her glasses clattered to the floor. I managed to avoid stepping on them as I held her down,

using my greater height and weight to keep her pinned. She writhed beneath me like a thing possessed, her lips pulled back from her teeth as she snapped at my face. A low growl came from her throat, barely human.

Possessed.

"Help me," I gasped.

Brad shut the apartment door and joined me, holding Jen's arms tightly against her sides. She tried to buck us off but was unable to.

I placed one hand against Jen's cheek. She turned her head to bite at my fingers, snarling like a dog, but I had what I needed.

"She's blight-ridden."

"I guessed," Brad said between clenched teeth. "Can you kick it out?"

"It would take time," I said, torn. It'd taken me almost an hour to cleanse Larry of his infestation. Longer to deal with Brad's. Seeing Jen like this broke my heart. But if she'd been sent here to distract me…

"What's the alternative?"

I leaned forward and exhaled onto Jen's face. The outraged expression faded from her eyes like a snuffed candle as sleep stole in and calmed her.

Hand trembling, I leaned down and picked up her glasses, putting them on the coffee table.

Brad loosened his grip reluctantly, as if expecting her to leap up and attack him again. When she didn't he straightened and, wincing, touched his cheek with one finger. It came away red. "Damn, she got me good. How long will she sleep?"

"I'm not sure." I hurried into the bedroom and returned with a wad of tissues, holding them to his cheek. "The only other time I've used my sleeping magic on someone actively possessed, I exorcised the blight straight away."

"That was me, wasn't it?" He put his hand over mine as I nodded. The tender gesture made me melt.

"On a regular human it lasts at least a few hours, but on someone a blight has actually taken over, who knows? The blight might grant some resistance."

"If we're not going to exorcise her straight away, then we'll need to restrain her."

"That would be safest, yes. So she doesn't hurt herself or anyone else."

We turned the apartment upside down looking for rope alternatives that wouldn't hurt Jen. The television's power cable was out, for example. Eventually we settled on the terry towelling belts from the two dressing gowns, tying her wrists and ankles and then placing her in the middle of the bed, her head on a pillow. Hopefully she wouldn't roll off. I wrote a note in big letters and propped it up on the bedside table, next to her glasses. Jen was short-sighted, so she should be able to see it.

Dear Jen,
Don't panic. You're tied up because you're blight-ridden. We'll be back soon and then I'll kick its blighty arse. Please try and stay calm.
Love Melaina.

"Do you think it'll work?" Brad said, reading the note.

"What?" I shrugged into my coat.

"I wouldn't stay calm if I were her."

"Me neither." I grimaced, locking the apartment door carefully behind me. "Let's hope she stays asleep."

"So," Brad said as we hurried to the elevator, "does Jen go out to Wattle Tree Park too?"

"She's never been there," I said, curling my hands into fists. My nails bit into my palms. "But I set her up on a date with an employee. A nurse named Ewan."

Which meant her possession was my fault. And if he'd done it deliberately I would kick his arse.

"Oh." Brad looked me up and down, taking in my scowl and aggressive pose. "I wouldn't want to be him right now."

I grunted a reply but didn't say anything, too preoccupied with my guilt. It wasn't until we were in the car, on our way to the nursing home, that I remembered what Brad and I had been talking about before we'd been interrupted. "What's your theory?"

"What theory?" he said.

"About my father."

"Is now really the time to talk about it?"

His evasiveness made me nervous. "Tell me. Please?"

"Okay, but remember I'm driving a car right now so, if you punch me, we might crash and die."

"Spill it!"

"I think ... that is, I'm pretty sure your father isn't your biological father."

I stared at him through wide eyes. "Of course he is. How else could I do what I can do?"

"I'm not saying he didn't affect your development, because clearly he did. Maybe it was the close contact he had with you when you were in your mother's womb. You basically all shared a body for nine months, right?" he asked. I nodded, swallowing against a sudden lump in my throat. "But the genetic material, the initial sperm to your mother's egg ... I think that came from a regular old human, probably in the old-fashioned way." When I didn't say anything, he reached out with one hand and squeezed my fingers. "Are you okay?"

"I'm ... I don't know. Mum always swore she never ... she told me Ollie was my father. You think she lied to me?" My voice sounded weak.

"She probably didn't think of it as lying. Maybe she figured it was like having a stepfather."

"But then who is my real father?" He didn't answer, and I stared at him. "You've got a theory, don't you?"

"I do. But I don't know for sure."

"Who? Please tell me?"

"I think it was Thomas. The guy at the funeral. Your uncle's childhood friend."

I remembered Thomas, looking down at me with blue eyes, eyes so like my own, as he declared me to be like a daughter to Uncle Ian. Why would he do that? If he'd really known my uncle, he had to know it wasn't true. Was it possible he was speaking for himself? Given Mum had refused to talk about how she got pregnant, and my uncle and his parents had assumed she'd been raped ... I could see why a young man still at university wouldn't have had the courage to admit he was the father.

Nausea curled in my stomach, drying my mouth and making my palms cold and clammy. What if he really *had* raped her? And Mum had lied to me about the full details of my conception to protect me from that?

"God," I whispered.

"I'm sorry, I shouldn't have said anything." Brad's hand was still in mine and he squeezed again.

"I asked you to." I remembered something. "Is that

what you and he were arguing about at the wake?"

Brad nodded, his cheeks turning red. "I'm sorry. I didn't mean for the conversation to go as far as it did, but I guess he'd seen me with you, because when I asked him if he had any kids, he... Well, he got angry and denied you were his. But then, he would, wouldn't he?"

"Yeah," I said, sighing. "Especially if he believed he'd been overheard. Uncle Ian may not be around anymore to beat him into a red smear, but Lacey's pretty frightening in her own right."

"I noticed," Brad said dryly.

I slouched down in my seat, staring out the window. If Brad was right ... was this what Leander and the other Oneiroi were so keen to discover? How Ollie had managed to affect the development of a human foetus—me—until by the time I was born I wasn't entirely human anymore? Ollie had suggested there was something special about Mum, something that had let it happen.

That she's a lucid dreamer, maybe?

I brooded over the idea until we reached Wattle Tree Park. The visitor parking was deserted at this time of night, so Brad was able to pull the car in right out the front. He turned to me. "Are you sure you want to do this now? We could come back first thing tomorrow."

Pushing thoughts of my father, or fathers, aside, I shook my head. The certainty something was happening right now weighed on me, filling me with an icy chill.

"Let's do it," I said, stepping out of the car.

Chapter Thirty

We walked past the vehicle entry—STAFF AND DELIVER-IES ONLY, the sign said—to the pedestrian gate. It wasn't locked, but the security guard sitting in the booth put down his phone and frowned at us.

"Can I help you, miss?" I didn't recognise him from my previous visits. Maybe he didn't work the day shift.

"I hope so," I murmured. Then I smiled brightly, trying to look harmless.

"Sorry, you'll have to speak up," he said, leaning closer.

And I exhaled onto his face, breathing my sleeping magic straight at him.

The guard blinked a few times before slowly lowering his head to the bench in front of him. He snored quietly.

"That was easy," Brad whispered behind me.

"For now," I said, nodding at the opaque plastic dome above the guard's head. "Although there's a camera behind that. Are you positive you want to come?"

He stepped past me to open the gate. "After you, ma'am."

"I'll take that as a yes, then."

"Well, I'm already on camera, so I might as well." He grinned, following me through, and closing the gate behind us. Despite his care, the metal latch clanged in the still night air. I winced.

The gardens around the home looked very different at night. The branches of the wattle trees seemed more twisted, the shadows lending them a sinister mien they didn't have during the day. A light fog had settled, wisping among the trees like a thing alive.

"I feel like I'm on a road through an enchanted forest," Brad muttered, glaring at the path. "And the Big Bad Wolf is out there somewhere."

"And the role of Little Red Riding Hood will be played by Brad Peterson," I said in a soft, teasing voice. But I knew what he meant. In-ground lights dotted the path at regular intervals, their steady white radiance making our shadows leap and shrink as we passed each one.

"Are you planning on putting everyone to sleep in there?" he said as we approached the sliding door.

"Have you got a better idea?" I said. He shook his head reluctantly and I continued, "I don't want to hurt anyone. At least the patients should all be asleep. Really asleep, I mean. And as far as I know the cameras are all on the outside of the building."

We nearly collided with the sliding door when it didn't open. I stood back and frowned at the sensor, waving an arm to get its attention, but nothing happened. My neck prickled, aware of the eyeless gaze of another camera mounted under the eaves to my right.

Brad pointed at a nondescript grey box on the wall beside the door. It was half-obscured by the soft golden foliage of a diosma. "We need a pass to get in after hours."

"Now what do we do? We can't just smash our way in." *Not in front of that camera.* I paced to keep warm. He opened his mouth to say something and I scowled at him. "I won't give up yet. I have a really bad feeling." I would feel like an idiot if nothing was going on, that was certain.

"I wasn't going to suggest leaving. I was going to suggest this." He rapped on the glass with his knuckles.

For a few moments nothing happened. Then, as he knocked again, a young Vietnamese woman in a blue nurse's uniform walked into view, head tipped to one side. Her name was Lien. We'd talked a few times, comparing notes about our studies, before I'd dropped out of university.

Lien's eyes widened when she saw us shivering on the other side of the glass. I raised a hand and waved to her, trying to look harmless. I wasn't sure how good a job I was doing but, after hesitating briefly, she pressed a button beside the door. The glass *wooshed* open and we hurried inside. "Thank goodness," I said, only slightly exaggerating my shivering. "It's freezing out here."

"What are you doing here, Melaina?" she asked. She didn't recognise Brad, if the nervous looks she was giving him were anything to go by.

"It's so exciting!" I said, grasping her hands in mine. "My mum called to say she's awake, and I just had to rush down here straight away!"

"She ... what?" Lien's mouth fell open with surprise. "She was still sleeping when I checked on her an hour ago."

She started to turn from me, to hurry down the corridor towards my mother's room, but I pulled her back to me as gently as I could. Then I put her to sleep.

Brad helped me catch her as her body crumpled to the floor, sweeping her up and carrying her back to her desk. He arranged her comfortably on the chair, leaning her head on her arm beside a computer keyboard and a complicated-looking phone covered in buttons. "We could get a few people fired tonight," he said quietly as he came back around to where I waited. His shoulders were tense, his brown eyes full of guilt.

"I know." I clenched my jaw for a moment. "Let's worry about it after we check on our people, okay?"

"Okay."

We walked together down the corridor. About halfway down, he turned to face a closed door. I'd never seen this door open before. "This is my grandfather's room," he said.

I glanced longingly at my mother's door—also closed, but they all were at this time of night—and then turned to nod at Brad. He eased the door open and we slipped into the room, feet silent on the heavy carpet.

My first impression of the room was that the medicinal stink was stronger here than in Mum's room.

My second was that there was something ... wrong ... about the place. Very wrong.

The room had the same layout as Mum's: bedhead and side table against one wall, wardrobe on the other side, and a chair and small table by the curtained window. The only lights in the room were from a lamp on the table, and a heart-rate monitor that beeped quietly on a small trolley by the bed. Both the monitor and a drip were connected to an emaciated old man who sank into the bed as though it were trying to swallow him up. If Brad hadn't told me this was his grandfather, I wouldn't have recognised him from the photo I'd seen. His skin was sallow and paper-thin, a tracery of veins on the back of his hands visible even in the poor light. His hair was clean but lifeless, like cobwebs abandoned by their spinner.

A chart hung from the end of the bed, the name Marcus Peterson printed at the top.

Brad reached out to take his grandfather's hand. Before I could think about it, I grabbed it, pulling it away. "Don't touch him!"

"What? Why?" Brad's eyes widened and his nostrils flared; he looked the angriest I'd ever seen him, blight possession excluded. But there was fear there too.

He was right to be afraid.

"I just ... I have a really bad feeling. Catch me if I fall, okay?"

And I reached my own hand out to touch his grandfather's papery skin.

I'd seen blights before. Immature ones, like the ones in Larry's and Jen's minds, and mature ones, like Brad's.

At least, I'd thought those were the mature ones. Until now.

I was inside the house from Brad's dreamscape once again. I recognised the floral wallpaper in the top hallway. But this place didn't seem to have suffered the surface damage of a frustrated blight's attention: the damaged walls and shattered furniture. Relief tugged a sigh from me and I took a single step. My boot thumped, unnaturally loud on the carpet. The sound rolled and echoed like thunder.

And it drew immediate attention.

A sunflower on the wall moved, *blinked*, and the centre opened—

—a burning black eye like a smouldering coal stared back at me, fringed by cheerful petals that slowly withered and turned brown—

—then *all* of the flowers moved and opened, and a dozen more eyes stared, moving as one to glare at me.

No, this place hadn't been damaged. It had been infested like maggots infest a wound. Infected like blood poisoning, sickness flowing to every part of the body. The danger was beneath the surface.

Even as the danger I was in struck me, the floor trembled beneath my boots, and then buckled. I screamed as I fell, shunted forward, towards the stairs. I clawed at the carpet, trying to find a handhold, something to stop my fall. Pain stabbed through my fingers as my nails tore. But the floor was slick, soaked with oil.

I hit the edge of the stairs hard, wheezing as the wind was knocked from my lungs. I threw my arms and legs out to grip the walls, willing myself to stop. *Needing* myself to stop.

And it worked. Beneath me, the stairs curled and roiled like a tongue trying to swallow. I was a fishbone, stuck in the gullet of a giant beast. From below, the sharp stench of acid burned my nostrils, making my eyes water. I couldn't see what awaited me, although the black, oily rust staining the walls hinted at its nature.

"Melaina!" Two voices cried in unison, panicked.

"Let us help you," one added. My father.

"You better," I yelled, then coughed until I was breathless. I closed my eyes and willed the two Oneiroi free.

For several heartbeats, nothing happened. Had they deserted me? Would my father do that? Would Leander?

Then the pair appeared at the top of the stairs, hovering

in the air like kites: wings spread but not moving. They each glowed faintly with an inner light, Leander's silver and my father's an earthy gold. Leander began down the stairwell but recoiled when he encountered the acrid air, coughing and shivering. He withdrew, bracing himself at the head of the stairs and reaching down towards me. "Give me your hand."

"Can't let go," I said through gritted teeth. The walls shuddered under my grip and then began to ripple, like a muscle contracting. Plasterboard shattered, a brittle shell over something malevolent, and tumbled into the void below me. Slick pink flesh glistened where the plasterboard had been. "Help me!"

Ollie snatched one of Leander's hands in his, locking their fingers together. "Brace me!" He leaned down into the stairwell's gulf, his other arm grasping at me. His fingers brushed my sleeve. Leander leaned a little farther, muscles straining, and Ollie's hand locked onto my arm. "Pull!"

Leander did, hauling back, dragging us both from the throat of the beast. Ollie and I coughed furiously. From below, a frustrated roar arose, carried on air that stank of rotten meat.

Then Leander wrapped his arms around both of us and yanked us out of the dream.

Back in the seamless fog of my own dreamless mind, I collapsed, shivering, to the ground. Ollie sat beside me, still coughing, presumably trying to get the taste of acid and decay from his lungs. I knew how he felt.

Leander stood over us, arms folded. His wings trembled faintly, telegraphing his distress.

"What the hell was that?" I gasped finally.

"A blight," Leander said.

"I've seen blights before—"

"A breeder blight. The source of blight larvae." He shuddered. "I've never seen one from the inside before."

"Like a queen bee?" I guessed. "That kind of thing?"

He nodded. "Only with less honey and more eating you alive."

"How do we fight it?"

"*We* don't. Taking out a breeder blight requires at least a dozen Oneiroi. The three of us don't have that kind of power." He leaned down and locked a hand around my father's forearm. "Once he's in custody I'll bring a team back to take care of it."

Ollie lifted his head in alarm, yanking his arm free of Leander's grip. "Wait a minute! You said you'd help me with Davina first. I'll go with you, but only after that."

Leander frowned as he looked between us. "I assumed that was her dream."

Ollie shook his head emphatically. "You think I'd let something like that take over her mind?"

I shuddered. "That was Brad's grandfather."

"Well, that explains where he got his blight infestation from," Leander said.

"Yeah. And I think I know how, too. From Ewan, one of the nurses here. He infected Jen too."

Ollie frowned, clearly trying to place the name, but Leander knew who she was. He narrowed his eyes. "Your flatmate? Is she okay?"

"Not yet, but she will be. Hers is only a baby blight by comparison. I can deal with it. Look, can I rely on you two to hang around without fighting? I need to go to Mum's room before I can touch her dream. And I need to tell Brad about his grandfather."

Ollie looked at Leander, who nodded reluctantly, say-ing, "Okay. I won't do anything so long as he doesn't try and escape."

"I'm here to help Davina," Ollie said, thrusting his chin out. "I won't run."

I nodded and left them without another word.

Chapter Thirty-One

I opened my eyes and blinked, confused. It took me a few seconds to realise I was looking at the side of a bedframe from ground level. Perhaps unsurprisingly, it was pretty clean under there. Cleaner than it was under my bed, anyway. Groaning, I rolled my head to look the other way. Brad knelt beside me.

"Are you alright?" He stroked my hair. "You touched him and just … collapsed."

"I'm fine," I said, trying to push myself upright. Brad steadied me with a strong arm. "Did I miss anything?"

"A nurse poked his head in but didn't come into the room. He didn't see us." Brad had laid me on the carpet on the side of the bed facing the window, not the door. Smart.

"How long was I out?"

"It felt like forever, but—" he glanced at his watch "—maybe five minutes? What happened? Is Grandad okay?"

I met his gaze and drew a breath, wondering where to start.

His face fell. "It's bad, isn't it?"

"Yeah, it's bad." Taking his hand, I explained as gently as I could what I knew. It wasn't much. I left off the graphic details of the infestation, hoping to spare him the knowledge of what the creature was doing to his grandfather's psyche. But, judging by his sombre expression, he was able to read between the lines. "I promise you, Brad, I'll make the Oneiroi deal with it as soon as I can. It's just … beyond me. I'm sorry."

He looked up at the profile of his grandfather's sleeping face, his eyes sad. "Do you suppose that's why he hasn't woken up since the accident?"

"It could be. I don't know. The blight has … well, it's got a strong hold on him. Very strong. The one in you didn't have the stamina to manage long stints in control."

"Do you think he's been walking around?"

"I doubt it." I gestured to the heart rate monitor. "The nurses would know."

"Yeah, but if one or more of the nurses are responsible for passing the infestations along … if it's been done intentionally rather than by accident…"

"I know." Brad's reminder about the staff's possible culpability brought my anxiety back in a nauseous rush. "Let's go check on Mum."

Brad stood and offered me his hand. I took it with a smile and let him help me to my feet, then fished around in the bottom of my bag for a caramel. The sugar would help take the edge off my dizziness.

While I was peeling the lolly, Brad cracked the door open and peeked through the gap, looking for signs of movement. "It looks clear," he murmured, opening the door wide and stepping into the hall.

There was an explosion of movement to the right of the door. Someone brought a full pitcher, heavy with water, down on Brad's head with a sickening thud. He fell forward, water drenching him as the pitcher fell.

"Brad!" I snatched the chart from the end of the bed and flung it to my right as I ducked through the doorway. Batting the chart away, Brad's attacker lunged at me. I scrambled to the left, stumbling over my boyfriend's outstretched legs. Fingers brushed along the edge of my coat but didn't gain a purchase. I whirled to face my attacker—

"Ewan!" I gasped.

"Surprised?" He grinned. His eyes were alert, not the dull look of the blight-ridden.

"Not really, no." I tried to keep my voice steady, but my heart pounded so loudly Ewan might be able to hear it. "I figured it was you when Jen attacked me."

"How is dear Jenny, anyway?" He took a step forward, standing over Brad like a hunter over his kill.

I moved back, holding my fisted hands in front of me in a posture I hoped looked threatening. "She's fine." I bared my teeth in a smile, my gaze flicking briefly to Ewan's hands. One of them was wrapped in gauze.

"That's good. I gave her a very special treat."

The blight. "She'd gouge your eyes out for calling her Jenny."

"Lucky she's not here then."

As Ewan spoke, Brad tensed beneath him. I tried not to look, but something in my reaction gave it away. Ewan shifted his weight to take a hasty step forward. Brad kicked upwards, bending both legs at the knee. His heels connected with the top of Ewan's calf, knocking him off balance. I darted in and shoved the nurse hard in the chest. He stumbled over Brad and fell to the carpet. Brad rolled, pinning him to the ground.

"What have you done to my grandfather?" Brad leaned down so his face was inches from Ewan's. "What did you *do*?"

"Nothing," Ewan said, smiling. "He was like that when I found him."

I stepped forward so Ewan could see me over Brad's shoulder. "But you've been spreading the blight eggs, right?"

He shrugged one shoulder as best he could, the movement restricted by Brad's weight on him. "Sure. Spreading the love."

"Love?" Brad growled, water dripping from his hair. His eyes were dark with fury, his fists balling in the front of Ewan's uniform until the fabric threatened to tear. "Nightmares? Sleepwalking? Making me into a weapon? Is that what you call love?"

"I never said it was love for *you*." Ewan smile was so serene that I opened my mouth to ask whom he loved, but Brad had spotted the bandage-wrapped hand.

"How'd you hurt your hand, *nurse*?"

Ewan clamped his mouth shut, but his gazed shifted to me. It was just for a moment, but it was enough. My hands clenched. "You started the shop fire!"

His grin was all the answer I needed. Serenity had put everything into that shop, had built it up over more than a decade to be a place she loved more than her own home. And he'd destroyed it. I stepped around his head, kneeling and grabbing a fistful of two-toned hair in my hands. "Tell me why." When he didn't answer I picked up the water pitcher and held it over his head. It was

empty now, but still solid. "Tell me or I'll beat the crap out of you right now."

His eyes widened as he stared at the bottom of the pitcher. I wondered what he saw in its glossy surface. His own reflection? An Oneiroi? I glanced at the dull surface of the plastic, but only my own features gazed back.

I looked crazed.

"I won't tell you." Ewan's voice trembled slightly. "He'd kill me."

"*Who* would kill you?"

But he didn't answer. I glared at him, my fingers tightening on the handle of the pitcher. Could I really strike a defenceless man in the head? Could I?

"What the *hell* is going on here?"

Standing at the far end of the corridor was Daniel, the usually shy nurse. His eyes were wide, horrified, as he looked from us to Ewan.

I dropped the pitcher to the side and leapt to my feet, rushing towards him. "Thank goodness you're here," I said, voice high with a panic that wasn't entirely feigned. "Ewan attacked Brad, hit him on the head with the pitcher. You have to call the police."

Daniel's gaze took in the scene—there was no denying Brad was soaked, and bloody streaks marred his cheek from Jen's attack. Daniel frowned, opening his mouth to ask the obvious question: why were we here at this time of night?

But by then I was in front of him. I exhaled gently onto his face, catching him as he crumpled and lowering him to the ground.

"Now what do we do?" Brad said.

"Tie Ewan up."

Hearing this, the nurse struggled. But he was more lightly built—thin due to a high metabolism rather than exercise, I guessed—and Brad held him easily.

I knelt over Ewan, my lips parted.

"Are you going to kiss me?" He froze, eyes wide.

"Dream on," I said, and put him to sleep too.

Brad stood slowly, leaving Ewan lying in the puddle of water. Wincing, he touched the top of his head with his fingers and inspected them for blood. "Are you okay?" I asked, reaching up to run my fingers through his hair as lightly as I could. There was a lump forming but his skin was intact. "Ouch."

"Yeah," he said, lifting Ewan. "Luckily I've got a head like a rock. Where shall we put him and the other nurse?"

"We can't leave them here?"

"If any of the residents wake up and find them in the corridor..." He shrugged, but I got the idea. We were probably already going to jail for our actions tonight. I wanted to achieve what we'd set out to do before the police arrived.

We decided to put the two men in the dark, empty rec room. Fortunately for us, the heavy door to each patient's room was almost soundproof, giving them privacy and conveniently screening them from the sounds of assault in the corridor. If the residents needed assistance, they had buttons to call the nurses. I fervently hoped none of them needed a nurse until we woke Daniel or Lien up as we were leaving. I had no intention of leaving those two asleep any longer than we had to.

Ewan, on the other hand... I bit my lip, wondering what to do about him.

I don't know what I'd expected to find when I eased the door to Mum's room open with trembling hands. Ewan's attack on Brad felt like a delaying tactic, a distraction, like the shop fire had been. Something to keep us busy.

But Mum's room was undisturbed. She lay in her bed, sleeping, arms folded on top of the blanket. A drip line ran into the back of her left hand, the only change from the last time I'd seen her.

I exhaled with relief.

"Were you expecting something different?" Brad asked, closing the door behind me with a soft click.

"Not sure. An evil scientist, maybe. Whoever Ewan's working for." I perched on the edge of the bed and touched the back of Mum's hand lightly. If she stayed unconscious for long enough, would her skin and muscle fade like Marcus Peterson's had?

Brad's next words sent a chill through me. "They still could be here. If they're a mothman like your father." He nodded at her sleeping form.

"I have to find a way in there," I said. "Are you going to be okay out here on your own? How's your head?"

"I'll be fine. I'll see if there's any painkillers in the nightstand." Brad brushed my lips with his. "I'm more worried about you. Be careful."

"I will."

I lay down awkwardly beside Mum, feeling a twinge of guilt as I put my boots on the blanket. She'd scold me for that … if she were conscious.

I took her hand and closed my eyes. It was time to see if I could wake her up.

Chapter Thirty-Two

I didn't step straight into Mum's dream. I couldn't. So I stepped into my own, to the place where I'd left my father and Leander.

They were still there, which surprised me a little. After all this time I didn't doubt Ollie's affection for Mum, so I'd been confident he wouldn't leave without trying to help. But I hadn't been sure Leander would let him.

They'd taken some liberties with my dreamscape. The fog had receded to show a pleasant park by the lakeside, bordered by shady European beech trees and carpeted with lush grass. The Oneiroi sat on the grass, cross-legged like a couple of schoolchildren as they talked quietly. They looked up, falling silent as I approached.

"You've been a while. Is everything okay?" Ollie said. The concern in his voice seemed genuine, but I realised it wasn't for me when he added, "Davina?"

"She's fine." My heart sank but I kept my voice even. "Physically, at any rate. Brad and I got jumped by the

nurse who's been spreading the blight larvae."

"Did you—"

"He's asleep. Probably dreaming of arson and puppies. What do I know?"

Leander's eyes gleamed, their colour intensified by the vivid greens of the grass and trees behind him. "Was he blight-ridden?"

"I didn't check. But if he was, it wasn't in control. I figured we should take a look at Mum first. I'll worry about Ewan later."

"Fair enough." Leander rose to his feet gracefully, while Ollie leapt, urgency in his every movement.

"You're both coming?" I asked, raising an eyebrow at Leander.

"I said I'd help Davina in exchange for Ollie turning himself in. I meant it." His expression softened. "Besides, she's your mother."

I tipped my head to the side, frowning at him. But before I could say anything, Ollie took our hands and pulled us sideways.

We didn't land in my mother's dream, but in the form-less mass of Erebus around it. Like the rural fringe surrounding a city, only without the cows or roads or, well, anything.

Because my method for travelling through dreams involved stepping straight into the mind of a sleeper, I'd never entered Erebus in its raw state—although I had glimpsed it from the outer edge of dreamers' minds. I wished I wasn't here now. It was ... nothing. Blackness. I blinked frantically and, if it weren't for the warm presence of Ollie's arm through mine, I might have panicked. His touch was the only thing I could feel. I moved my feet experimentally but there was no surface beneath me. Even the air brought no sensation—the temperature was neither hot nor cold, and not a puff of a breeze stirred it.

Sparks of light winked into existence in the distance. Was my mind playing tricks on me? Unable to process the lack of input, was it conjuring images of its own? But slowly my eyes adjusted and I was able to make out the dim form of Ollie hovering beside me, and Leander beyond him. The faint lights looked like pinpricks in an all-encompassing sheet of black velvet. Like distant stars, some were clustered together, part of a galaxy, while others stood far apart from the rest, isolated spots that almost vanished in the blackness.

"What are they?" I breathed.

"They are human minds. Dreaming," Ollie said.

"That's what we look like to you, from the outside?"

"Not you." Leander drifted closer, so he could see my face. He wasn't clinging to Ollie like I was, but then, he had wings. I wasn't sure what would happen if I let go—whether I would fall forever through the darkness until I went mad, or just float away like an untethered astronaut. Or both. I didn't want to find out. "Compared to your mind, these are like ... fireflies to a bonfire."

"Fireflies are pretty," I said, craning my neck to stare at the expanse of minds. They went in all directions, not just around me horizontally but above and below, too. Their locations in Erebus must not directly correspond to their locations on Earth.

"But you can warm yourself at a bonfire."

I looked back at Leander, but he had turned away from me to examine the wall.

It loomed to my left, like something out of a fairytale—if

fairytales drifted in space like a giant, vine-covered satellite. Ollie manoeuvred us closer, tilting his wings like the rudders on a ship, until the plants became clearer. They were climbing roses, although the flowers weren't in bloom. Wicked thorns sprouted every few inches.

"Those look sharp," I said.

"She liked the story about Briar Rose. You know, the princess who sleeps in an enchanted castle till her prince comes to save her?"

I raised an eyebrow at him. "I think every girl born in the last fifty years knows who Briar Rose is, Dad."

He beamed at me.

"What? What'd I do?" I knew I sounded suspicious but I didn't care.

"You called me 'Dad'."

"Oh. Yes. So I did." I would've busied myself tying a shoelace but I couldn't reach my boots, so I stared back up at the wall.

"Are you two finished?" Leander asked. I nodded, thankful for his interruption, and Ollie's lips pressed together. "Good. Show us where this entrance is."

"Was," Ollie corrected. But he led us partway around the wall, and down a little, until we were at its base. There was nothing to mark the location as different from any other spot on the wall: it had the same, featureless grey stone. The same tangled, spiked vines of the climbing rose spiralling upward. But Ollie pointed.

"You're sure?"

The look he gave Leander was scathing. "Of course I'm sure. See how this handful of stones here is lighter than the rest?" I squinted, but in the faint light they all looked the same to me. "I used to be able to press here—" He placed his palm, fingers wide, on the spot "—and the wall would open for me. Now? Nothing." He demonstrated.

"Maybe it rusted shut from lack of use," I said hopefully.

"Stone doesn't rust." Leander came forward and peered at the stone.

"The magical equivalent then," I said through gritted teeth.

He touched the wall and closed his eyes. "There's definitely been another Oneiroi here, and recently."

Ollie's mouth fell open. "You can sense that?"

"There's a reason I work for the Morpheus." He looked at me as he said it, and I remembered my ill-timed joke a week-and-a-half earlier, about him being bad at his job. The memory made me hang my head. Looking at this wall—the sheer impossibility of searching its entire surface for a hidden entrance—there was no way he'd ever have been able to catch Ollie while he hid inside.

But now someone else was inside. And they'd shut us out. "Can you get in?" I said.

Leander hesitated, then shook his head. "If I could have before now, I would have, and your father wouldn't be here. Knowing where it is doesn't help. Not enough."

Ollie's wings drooped.

I wasn't so ready to give up. Whoever was in there was responsible for the blights, the shop fire, even Uncle Ian's death. I *knew* it. I wouldn't lose anyone or anything else to him. Or her. "Hang on. This wall's built from Mum's dreams, right? Leander, between your power, and the fact she trusts Ollie and me, we might be able to coax it to change for us."

"I've tried changing it," Ollie said. "It doesn't work."

I sighed, and would've folded my arms except that one

was still hooked through Ollie's. I settled for putting my free hand on my hip so I could glare at the pair of them. "That's because you're both lazy."

"*What*?" they said together. "How am I getting blamed here?" Leander added.

"It's true! You're both so used to having complete control over a dreamer's dream that if you can't waltz in and change it on a macro scale, you don't realise you can still make minor alterations. Accept the dreamer's paradigm, then work with it."

"That's what you do?" Ollie gave me an unreadable look.

"Yes. The only dream I have total control over is my own. Take me closer." I pointed to the base of one of the climbing roses, a thick mass of barbs and tangled vines. "Hello," I said softly to the plant, reaching out and placing a finger carefully between the thorns. The trunk was cool and pliable, but strong. I closed my eyes and fed a little energy into the plant, willing it to do what I wanted.

The Oneirois' gasps told me I'd been successful. Grinning, I opened my eyes again to see a fresh green tendril had sprouted from the trunk, pliable and tender. Even its thorns were soft, not yet hardened into brutal spikes. It curled around my fingertip as though embracing it, like a baby gripping its mother's hand.

"See?"

"Yes." Leander leaned closer, examining the tendril with fascination. "You think we could..." He gestured up at the wall.

"Not bring the whole thing down, but..." I looked up, thinking. "Maybe we could convince the plant to force a hole in the brickwork. Vines can do that to buildings if they aren't controlled. Pull everything apart."

"It's worth a try," Leander said, looking at Ollie. "Unless you have any better ideas?"

My father shook his head. "How do we do this?"

"I'll take point," I said. "Leander, give me your hand." He hesitated before reaching out for me—but, to his credit, it was only for a moment. I considered making a joke about it, but his solemn expression convinced me otherwise.

With Ollie holding one arm and Leander the other, I couldn't reach out to touch the plant again. But it shouldn't be necessary. I could feel their power flowing into me, a pair of lights that I twined together into a knotted rope, silver and gold bound together with my own energy—a vibrant blue. I examined the dense growth just above where the roots dangled free into the air, drawing sustenance from Erebus as they would the ground. That dense point was the plant's heart. And I pushed my will into it, gently but persistently, like water flowing into the soil until it was so saturated it started to pool on the surface.

The plant trembled at first, as if caught in a nonexistent breeze. Then one, two, three new branches burst forth from the trunk, ripening from tender to mature in heartbeats. They clung to the brickwork. Rustling faintly, one, then another, worked its way into a gap between two bricks, pushing in gently but implacably. Leander reached out and moved the tip of the third so it joined them. As if in response, the stems thickened and bristled with thorns, but pushed harder into the gap, as if they were reaching for water, or nutritious soil.

The sound of the first brick cracking seemed impossibly loud in the hush of Erebus. Another brick followed

it: cracks shivered across the stone surface as if it were made of glass.

Soon the cracks covered an area of the wall about a metre square. The two Oneiroi each pushed with one free hand, shoving the broken masonry inwards. It tumbled from sight, leaving a jagged hole.

The three of us exchanged a look. "Do you want to go first?" I asked Leander.

He shook his head. "I'd rather keep Ollie where I can see him."

"So long as I'm not last," I said, exasperated. "I need one of you out here to support me."

"Ollie first, then you, then me," Leander said.

"Let's go."

My father peered past me to confirm Leander was still holding my arm and then let go, drifting towards the hole. He gently extracted the trailing vines, laying them along the outside of the wall, and then folded his wings down his back so he could crawl through the space. It was wide enough for his shoulders, but his wings were a hair's breadth from the top of the gap.

"Do you really expect him to try and escape?" I asked softly as my father's bare feet disappeared into the hole.

"No. But the Morpheus will... Well, if Ollie escaped my custody it wouldn't be good for me. Why risk it? You're next." He manoeuvred me until I could scramble into the hole.

I crawled in, grateful for something solid under me instead of the unnerving feeling of hanging in space, at the mercy of the Oneiroi for my safety—even if the uneven surface of the wall bit through my jeans and into my knees in several places. I willed the denim to thicken and was relieved when it complied.

After crawling forward for a few seconds I noticed the already dim light was fading around me until I was in pitch blackness. Biting my lip, I placed each hand gingerly on the cool brickwork before committing my weight to it. How far in front of me was my father? The only sound was the scuffling of my own movements.

And then there was nothing beneath me. I pitched forward with a scream.

Chapter Thirty-Three

I landed hard, breath knocked from my lungs to
leave me gasping for air. It was still dark. I ran a
cautious hand across the surface beneath me. It was
fuzzy, and extended as far as I could reach.

With a fitful buzz, the fluorescent lights above me
flickered on. I sat up, blinking. I was in what looked like
the rec room at Wattle Tree Park, sitting on the peach-
fuzz carpet near the silent television. I couldn't see the
hole through which I'd crawled, or any sign of the wall
we'd come through.

"Ollie?" I stood, brushing flecks of masonry off my
jeans. "Are you here?"

When there was no answer I walked to the door, opened
it … and caught myself before I stepped out into blackness.

The rec room floated in a black space that resembled
the nothingness of Erebus. But the air tingled across my
skin, and a faint breeze carried the rosewood scent of
my mother's favourite soap. I was inside her dream, not

Erebus, but something was very, *very* wrong.

Holding the doorframe with white-knuckled hands, I leaned out.

Around me floated fragments of my mother's dreams. Some were of places I recognised—such as a patch of wattle grove drifting slowly below me, maybe fifty feet beneath the toes of my boots—while others were fantastical locations or dreamlike versions of real places that, as far as I knew, Mum had never been. The lights of the Eiffel Tower cut through the gloom in the distance, an ornate arrow; a deserted fairground whose rides blinked, cheerful but motionless, hovered to my right. Other patches of dream were shadows against the greater darkness, containing no source of light to make them stand out.

Mum's dreams had fractured into pieces and drifted like leaves pushed around by faint puffs of breeze on a still pond ... if the surface of the pond were rendered in three dimensions.

The sight wrenched my heart. It was beautiful and strange, but what did it mean for my mother's psyche? I'd never seen anything like it.

A furious, wordless cry cut through the dimness.

One of the dark shadows flared with a light so bright the other dream fragments cast shadows like the fingers of a giant hand, stretching across the sky. I shielded my eyes. When the flare dimmed I could see the source. It was an old-fashioned children's playground—the sort with a worn wooden fort and a metal slide that would burn your legs on a summer day, not a new one with plastic-sheathed play equipment. The fort had been built around the slender trunk of a ghost gum. Tanbark covered

the ground beneath it and occasionally, as the dream fragment moved, the bark showered, rattling, over the edge.

On the fort's top platform, two figures wrestled. Judging by the wing colour, one was my father. I didn't recognise the other, although he was clearly Oneiroi; from this distance all I could see were orange wings veined with black, like those of a Monarch Butterfly.

As I watched, the stranger pinned Ollie to the platform. I couldn't see my father clearly past the timber railing, but he lay still, either unconscious or restrained. The other Oneiroi stood, legs apart in a fighter's stance, looking down at Ollie's unmoving body. The stranger's Monarch wings flared behind him, the orange nature's warning of danger. He wore a skirt that was little more than a loincloth. Tattoos covered his skin, twisting in Celtic-style knotwork. They were inky black, the same colour as his shoulder-length hair.

A hint of movement caught my eye: light reflecting off white wings. Leander, drifting silent as a ghost from above, a determined look on his face as he wafted down towards the strange Oneiroi. He was roughly level with me, the fort below him. Our eyes met briefly and he held a finger to his lips in warning.

I held my breath.

The Oneiroi spotted Leander when he was scant metres above the fort. He smiled, showing white teeth, and made a shooing gesture. Struck by an invisible force, Leander flew to the side, into the trunk of the gum. The fort shuddered with the impact of his landing, and the tree branches swayed. Leaves rained down.

Leander was powerful. Whomever this stranger was,

he was stronger.

Leander struggled to stand, and the other Oneiroi touched his shoulder lightly. Vines twisted around Leander, barbed vines that cut into his flesh and shredded his wings even as they pinned them to his back. He screamed.

I had never felt so helpless in my life. If I had Oneiroi wings I could fly across the void of Erebus to help them. But no amount of trying to conjure them had ever worked.

"One, two..." The voice carried, the entire dream resonating with it: warm and thick as a snow leopard's coat, and containing the same promise of danger. The strange Oneiroi stood over the others, hands on his hips as he glared down at them. "I detected a third presence. Was it the daughter? Where is she?" He began to turn, scanning the dream fragments around him. Heart thundering, I ducked back in through the doorway and pressed my back against the inside wall. His voice carried over the roaring of my pulse in my ears. "Are you here, little girl? Melaina Armstrong?" He said my name slowly, as if he were tasting each syllable.

"What have you done to Davina?" Ollie demanded, coughing. "Where is my wife?"

There was a pause ... long enough for me to imagine the Oneiroi flying up to my hideout like an eagle honing in on a mouse. And then he spoke, his voice no closer. "She's sleeping."

I exhaled, my breath trembling.

"But where is she? She's a lucid dreamer!" Ollie said. Was he trying to distract the Oneiroi from hunting me? The door still hung ajar. I peeked through the crack where it met the doorframe.

"Not right now, she isn't." The Oneiroi looked down at Ollie. "I've been looking through her dreams to find out how you did it, but now, *here you are.*" I could hear the satisfaction in his voice. "So tell me."

"How I did what?" My father struggled to prop himself up against the fort railing, and lifted his chin to glare at the orange-winged stranger. "Who are you?"

"He's Ikelos." Leander's voice was tight with pain. "The exile."

"The Morpheus's brother?" Ollie's mouth dropped open.

"And how *is* my brother?" Ikelos said. His back was to me again, displaying those gorgeous wings to full benefit, so I couldn't see his face. But his words were clipped. "Is he well?"

Ollie gasped a laugh. "As if I'd know. I'm an exile too."

"Yes." Ikelos leaned forward, blocking my view of my father. "And we need to discuss the reasons why."

Leander looked at me—at where he knew I must be hiding, safe behind my door—and his eyes were wide, imploring. *Do something.*

But what? Ikelos was the brother of the most powerful Oneiroi in Erebus, and obviously that strength ran in the family. He'd tossed Ollie and Leander around like a dingo with a pair of baby rabbits. He was running Mum's dream as if it were his own.

It wasn't, though.

The idea hit me with enough force that I gasped aloud, and then bit my lip and stared at Ikelos. He didn't react. Ollie was talking agitatedly, demanding to know if Mum was alright.

They *were* keeping him busy for me.

And if I could find Mum in the dream, wake her up so she had a presence within it, I could work with her to take charge of her dream—the way I had with Brad, cleansing his blight infestation. Ikelos had said she wasn't a lucid dreamer *right now*. He'd stripped her of the ability, somehow put her into a deeper dream, giving himself unfettered control.

I needed to find where she was sleeping.

Walking as softly on the carpet as my heavy boots would allow, I crept to a window on the opposite wall of the room and peered out.

More dreams were scattered across my field of vision, drifting slowly like parts of a bizarre children's mobile. A small slice of beach, complete with a sandcastle, floated upwards in a bubble to my right. It was shrouded in shadow due to the lack of a sun, and the waves sloshed around, excised from a greater ocean. A rose garden I didn't recognise hung nearby, ephemeral bees hovering over the flowers with mindless industry. Beyond the garden, a slice of a mountainside slicked with flowing lava cast its own baleful light; the lava spilled off the edge and into space in a deadly waterfall.

It wasn't till I craned my head and leaned out to peer directly down that I saw her.

The wattle grove I'd noticed earlier had passed underneath my drifting room. Or maybe we'd passed over the grove—with no fixed point of reference it was impossible to say. Looking down from above, I could see a ring of healthy trees in full bloom, smothered in small puffs of yellow. But in the centre of the ring was a drooping shape, an unusually broad trunk bristling with bare branches. Only one branch had any leaves. It reached for the non-existent sky, straight

towards me, shaped like a hand. The twiggy fingers were outlined with blossoms. Sitting on the branch, looking at the tree expectantly, were two ephemeral magpies.

"One of the wattle trees out there is dying. Do you think I should tell someone?"

"Whenever I come out here, they come to investigate."

It was her. I knew it as surely as if she'd placed a flashing sign there for me to read. But my surge of elation quickly turned to panic. I knew where she was, but she may as well have been on the moon. I was trapped on a different fragment of dream, unable to travel between them.

Although...

I couldn't summon Oneiroi wings, but maybe I could come up with an alternative. The space between us wasn't the true void Erebus; it was part of Mum's dreamscape. Malleable.

Feeling a smile tugging at my lips, I closed my eyes.

When I opened them, a shape hung suspended outside the window. It resembled a hang-glider, although the wingspan was smaller than those of the gliders I'd seen flying off the escarpment out near Lake George, and the wings were intricately detailed, like a dragon's. The fabric was black, in an attempt to camouflage me against the skyline.

I liked to travel in style.

I scrambled onto the window frame. The hand that reached for the control bar shook as I grabbed the cool metal to pull it closer. One outstretched wing thumped against the wall. I paused to listen, biting my lip to keep in a string of curses. But I could still faintly hear voices. Ikelos shouted something, and then someone screamed: a voice full of pain. Below me, the dying wattle tree trembled.

Oh god. Was Ikelos torturing my father? I had to be quick.

I fumbled with the leather strap hanging from the A-frame. It slipped through my nervous fingers before I separated the halves of the loop and slid it over my head and down around my hips. Then I leaned forward into the frame, gripped the bar with both hands, and pushed off from the wall.

The glider shot straight out into the null space, the wing fabric rustling above my head. I hoped it wasn't as loud as it sounded, although it was hard to tell over the frantic gasping of my breath. I'd always thought hang-gliding might be fun: soaring like a bird over the land-scape, flying high on thermals and racing over paddocks full of oblivious sheep.

This wasn't like that.

When I glanced down between outstretched arms, I'd already passed right over the wattle tree stand. Below me was empty, featureless darkness. My head spun and I looked up again ... just in time to avoid crashing into the rose garden dream fragment. I pulled up and the glider responded sluggishly. My boots grazed the tops of bushes, scattering bees and scarlet petals behind me.

Look where I'm going. Good plan. The last thing I wanted to do was to fly into that lava waterfall.

I leaned to the left and, once I'd cleared the rose garden fragment, tilted the glider's nose down, towards the wattle grove.

That was when Ikelos noticed me.

I don't know whether he'd caught a glimpse of move-ment against the darkness, heard the glider's wings as I turned, or maybe noticed the bees' agitated buzzing,

but something alerted him to my presence.

"*You!*"

He leapt into the air and sped towards me, much faster on his butterfly wings than I was in my cumbersome airframe. I tried to dodge him, turning right and then, as he loomed over me, left. But he crashed into the top of the glider. It shuddered and dropped several feet. A copper taste filled my mouth as I bit my tongue.

He tore through the glider fabric as easily as a child through wrapping paper. Talons glittered at his fingertips. He looked down and smiled at me, strange eyes glittering with malice. Then he bunched himself to fly away. The glider began to plummet—

—I willed the shredded fabric to catch on one elegant foot as he leapt into the air—

—and we fell, bound together by the glider's carcass.

If I was going down, Ikelos was coming with me.

Something broke my fall. Wattle tree branches bent and then tore free of the trunk as if I were peeling a banana. The glider frame caught in a branch, stopping with bone-jarring force. I swung forward on the leather strap, knocking my head on the bar.

Blinking stars away, I glanced down. My feet dangled barely two feet above the ground. A startled cricket stared up at me before bounding away.

The crashing sound of movement coming from above loaned me strength. I hauled myself forward, pulling my legs through the strap, and swung to the ground. A shadow loomed. Ikelos had torn himself free of the wreckage and hovered, orange wings spread wide. He howled. The roots of the trees writhed underfoot, scattering clumps of dirt as they punched through the grass and sought to entangle me. I jumped the first, but the toe of my boot caught on the second and I fell, face first, to the ground. The roots twined around my ankle. The boot leather absorbed some of the pressure but it still hurt enough to make me cry out. I kicked at the roots with my other foot but they wouldn't budge.

Ikelos landed lightly in the grass beside me and glared, pursing perfectly formed lips. "You really *do* have an Oneiroi's gifts. How marvellous."

I turned to the side and spat out a mouthful of dirt and blood. "You weren't sure?"

"My blight said you did after you so rudely cast it out. But one can't always trust a blight. They're idiots." He grabbed my hair, yanking my head back and to the side so I had to look him in the eye. His irises were a curious dark orange. It was like staring into the heart of a bonfire. "A half-Oneiroi who can walk in the human world," he said softly, running his free hand down my cheek. "What I could do with that power..."

Revulsion crawled through me and I shoved his hand away. His lip curled, and roots slithered around my wrists, trapping them on either side of my head. His grip in my hair tightened. "How did he do it? Your father?"

"I don't know," I gasped. "I wasn't there."

"Funny." But Ikelos didn't sound amused.

My father's voice came from above. "Let her go!" He sounded close. I couldn't turn my head far enough to see, but Ikelos looked up and clenched his fist in my hair until my scalp burned and tears prickled my eyes. I bit my lip to stop the whimper escaping. I wouldn't give him the satisfaction.

Leander's voice came from further away. "Let her go,

Ikelos."

The Oneiroi growled low in his throat and leapt into the air with such violence that dirt sprayed in my face. I rolled as far onto my side as I was able so I could look upwards, catching glimpses through the dense foliage.

Ikelos bore down on my father, who flitted out of the way again and again, nimbly avoiding each furious lunge from the bulkier, orange-winged Oneiroi. One of Ollie's hands dripped with blood. I remembered that pain-filled scream.

He *had* been tortured.

He'd been tortured and he hadn't fled. He'd come to lead Ikelos away from me.

Something melted in my heart: an icy core of distrust and sadness at what I'd always believed to be Ollie's indifference. I'd dismissed the explanations of why he'd never come into my dreams, written him off as a selfish and neglectful father.

That cold core vanished in a final wisp of mist, leaving gentle warmth in its place. And, as I watched Ikelos pursue Ollie across the sky, that warmth turned into a hot fury.

With a wordless scream, I directed the power of my rage at the roots trapping my ankle, my wrists. Without Ikelos's attention they had ceased to act independently, but they still bound me to the earth.

Until my rage struck them, and they exploded in a shower of splinters.

Ikelos turned back to look at me, mouth falling open in dismay.

I lunged towards the dying wattle tree.

My palm struck the trunk, fingers splayed across its rough surface. The scent of rosewood washed over me, and the trunk split like a chrysalis disgorging a butterfly. Overhead, the magpies carolled a welcome.

My mother stepped out, young and beautiful. She held her hand out, pulled me to my feet. Together, we turned to face Ikelos as he plummeted through the trees, landing hard before us. Branches swayed. Yellow blossoms rained down around him as he stepped forward, his face a mask of fury.

Fury that had nothing on my mother's.

"*Stay the hell away from my family,*" she snarled, her fingers entwined through mine.

Drawing on her strength, I flung my free arm out, pointing at Ikelos. A wave of force gathered around my fist and shot towards him with a crack and the tang of ozone, blasting him out of the grove. His wings fluttered desperately, shredded by the hailstorm of broken wattle branches and sharp-edged leaves, as he tried to control the arc of his fall.

The Oneiroi's roar as he landed in the molten lava of the volcano tore through the air like thunder.

Chapter Thirty-Four

*S*omeone blurry leaned over me.

I blinked, lifting a hand to rub my eyes, and the person resolved into a woman. She had her hair in a bun and wore a serious expression. "Welcome back," she said.

"I didn't go anywhere. I've been right here the whole time." My voice sounded strangely slurred. I looked around. The movement sent a spike of pain through my head and I winced. "Uh, where is here?"

"You're at Wattle Tree Park. You collapsed. Try not to move." She stood and took a few steps back to talk to someone. She wore green overalls: a paramedic uniform.

I was in the corridor outside my mother's room, lying on the soft carpet. I recognised the pot plant that loomed by my head, a palm with distinctive yellow-and-green fronds. Voices murmured nearby, but I couldn't see who was talking, so I tried to sit, ignoring the pain that rattled around in my skull. The wave of dizziness nearly knocked me back, but Brad came out of a bathroom and hurried to my side, helping me up.

"Are you okay?" he said.

"Dream headache. I need some sugar."

He slipped me a caramel and I gave him a weak smile, unwrapping it with shaking hands.

As I chewed slowly on the lolly I looked around the corridor. There were several police officers there—fortunately the ever-suspicious David Nelson wasn't among them. Daniel talked to one of the officers, looking confused.

"Are we under arrest?" I whispered, the caramel sticking to my teeth.

Brad shook his head, sitting beside me. I leaned my head on his shoulder so he could murmur into my ear. And also because it was comfortable. "I told the police we figured out Ewan was drugging a couple of the patients. We came down here to try and stop him."

"How did you explain...?" I indicated Daniel with a flick of my fingers.

"He doesn't remember much. Neither does Lien. I told them Ewan drugged you lot and knocked me unconscious." He brushed the lump on his head.

"Stop poking it. Did the paramedic check you over?"

"Yeah, they said I'm okay."

"Are you?" I narrowed my eyes. "What if you have a concussion?"

"Don't worry about me."

I opened my mouth to argue and he planted a quick kiss on my lips to silence me. Then he changed the subject, murmuring in my ear, "Luckily for us, Ewan's raving like a lunatic. About nightmare monsters and his dark lord and how he'll get us all. They took him away in an ambulance not long ago."

I sighed, relieved. The movement hurt less: the sugar was already helping, the zing of energy easing the thumping behind my eyes. "Do you think we're going to be arrested?" I remembered Jen, lying asleep—hopefully—on my hotel bed. The sooner we could get back to her, the better.

"No. But they might charge us with trespassing," Brad said, frowning. My heart sank. If I got charged it wouldn't make much difference to my customers, but he could lose his job. He lowered his voice even more when he next spoke. "How'd it go? Your mother ... well, she's still asleep."

He was concerned for Mum, not his job. That was what the frown meant. A bubble of warmth swelled inside me. "I know. She'll wake up tomorrow morning. You were right; there was an Oneiroi. Ikelos. We kicked his butt." Sort of. "Mum and Ollie are saying goodbye." The bubble popped.

"Goodbye?"

"He promised to go with Leander in exchange for Leander's help with Ikelos. Leander agreed to give them one last night before he arrested him." Hot tears burned my eyes as I remembered Mum's reaction to the news, the way she'd crumpled into Ollie's arms.

"Hey," Brad said, kissing me on the cheek. "Maybe they'll just talk to him and let him go."

"Maybe," I said, but I didn't really believe it. He'd been evading the Morpheus for more than twenty years. That alone would land him in hot water.

Or lava.

I grimaced.

"Excuse me, sir," the paramedic said, frowning as her sharp gaze caught my expression. She bore down on Brad in a green-clad fury. "The young lady really shouldn't be sitting up yet."

"I'm alright," I protested. "Really. I'm starting to feel better already."

At the sound of my voice, one of the police officers detached himself from the group and strode over. The paramedic gave him a pointed stare as he reached me. "Excuse me, miss? Can you answer a few questions?"

I glanced at Brad, feeling anxious, and he squeezed my hand. "I'm not going anywhere," he said.

"Good." I smiled as I thought about how much I wanted to kiss him right then, and what I would do to him later. "Don't you dare."

The end

Acknowledgements

Lucid Dreaming has been a long time coming, and so many people have helped out along the way that I'm actually a little worried I might forget someone. If I do, please forgive me!

Firstly, thank you and confetti cannons to everyone who helped during the drafting of Melaina's story: to Peter, my enduring bad-guy consultant; to Shane for his nursing advice; and to Fad for answering questions about police procedure. Any errors of fact or bad guy failures are my fault, not theirs. To everyone who read the drafts in various states and gave me valuable advice and encouragement—Stacey Nash, Kim Last, Craig Lawrie, Rena Rossner and Dannie Morin in particular—thank you and squishy hugs.

Also, thank you to my wonderful editor, Lauren K. McKellar, who asks all the hardest questions, talks to me about ellipses and spots even the tiniest inconsistencies. This book wouldn't be half of what it is without you.

The cover is brought to you by the aforementioned Kim from KILA Designs, who patiently bore with me while I threw random design ideas at her and then produced something wonderful. Bless your socks, lady!

Thank you to my friends and family for putting up with my frequent absences and blank stares, for feeding me coffee and Bad Chicken, and for being my cheer-squad: Mum, Dad, Kristy, Ali, Craig, Karen, Mikey, Peter, Cassandra, Nicole, the BC09 girls and the AOR girls. Also, a special mention goes to Bec, who puts up with my irrational love of hyphens.

And finally, thank you to my son, Nathaniel, who asked me why I "worked" in the study after he went to bed, and then said when he grew up he'd be an editor so he could help me proofread my work. Sweetheart, with your imagination I have no doubt *I'll* be proofreading *yours*. Love you, little guy.

About the author

Cassandra Page is a mother, author, editor and geek. She lives in Canberra, Australia's bush capital, with her son and two Cairn Terriers. She has a serious coffee addiction and a tattoo of a cat—despite being allergic to cats. She has loved to read since primary school, when the library was her refuge, and loves many genres—although urban fantasy is her favourite. When she's not reading or writing, she engages in geekery, from Doctor Who to AD&D. Because who said you need to grow up?

www.cassandrapage.com

Review for
Isla's Inheritance

"Witty, fun, and faerily spooky, this first instalment is perfect for fans of the fae and those who like their urban fantasy a bit light-hearted. I was literally laughing out loud at several points in the book. However, things are not all fun and games and witty banter. There were some serious creep-out moments, and wonderful twists and turns in this beautifully Australian urban fantasy."

– 5 star review, Carissa at Amazon

www.ingramcontent.com/pod-product-compliance
Lightning Source LLC
Chambersburg PA
CBHW030023180626
46810CB00001B/177